A former history lecturer, A. E. Marston was born and brought up in South Wales and educated at Oxford University. Since 1966 he has worked as a full-time writer. He has written over forty original plays for radio, television and the theatre, as well as children's books, literary criticism and novels. A keen sportsman, he lives in rural isolation in Kent.

Also by A. E. Marston

The Wolves of Savernake
The Ravens of Blackwater
The Dragons of Archenfield
The Serpents of Harbledown

The Lions of the North

A. E. Marston

HEADLINE

First published in 1996
by HEADLINE BOOK PUBLISHING

First published in paperback in 1996
by HEADLINE BOOK PUBLISHING

10 9 8 7 6 5 4 3 2

ISBN 0 7472 5415 X

Printed and bound in Great Britain by
Clays Ltd, St Ives plc

HEADLINE BOOK PUBLISHING
A division of Hodder Headline PLC
338 Euston Road
London NW1 3BH

To Anne Williams,
Mother Superior of the Convent of St Eadline

Be sober, be vigilant, because your adversary the devil, as a roaring lion, walketh about, seeking who he may devour.

Peter V:8

Domesday Yorkshire

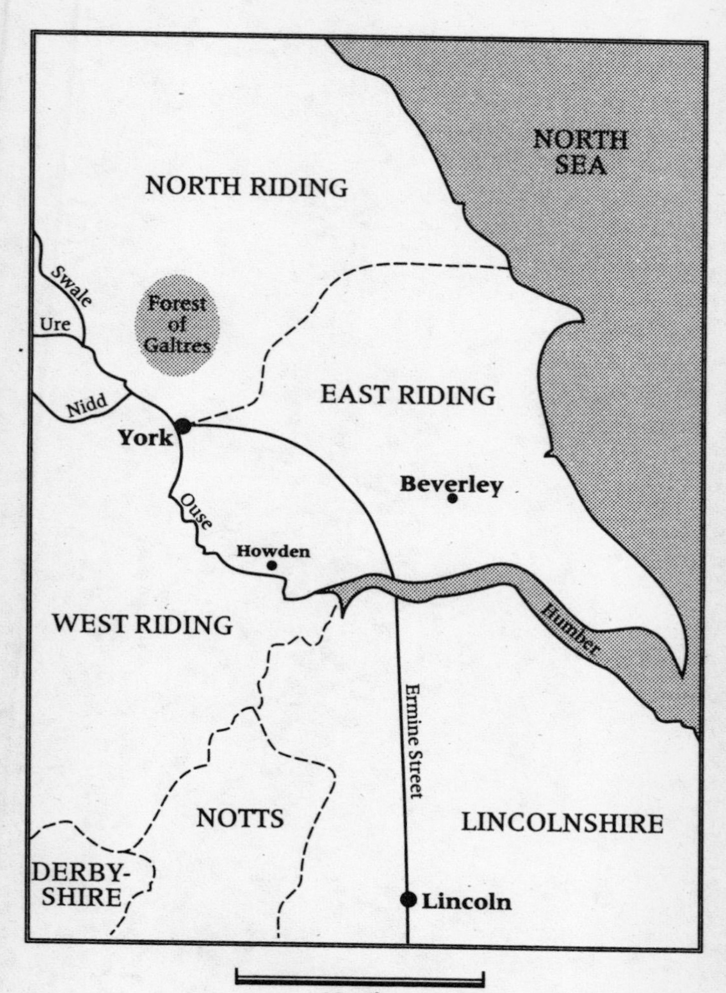

Prologue

The two men were courting danger. They knew that. Throughout all their discussions it had been an invisible presence at their shoulders, but it remained silent when their brave words instilled a heady confidence. Strength of purpose had brought them to the city and enabled them to conduct their reconnaissance with care and precision. Bright sunshine had blessed their enterprise; the swirling crowds were an ideal cover for them. It all went as planned.

Darkness changed everything. The populous streets slowly emptied. The teeming wharves became deserted. The boisterous taverns closed for the night. The last of the day's cacophony gradually died away. Even the competing smells of the city seemed to lose their pungency. York was no longer the bustling marketplace which had opened its gates to them at first light with a smile of welcome. A chill wind began to blow. They found themselves locked inside a cold and hostile prison.

Danger could now be seen and heard on every side. It conjured fearsome shapes out of the gloom and assaulted their ears with strange and unexpected cries. Danger could also be felt, tingling in their blood, pressing in upon them with gentle but persistent force, weighing down their bodies, fettering their ankles. Their courage was put to the test.

It was the older of them whose resolve began to weaken.

'We need more men,' he said.

'No,' said his companion. 'Two may succeed where twenty would surely fail.'

'Twenty? Ten times that number could not storm the castle.'

'We are not trying to storm it. We come but to look.'

'The walls are too high to scale.'

'That is why we brought the rope.'

'The castle has a garrison. There will be guards.'

'Then we must elude them.'

'What if they catch us?'

'They will not,' insisted the other, 'if we stay alert and act boldly.' He grabbed his friend's arm. 'What ails you, man? Have you so soon lost your nerve? I have not come all this way to turn back now with the task undone. Think how many depend on us. I'll go alone if the dark brings out your cowardice.'

'I am no coward!' retorted the other, stung by the charge. 'It was my idea to come here in the first place, and I stand by that. I merely counsel caution.'

'Say no more. Let's about it.'

The younger man was nineteen, tall, sturdy and lithe. His beard and hair were bleached by the sun, his face bronzed and weathered. Five years older, his companion was shorter and more compact. Though he could move swiftly, he did so with a pronounced limp, executing a curious dance on his toes. His beard was fuller and already salted with grey. Both of them wore tunics and gartered trousers. Each had a dagger concealed in his belt.

As they flitted through the streets, they felt the first drops of rain. They were on the west bank of the Ouse, the river that flowed through the heart of York before greeting its tributary, the Foss, with a liquid kiss beyond the city walls. When they came round the angle of a house they halted in their tracks. Directly ahead of them, rising into the night sky like a small mountain, was the castle they had so meticulously studied during daylight hours. It looked indomitable. Its sheer bulk taunted them.

Rain now began to fall in earnest, but the younger man ignored it. His eyes traced the outline of the stronghold with the calculating ardour of a lover appraising his mistress before their first embrace.

'There it is!' he whispered.

'If only we knew what is inside.'

'We *do* know.'

'We may only be guessing.'

'We know,' affirmed the other. 'My father helped to build this place. He described it to me in great detail.'

'It has altered since then.'

'Not much. They lavished their time and money on *that*.' He pointed across the river to an even bigger castle that climbed out of the shadows. The two citadels were monuments to military might, twin sentinels that protected York from attack without while discouraging any thoughts of insurrection within.

'Two Norman castles,' said the older man ruefully. 'York is doubly cursed. I would love to torch them both.'

'Think only of one tonight. This is our target.'

'I am ready.'

'Are you sure?'

'Yes,' said the other, mastering his apprehension.

'I need a strong man at my side, not a fearful one.'

'I am with you.'

'That heartens me.'

They embraced in a brief display of friendship, then steeled themselves for the task ahead. The younger man led the way furtively through the dripping darkness.

The castle loomed malevolently above them. Fronted by a deep ditch, its walls were high earthen banks surmounted by a wooden palisade. Night painted out the gaudy colours in which the timberwork had been daubed. As they slithered down the bank, they found the ditch filled with accumulated refuse. One man swore under his breath as his foot slipped on human excrement, the other was startled when he trod on the putrefying body of a dead dog. They held their breath and scrambled up the bank towards the palisade.

The young man uncoiled the rope he had been carrying over his shoulder. It already had a loop tied in the end. He swung it a few times before tossing it high above him. It bounced harmlessly off the wood and caught his companion a smarting blow across the face as it came snaking back down. The rope was pulled in, partially coiled, then swung in the air before being hurled upwards again. The aim was true this time. The loop settled over one of the upright timbers which had been sharpened to a spike.

They waited for a few minutes to make sure that the thud of the rope had not aroused any of the guards on the ramparts. Satisfied that they were unobserved, the younger man tested the rope before shinning up it with speed and agility. When he reached the top, he peered over the palisade to take inventory of the manpower. They were in luck. Only a handful of sentries had been posted on the walls and they were too busy complaining to each other about the wet weather to notice the lone figure who now rolled over the palisade and crouched on the rampart.

A tug on the rope signalled a second ascent. The man with the limp had strong arms and he was soon hauling himself over the palisade to kneel beside his accomplice. Torches flickered in the courtyard below to illumine a large oval area dotted with wooden buildings. Raucous laughter identified the guard house, and the stables were also easy to locate. Barracks and storerooms lay under the wall. Sheep and cattle were kept in separate open pens. A low fire still burned in the armourer's forge.

The keep was at the far end of the bailey. Constructed of solid oak and sitting atop a huge mound, it was encircled by a ditch which was in turn defended by a palisade of sharpened stakes. The soaring tower looked impregnable.

'We'll never get in there,' hissed the older man.

'We must.'

'But *how*?'

'Watch me.' The younger man retrieved the rope and coiled it up again. Though the thickening rain hindered their movement and obscured their vision, it also came to their aid. Grumbling guards shuffled away to take cover. The intruders were able to scurry along the rampart without fear of being seen. When they were close to the keep, they sat hunched against the palisade while they took their bearings. A strange odour drifted into their nostrils.

'What's that foul smell?' said the younger man.

'Normans.'

'I've never known such a stench.' He surveyed the keep for a full minute. 'I'll go first. Wait until I'm inside before you leave the rampart.'

'God go with you!'

'Amen!'

He checked to see that nobody was looking, then hurried down the wooden steps into the courtyard. Moving towards the rear of the keep, he chose a part of the palisade that was largely obscured from the bailey. It was lower than the wall they had already scaled and his rope found its target on the first throw. Within a second, he was up and over the initial line of defence.

The older man was about to follow when a great roar went up from beyond the palisade. The noise was so loud and so savage that it seemed to fill the whole castle. His friend cried out in terror but his voice was drowned beneath a second blood-curdling roar. Guards came running, lights appeared at windows in the keep, and the animals in the courtyard were restive. Wanting to rescue his companion, the figure on the ramparts was frozen by fear.

He caught one last glimpse of his friend. The younger man clambered up the inside of the palisade and tried to climb over it but something caught him from behind with a triumphant roar and began to drag him back down. As the courtyard filled with soldiers, the older man looked to his own safety. His accomplice was beyond salvation. Impaled on the sharp stakes, he was howling in agony as unseen tormentors attacked him from below.

The man on the ramparts took to his heels. With the roaring still in his ears, he flung himself unceremoniously over the palisade and dropped through the darkness into the filth of the ditch. Bruised by the fall, he yet had enough strength to drag himself to his feet and limp off in the direction of the river. His mind was ablaze, and he was further impeded by the weight of the terrible news that he bore.

The lions of York were still dining noisily behind him.

Chapter One

'Who *is* he?' demanded Canon Hubert with frank disdain.

'Tanchelm of Ghent,' said Gervase.

'I know his name and his country of origin. But what of his character, his rank, his fitness for this important work? In short, what manner of man is this Tanchelm of Ghent and why is he being allowed to interfere in our affairs?'

'He is coming to aid and to advise us, Canon Hubert.'

'We need no aid,' argued the other vehemently. 'We require no advice. Did we not discharge our duties ably enough in the Savernake Forest? Were we not decisive in our handling of the irregularities in the Blackwater Estuary? Have we not earned praise for our success in Archenfield?'

'We have indeed.'

'All that was achieved on our own, Gervase.'

'True enough.'

'Then answer me this. If we can manage perfectly well without him in Wiltshire, in Essex and in Herefordshire, why are we saddled with Tanchelm of Ghent when we ride to that heathen wasteland known as Yorkshire?'

'It is the King's express wish.'

'We do not *want* another commissioner.'

'Royal command overrides our own inclinations.'

Canon Hubert sulked in silence. He was sitting astride his donkey, close to the half-built cathedral up on the hill. It was shortly after dawn and the city of Lincoln was already bursting into life below them.

Gervase Bret, also mounted, hid his amusement behind an expression of studied neutrality. The young Chancery clerk remembered only too well how long and how vociferously Hubert had resisted the summons to take up his present role, contending, with righteous indignation, that he had been called to serve God in Winchester rather than to oblige the Conqueror by journeying to inhospitable corners of his kingdom. Yet this same reluctant canon was now boasting about their earlier triumphs and strongly resisting the addition of a new member to their commission. Canon Hubert did not want to share any of their glory with a stranger.

He came out of his silence to repeat his question. 'Who is Tanchelm of Ghent?'

'I do not know,' admitted Gervase. 'All I can tell you is that he has substantial holdings in this county.'

'Then why does he not stay to look after them instead of obstructing our deliberations?'

'He has been sent to assist us, Canon Hubert.'

'Unnecessarily.'

'I disagree. We have a large number of cases to examine, some of them so tangled that we may be grateful for an extra pair of hands to help unravel them. This is by far our most onerous assignment. We must look to spend at least a fortnight in the North Riding alone.'

Hubert emitted a groan of despair and rolled his eyes towards heaven in supplication. The adipose canon was not enjoying the journey to Yorkshire. He was a poor traveller at the best of times, and they had been on the road for over a week already. Lincoln seemed like a beacon of hope after the interminable ride from Winchester, and he had expected to be welcomed and soothed by Bishop Remigius himself. Instead, since the bishop was absent from the city, Hubert had spent the night at the home of one of the secular canons. Having arrived in Lincoln too late to see anything of the place, they were now leaving too early to permit anything but the most cursory exploration. It was galling.

There was another reason for Hubert's deep frustration. It came out through the gate of the nearby castle. Ralph Delchard rode at the head of a troop of fifteen men-at-arms from his personal retinue, but it was not the sight of the Norman lord which offended Hubert. He was accustomed to the mocking joviality of his fellow commissioner by now. What he could not get used to – still less approve – was the presence at Ralph's side of an attractive and gracious woman.

Golde had drifted into their lives during their stay in Hereford, and she would assuredly have drifted out again if circumstances had not thrown her and Ralph Delchard together. She was now his constant companion. Gervase was very fond of her, but Hubert regarded the Saxon woman as an irritating encumbrance and a symbol of moral decay.

'Good morrow!' called Ralph. Golde offered a warm smile by way of greeting.

Gervase gave them a cheery wave but Hubert merely grunted in acknowledgement. Brother Simon, faithful scribe to the commission, could not even manage a grunt. He lurked in the shadows a short distance away and watched Golde with mute disquiet. Women of all kinds unsettled him, and he had taken the cowl partly as a means of isolating himself from the terror of their tenderness. What scandalised him was that Golde had such a close and candid relationship with a man to whom she was not married. In Simon's codex, she was anathema. He was being forced to travel alongside someone who deserved excommunication.

'Where is our new colleague?' asked Ralph, reining in his horse. 'He should have been here at first light.'

'Let us ride on without him,' urged Hubert.

'We have orders to wait.'

'Our embassy will brook no delay.'

'He will not be long,' said Gervase. 'Tanchelm dwells nearby. And it would be foolish to continue without the additional escort that he will surely bring.'

'Wise words,' agreed Ralph. 'The road to York is a long one and many bands of outlaws haunt it in search of easy prey. We will need all the swords that we can muster in order to ensure our safe passage.' He beamed at Golde. 'And to guarantee the lady complete protection.'

'I fear nothing when I am at your side, my lord,' she said softly. A spluttering noise drew her attention to the figure in the shadows. 'I did not see you there, Brother Simon. Good day to you!'

To be in Golde's company was ordeal enough for him; to be addressed directly by her was like a sudden descent into Purgatory with no intervening stops. Brother Simon shut his eyes tight, crossed himself and began to pray vigorously. Ralph came across to tease him but the clatter of hooves diverted his attention away from the Benedictine monk.

Clad in helm and hauberk, with his cloak trailing behind him in the wind, a tall, stately man in his forties was cantering up the hill on his destrier. At his back, riding in formation, were a dozen soldiers with an array of weapons. Sumpter horses were pulled along behind the cavalcade, which scattered pedestrians in the narrow street. When they reached the waiting commissioners, the newcomers came to a halt and drew up in a semicircle. Their leader nudged his mount forward and bestowed a disarming smile upon them.

'Welcome to Lincoln!' he said affably. 'I am Tanchelm of Ghent.'

Aubrey Maminot was a genial man of middle years with an almost boyish eagerness about him. Time had silvered his hair and etched lines into his face, but it had stolen none of his restless energy. As he discussed preparations with his steward, he paced up and down the hall at the castle, his gown billowing and his heels clacking on the oaken boards.

'Venison served with frumenty,' he decided.

'Yes, my lord.'

'Or maybe lamb would be more to their taste.'

'We will have both, my lord. With a dozen other dishes beside them.'

'Spiced rabbit must be on offer as well,' said Aubrey. 'I want my guests to be well fed during their stay.'

'When will they arrive?'

'In a day or two at most.'

'And how many of them will be staying at the castle?'

'That remains to be seen, Bodin. Ralph Delchard's letter spoke of five or six, but they will bring a sizeable escort as well. I want them to have all the comforts of the castle. Ralph is an old friend of mine and deserves the best that we may offer here in York.'

'I understand, my lord.'

'They will banquet in here on their first evening.'

'Everything will be put in readiness.'

Bodin was a dark and slightly sinister individual, but Aubrey had always found him a most efficient steward of his household. Quiet, watchful and discreet, Bodin had a quick mind which enabled him to adapt to the ever-changing whims of the castellan. If five or fifty guests arrived at the gate of the castle, he would be able to accommodate them.

'How long will they stay, my lord?' he wondered.

'As long as they choose.'

'Of course.'

'My home is theirs while they are in the city.'

Bodin gave a polite bow and backed away, electing to make the kitchen his first call. Aubrey Maminot continued to strut around the hall with proprietary zeal. Razed to the ground on more than one occasion, the castle had been rebuilt with greater solidity and a sense of permanence. Its castellan liked to think that he had transformed the keep into something more than a mere fortress. The hall and the apartments had touches of style and luxury that were not usually met with so far north.

As he glanced across at the long table, he imagined it laden with a magnificent banquet, set out with exquisite taste, steam rising from a selection of appetising dishes that would tempt the most jaded palate. For a few moments, the room seemed to fill with music, song, dance, and the happy laughter of his guests. It would be good to share a goblet of wine and a wealth of reminiscence with Ralph Delchard. He chuckled as he recalled the last occasion on which he had met his friend. A knock on the door invaded his reverie.

'Come in!' he snapped.

The door opened to reveal a short, stocky figure in a sleeveless coat of toughened hide which showed off his taut muscles. Black hair and a black beard framed a handsome face with a Mediterranean swarthiness. Broad wristlets of studded hide set off the matted hair on his forearms. The man somehow combined the appearance of a serf with the arrogance of a lord. Legs set apart, he stood there with his hands on his hips.

Aubrey Maminot smiled at his visitor with an almost paternal affection and bustled across to him. 'Ludovico!'

'You sent for me.'

'I wanted to know how they are.'

'Fine, my lord. Fine.'

'Have they settled down?'

'They are sleeping. I did not disturb them. I will feed them later when they wake up.'

'Call me. I would like to be there.'

'Yes, my lord.'

There was no trace of obeisance in Ludovico's manner. Secure in his position and confident of Aubrey Maminot's indulgence, the little Italian had an air of independence about him that was envied by the rest of the castle. He also had a success with the ladies that aroused a darker envy among some of the men. Because he could offer a service that nobody in York could match, Ludovico basked in his master's favouritism and wallowed in the female attention that he invariably excited.

'Who was he?'

'We do not yet know,' confessed Aubrey.

'What was he doing in the castle?'

'That, too, remains a matter for speculation.'

'How did he get inside?'

'There, we are on firmer ground,' said Aubrey with a flash of anger. 'He scaled the wall by means of a rope and walked the rampart unchallenged. The captain of the guard has been disciplined. The dolt had the temerity to blame the heavy rain last night. I expect vigilance in all weathers.'

'Was the man alone?'

'No, Ludovico. He had an accomplice. A figure was seen hurling himself over the top of the palisade. When they searched outside with torches, they found the place where someone had landed heavily and slithered down into the ditch. His only concern was to save his own skin. He obviously abandoned his friend to his grisly fate.'

'The intruder paid dearly for his boldness,' said the other. 'He came up against a line of defence that can never be breached.'

'Thanks to you.'

'And to you, my lord. Who brought us here?'

'I did,' said Aubrey with a complacent grin, 'and it was the most sensible decision I ever made. I know that you miss Italy and hate our Yorkshire winters, but I tell you this, Ludovico. With the three of you beside me, I sleep so much more soundly in my bed.'

'That is why we are here, my lord.'

'It is part of the reason.' Aubrey became brusque. 'I have instruction for you. Important visitors will soon arrive at the castle. They are here on royal business and must be given every assistance. But they need entertainment as well.'

'I follow, my lord.'

'The animals must be on their very best behaviour.'

'Leave that to me.'

'I always do, Ludovico.'

'Have they ever seen lions before?'

'No,' said Aubrey, cheeks glowing with pride. 'Not like mine. Nobody has ever seen lions like mine!'

Tanchelm of Ghent was an amiable man who went out of his way to befriend his companions. Introduced to them in turn at Lincoln, he quickly identified Canon Hubert as the person who would be most difficult to win over. As they left the city and rode north along Ermine Street, he fell in beside Hubert's donkey and struck up a conversation.

'I must offer my profound apologies,' he began.

'Apologies?'

'For foisting myself upon you like this. It is not by choice. King William gave order that I should join your commission. Left to myself, I own, I would much rather have stayed on my estates, immersed in my books.'

'Your books?'

'I am a reading man, Canon Hubert. I would willingly put a soldier's life behind me for good and spend the rest of my days in the simple joys of study and meditation.'

'Indeed?' Hubert was impressed. Tanchelm of Ghent was a Flemish mercenary who had fought beside the Duke of Normandy at Hastings and been richly rewarded. The likelihood was that he would be a boorish warrior with a compulsion to take control and to have everything on his terms. Instead, he turned out to be an intelligent and sensitive man who spoke Norman French without a whisper of a Flemish accent. When Tanchelm described some of the titles in his library, the canon was even more impressed.

'You have read Boethius?' he said in surprise.

'Many times.'

'And the Venerable Bede?'

'I can quote parts of *Historia Ecclesiastica* verbatim.'

'I wish that all soldiers exchanged the sword for the

written word quite so readily,' said Hubert with a meaningful glance at Ralph Delchard up ahead of him. 'But some, I fear, are beyond recall.' He turned to look shrewdly at Tanchelm. 'May I ask what your appointed role is, my lord?'

'To lend what assistance I may.'

'Yes, but in what capacity?'

'The King advises me that I sit in commission as an equal partner with you, but I realise that that would be an act of gross presumption on my part.'

'Presumption?'

'You are all experienced,' said Tanchelm respectfully, 'while I am a mere novice. You have sat in judgement before; I have little knowledge of legal matters. I have so much to learn, Canon Hubert, but I am a willing pupil. I have that in my favour. Be patient with me and I will soon grow to be of some practical use to you.'

'I am sure that you will, my lord.'

'In the meantime, overlook my folly and pardon my ignorance. Have no fear that I will challenge your decisions. I defer to you and the others at all times.'

'That is very reassuring.'

'My presence may lend additional weight to the commission, but I cannot promise that my voice will supply any illumination. I am content to be guided by wiser heads.'

Canon Hubert was delighted to hear these remarks, and he questioned Tanchelm closely to make sure that the sentiments he was expressing were genuine and not simply a means of ingratiating himself. Prompt with his answers, their new colleague seemed quite sincere. His soft-spoken manner endeared him to Hubert, who spent much of his time battling with the blunt and assertive Ralph Delchard. It was refreshing to meet a soldier who did not treat an argument as an excuse for a verbal cavalry charge. The canon began to see Tanchelm as a potential ally against the nominal leader of the commission. Only one more query needed to be raised.

'Why do you think that you were chosen for this work?'

Tanchelm gave a wry smile. 'You must ask that of the King himself, for he did the choosing.'

'You must have some idea why his eye settled on you.'

'I have done him good service in the past.'

'As a paid soldier?'

'Yes,' conceded the other easily. 'I do not deny that I fought for money. It is a more tangible reward than honour. My wealth enabled me to buy the time to educate myself, so I feel that the end more than justified the means. But I have not only been employed on the battlefield, Canon Hubert.'

'Oh?'

'I speak five languages. A legacy of having lived and fought in a number of countries. The King has seen fit to use me, in a small way, as a kind of ambassador.' He gave a shrug. 'I can only think that my mean skills in foreign courts recommended me for this assignment. Beyond that, my sole qualification is the one that we all share.'

'And what is that?'

'We are outsiders,' said Tanchelm. 'None of us was

born or brought up in Yorkshire. We have no personal interest in the county which could blur our perception or sway our judgement. That is vital.'

'Impartiality is our touchstone.'

'Even so.'

Hubert inhaled deeply. 'Let me tell you why *I* was selected to assist in the compilation of this Great Survey . . .'

Modesty had never gained more than the most superficial purchase on Canon Hubert and, as a result, his crushing self-importance went largely unchecked. He trumpeted his virtues for a mile or more without the slightest sense of his own vanity. Tanchelm showed remarkable patience and forbearance. Hubert warmed to him even more.

When they stopped to take refreshment, Tanchelm strode across to join Ralph Delchard and Golde. Locked together in their own private world, they had ridden at the head of the column and set a steady pace. It was now time to relax and to mix with their fellow travellers. They gave Tanchelm a smile of welcome.

'What do you think of Lincolnshire?' he said.

'It has much to commend it,' replied Golde.

'No,' said Ralph, shaking his head. 'The county is too flat and too featureless for my liking. All this undrained fenland. The place is virtually a peninsula. Why on earth did you choose to live here?'

'I like it,' said Tanchelm. 'More to the point, so does my wife. She would not live anywhere else.'

'Why not?' wondered Golde.

'She was born here.'

'Your wife is a Saxon?'

'No, my lady. She comes of Viking stock. We are standing at the very heart of the old Danelaw. Look at the names of the places around here, listen to the speech of the people. The Danes left heavy footprints in this county.'

'I'm surprised they did not sink up to their waists in water,' said Ralph. 'I do not like wet terrain. It makes me feel seasick.'

They chatted happily until they were ready to mount and move on. Ralph and Golde again led the way, and Tanchelm now took up a position at the end of the cavalcade, where Gervase Bret and Brother Simon were absorbed in earnest discussion.

He nudged his horse gently between them. 'Do I intrude?' he said.

'Not at all, my lord,' said Gervase. 'Ride with us.'

'I would hate to interrupt a private conversation.'

'It was more of a friendly debate, one which Brother Simon and I have been having for some time.'

'May I know its substance?'

'The Benedictine Rule.'

'A worthy subject for argument.'

'I was destined for the cowl myself at one point, but I drew back from taking my vows. Brother Simon has just been reminding me of some of the rewards of monastic life.'

'They are beyond my reach, alas.' Tanchelm turned to Simon with a half-smile of regret, but the monk was far too timorous to make any comment. The presence of this soldier and his men-at-arms was reassuring at one level, but it was also overwhelming. Brother Simon was travelling in the company of over thirty people, yet there were only two of them – Canon Hubert and Gervase Bret – with whom he had anything in common. He felt lost and vulnerable.

Seeing his profound discomfort, Gervase tried to steer the conversation away from the hapless monk. 'We are pleased to have you with us, my lord,' he said.

'It is an honour to sit in commission with you.'

'That is an opinion you may care to revise when you have spent endless days in a draughty shire hall, listening to property disputes. It can be tedious work.'

'The boredom is not unrelieved,' said Tanchelm. 'From what I hear, your investigations have a habit of throwing up a certain amount of excitement.'

'Unhappily, yes.'

'You have something of a reputation.'

'Who told you that, my lord?'

'I have many friends in Winchester. In any case, it was implicit in the orders which I received from the King himself.'

Gervase was astonished. 'King William spoke of us?'

'Yes,' said Tanchelm. 'By name. He holds you in high regard. Why else should he choose to send you to Yorkshire? There are other teams of commissioners, dispersed throughout other counties to look into questionable claims sent in to the Exchequer. Yet they were not singled out for the long journey to York. That reward fell to you.'

'It could also be seen as a punishment.'

'The King trusts you, Master Bret. He has always

been able to recognise able lieutenants. That is how I know that Ralph Delchard, Canon Hubert, Brother Simon here and your good self must be a formidable team.' He gave Gervase a smile of admiration. 'I repeat, it is an honour to join you.'

Ermine Street, the great highway between London and York, showed scant respect for any variations in contour. It arrowed its way north with Roman straightness, dealing with obstacles in its path by cutting through them. They were able to make steady progress before spending the night at a small village in the north of the county.

Inclement weather delayed their start on the next day and enforced a change of route. When they reached the Humber Estuary, they found it so broad and uninviting, so wild and so windswept, that Ralph Delchard, a reluctant sailor, abandoned the plan to cross by means of the ferry and instead struck west along the bank of the river. The detour slowed them still more and sapped the vestiges of their good humour. By the time they finally reached Howden in the East Riding, they were bedraggled and dispirited.

Like everyone else in the party, Golde fell asleep the moment she climbed into bed. They were staying at the local manor house, a long, low building with a thatched roof and a sunken floor. A fairly primitive structure, it made no concessions to comfort and had a musty atmosphere that made them cough when they first encountered it, but it nevertheless seemed like a palace to travellers on the verge of fatigue.

Golde was sharing a small bay with Ralph. When she awoke in the night, she was alarmed to find that he was no longer beside her. She dressed quickly and went in search of him, feeling her way to the door in the gloom. He was nowhere inside the building. Golde eventually found him at the rear of the house, sitting pensively on a chopping block and staring straight ahead of him. The storm had abated and a crescent moon now picked out everything in sharp profile.

She ran across to him on tiptoe and touched his arm. 'What ails you?' she said.

'Nothing, my love.'

'Then what has brought you out here?'

'I could not sleep.'

'After a day like the one we had?'

'I felt the need for some fresh air.' He stood up and slipped an arm around her. 'But there is no need for you to be out here at this hour.'

'I want to be with you.'

'Rest while you have the chance. I am used to a long day in the saddle. You are not. Go back inside.'

'Only when you have told me the truth.'

'About what?'

'This, Ralph. Sitting out here alone in the darkness. It is not like you. Something is troubling your mind and I will not leave your side until I know what it is.'

'Golde . . .'

'Do not think to fob me off with an excuse.'

'It is nothing that need concern you.'

'Everything about Ralph Delchard concerns me,' she said firmly. 'I left my home and my sister to be with you, and I have never had a moment's regret about that decision.'

He grinned. 'Not even this afternoon in that downpour?'

'Not even then.' She kissed him lightly. 'Now, tell me.'

Ralph heaved a sigh. 'There is not much to tell.'

'Then it will not keep us out here much longer.'

He pulled her close and held her in both arms. Golde had brought a happiness into his life that he had never thought to experience again. In the short time they had been together, she had rekindled something in him which had lain dormant since the death of his wife and which no other woman had been able to reach, let alone ignite. Golde was right to remind him of the sacrifices she had made in order to follow him. Having committed herself so completely, she was entitled to know what was worrying him, however painful it might be for him to tell her.

He sat her on the block of wood and knelt beside her. 'I hope you will not despise me,' he said quietly. 'It is not a pleasant tale.'

'I love you, Ralph.'

'My story may test the strength of that love.'

'You will not find it wanting,' she promised. 'No more evasion. What brought you out here tonight?'

'Guilt.'

'I do not understand.'

'How could you, Golde? Only those who were actually here could really understand the full horror of that time.'

'What time?'

'When I last visited this God-forsaken county.'

'You have been to Yorkshire before?'

'Oh, yes,' he said soulfully. 'I came once before. Many years ago, at the heels of the Conqueror himself. And we left the most dreadful legacy of our visit. As soon as I stepped on to Yorkshire soil again, the guilt rose up in me until I could hardly contain it.'

'But why? What did you do?'

'We wreaked havoc. We came to put down a revolt but we stayed to exact the most hideous revenge. I have never seen the Conqueror so angry. He was shaking with fury. The rebels dared to challenge his kingship for the third time in a row, and he vowed that they would never be able to do it again.'

'I recall it now. The King executed their leaders.'

'He did much more than that, Golde. He ordered us to lay waste the whole county. And when Yorkshire was torn asunder, we were to visit the same grisly fate on Northumbria. That was our appointed task – the Harrying of the North.'

'News of the terror even reached us in Hereford.'

'We committed every crime of which man is capable. We did not just kill our enemies, we destroyed everything in our path. We tore down houses, burned crops, slaughtered animals. King William can be a cruel man when roused, and Yorkshire bore the brunt of his cruelty. We starved this county into submission, Golde. The famine was unending. Men, women and children died of hunger in their thousands. The place was a wilderness.' He stood up. 'And the shameful truth is that I helped to make it like that.'

'I can see why it sits heavy on your conscience.'

'I shudder when I think of what we did. It is not something of which I am proud. It makes me feel sick. Now that I am back, I am aching with remorse.'

She rose. 'What are you going to do about it?'

'I do not know.'

Golde was moved. He had risked her contempt by admitting his part in a vicious act of vengeance, but he was making no bid for her sympathy. His anguish was something that he alone had to bear. It could not be soothed away with kind words from her. Golde was grateful for his honesty. She was shocked by his confession, but she was also touched that he felt able to reveal a more sensitive side to his character. They stood there without saying a word. Ralph grappled with his remorse while she tried to assimilate the full import of what he had told her.

The silence did not last long. A violent explosion of noise made the pair of them leap involuntarily apart. A quiet night was suddenly alive with noise and movement. Men were shouting, swords clashing, horses neighing, and a dog barked incessantly. Sounds of a fierce struggle came from the stables. Ralph reached instinctively for Golde and shielded her with his body as he hustled her to the safety of the house.

Once she was out of danger, he drew his dagger and moved towards the gathering pandemonium around the stables. All he could see was a mass of bodies and horses, swirling about in darkness. The clamour had woken everyone in the house and servants came running with torches. Soldiers billeted in neighbouring dwellings had also been roused from their slumbers, but they reacted too slowly to the emergency.

As Ralph moved in, a voice gave a stern command.

'Away!'

Before he could get any closer, he was caught in a stampede and buffeted to the ground by plunging animals. As he rolled over in the mud, he heard triumphant jeers rising above the thunder of departing hooves.

'Damnation!' he roared. 'They've stolen the horses!'

He was back on his feet in an instant, cursing the thieves, calling for light and slashing the air with his dagger to relieve his anger. The whole household seemed to be converging on him. The stables were no more than a series of ramshackle huts at the side of the property. Ralph had left two of his men-at-arms to sleep in the straw so that they might guard the area, and his immediate concern was for them. He grabbed the first blazing torch that reached him in order to see what had befallen his sentries.

Commotion was still at its height. The remaining horses were highly disturbed, the chickens squawked, the dog yapped louder than ever and Canon Hubert's donkey brayed with such ear-splitting force that its owner came trotting out of the house to join the throng. Ralph found the first of his men lying prostrate by the open door of the stables. Blood oozed from a gash in his temple but he was only dazed and seemed otherwise uninjured.

More torches came to illumine the whole stable area. Knocked unconscious, the second of Ralph's guards lay face down in the straw. When they turned him over, they saw no apparent wounds on him. Ralph was relieved to find both men still alive. Gervase Bret, armed with a sword, pushed his way through the crowd to get to his friend.

'What happened?' he asked.

'Robbers.'

'How many of them were there?'

'Six or seven,' said Ralph. 'It was impossible to be certain. They overpowered my men and made off with some of the horses. *And* our supplies,' he added with a fresh surge of rage as he noted the empty stall where their packs had been stored. 'Hell's teeth! I'll run every last one of them to ground and hack him into small pieces!'

The tumult was slowly fading. The horses were calmed, the chickens settled down, the dog was silenced by a kick from its master, and the donkey stopped braying when a providential carrot was thrust into its mouth by the resourceful Canon Hubert. Everyone was waiting for a decision from Ralph Delchard. He was no penitent now, reflecting with sadness on the Harrying of the North. This outrage had turned him into a stern and implacable warrior who met every reverse with a swift counter-attack.

'Saddle up!' he yelled. 'We ride after them!'

The soldiers responded until another voice intervened.

'Stay!' shouted Tanchelm, holding up a hand. 'Do not be so hasty. This needs more thought.'

Ralph was peremptory. 'I lead here,' he asserted. 'I will not have my orders countermanded.'

'That is not what I am doing.'

'Then stand aside and hinder us no longer.'

'I merely counsel a moment's consideration.'

'The more we talk, the further away the rogues will ride. Stay here with your own men, my lord. I have swords enough to deal with this villainy. Nobody steals from me with impunity!'

Before Tanchelm could protest, Ralph barked a command to the captain of his men-at-arms, then ran into the house to put on his hauberk and to apprise Golde of what had taken place. His horse was tacked up and waiting by the time he reappeared and he swung himself up into the saddle. With ten men at his back, some of them bearing torches, he rode off into the night at a canter.

Golde came out to tend the wounded man, stemming the blood and bathing his temple with a piece of cloth dipped in a bowl of water. The victim was soon able to give them a hazy account of what had transpired during the scuffle. His companion, whose bare head had been struck from behind with a wooden stake, would take much longer to recover. Gervase made sure that both men were being looked after before he moved across to join Tanchelm of Ghent. The latter was still staring after the posse.

'They are wasting their time,' he sighed.

'My lord, Ralph is a cunning hunter,' said Gervase.

'He would need the eyes of an owl and the speed of an eagle to catch this prey. It is futile. The thieves will know how to shake off pursuit and where they may hide without any chance of being found. This is their territory. They hold all the advantages.'

'Ralph would never forgive himself if he did not at least try to recover what was stolen. He will see the theft as a personal insult that must be answered.'

'I admire his bravado,' said Tanchelm, 'but I fear that it is tinged with madness. He did not even pause long enough to see what exactly was taken.'

'Our men were attacked, our property stolen. That is surely grounds enough for leading a posse, is it not?'

Tanchelm shook his head. 'Two guards were attacked, I grant you, but they were only knocked senseless when they might just as easily have been killed. Does not that tell you something about our nocturnal visitors?'

Gervase shrugged. 'Only that they were thieves rather than mindless butchers.'

'Most outlaws in this part of England are both.'

'Are you suggesting that they showed a degree of mercy? That does not lessen the severity of their crime, my lord. They stole our horses.'

'But not at random.'

'What do you mean?'

'They knew precisely what they wanted and took only that.' He pointed to the stables. 'Did you go inside and see what we lost? Have you reckoned up the cost? Five sumpter horses and the remainder of our provisions. That was their chosen target.'

'How did they know what was here?' said Gervase.

'They watched us. Hostile eyes have been upon us since we came into this county. They watched and they waited for their moment. Their strike was decisive.'

'That is certainly true. But why pick on us, my lord? We ride with a large escort. Others travel in smaller groups as more inviting quarry. Why did they select us?'

Tanchelm stroked his chin. 'I can think of two explanations. The first is that our purpose in coming to Yorkshire was known and our identity recognised. What happened tonight was merely a warning to us.'

'A warning?'

'Administered by someone who stands to lose heavily by our presence here. You have seen the cases we have to look into, Master Bret. Some involve sizeable amounts of land. If our judgement goes against them, a number of people could be far poorer as a result of our visit. They are trying to intimidate us in advance.'

'Then their plan has foundered,' said Gervase sharply. 'We would never bend to that kind of pressure. It will take much more than a raid on our horses to frighten us. But you said there were two explanations.'

'Yes,' said Tanchelm with a smile. 'The second one is much simpler. On balance, I must admit that I favour it.'

'And what might it be, my lord?'

'They stole our food for a very obvious reason.'

'Go on.'

'They were hungry.'

Chapter Two

The brooch was strikingly beautiful. Craftsmanship of a high order had gone into its design and execution. Two inches long at most, it was made of decorated gold so subtly worked into the shape of a lion that the creature seemed almost to be alive. The tiny diamond eye glinted with ferocity and the claws reached out with savage intent, yet the animal remained somehow tame and unthreatening. It was truly the king of the beasts in miniature, and the man who had commissioned it was overjoyed with the result. Holding it in the palm of his hand, he stared down at it with open-mouthed awe.

Hunched obsequiously, the jeweller watched him closely. 'Are you pleased, my lord?' he asked nervously.

'Oh, yes. Oh, yes.'

'I followed your instructions to the letter.'

'That is evident.'

'It was a privilege to create such a piece.'

'Exquisite,' said the customer, turning the brooch over to examine the rear. 'A work of art.'

'Thank you, my lord. The pin, as you see, is exceedingly delicate, so that it can pierce any material without causing damage. Your lion will scratch but never tear.'

Aubrey Maminot chuckled. He was so taken with the brooch that he was even prepared to tolerate the jeweller's feeble sense of humour. They were standing in a shop in Hornpot Lane, a busy little thoroughfare that wound its way down from Petergate, and had once been largely the preserve of craftsmen who worked in horn, antler, ivory and animal bone. Jewellers now developed their skills with gold, silver, amber, jet and semi-precious stones. Norman overlords were the bane of York, but they had money to spend.

'Will you take it with you, my lord?' said the jeweller.

'Of course.'

'I can deliver it by hand to the castle, if you prefer.'

'It will be safer in my keeping.'

'Yes, my lord. As you wish.' The jeweller took the brooch and wrapped it gently in a piece of material before slipping it into a leather pouch. With a simpering smile, he gave the pouch to the customer. 'Only one thing remains, my lord.'

'Yes,' said Aubrey happily. 'I must present the gift to the lady for whom it was fashioned.'

'I trust that your wife will be satisfied with it.'

'Have no qualms on that score.' Aubrey turned to go but the jeweller shuffled after him.

'My lord . . .'

'What is it now?'

'There is the small matter of payment.'

'The price was agreed beforehand, was it not?'

'It was indeed.'

'And my credit is good, I believe?'

'Above reproach, my lord.'

'Then why this unseemly rush?' said Aubrey fussily. 'I will acquaint my steward with the nature of this transaction and he will bring the money accordingly.'

'When might that be?' asked the other tentatively.

'Soon, my friend. Very soon.'

Aubrey Maminot swept out of the shop with his golden lion. He felt that it was a gift that would melt any woman's heart and he was anxious to bestow it on the recipient at once, but another priority called. Word had reached him that his guests would be entering the city within the hour. It was vital to be at the castle to welcome them. Putting the brooch in his purse, he mounted his horse and cut a path through the jostling crowds.

Long before they reached York, they saw it beckoning to them on the horizon. Its sheer size and solidity were reassuring to the travellers, who had been on the road for two days without seeing anything larger than a village. The two castles rose above the city walls to guarantee their safety and, as they rode ever closer, they could pick out the soaring grandeur of York Minster. Canon Hubert's heart lifted at the sight, and Brother Simon – still riding at the rear of the column in order to be at the furthest point from what he saw as the contaminating presence of an immoral woman – sent up a silent prayer of thanks and consoled himself with the thought that he could cleanse himself in the spiritual haven ahead of them.

Ralph Delchard was in a sombre mood. His search

for the horse-thieves had been fruitless and daylight brought no comfort. It was a grim ride north for him. More than fifteen years had passed since his last visit to Yorkshire, and yet the county still bore signs of the devastation inflicted upon it. When Ralph saw the scarred landscape, the undernourished livestock, and the pitiful remains of abandoned hovels, his guilt stirred again. A whole generation had suffered in the wake of the sustained destruction in which he took part.

What troubled his conscience most was the sight of the people themselves, living reminders of a past that they would never outrun. Proud of their Anglo-Danish heritage, they saw the Normans as cruel usurpers. As the long cavalcade of armed soldiers wended its way to York, everyone in the fields looked up at it with the resentment of the vanquished and the resignation of the forlorn.

Seated beside him on her palfrey, Golde grew weary of his brooding silence. They were riding a few yards ahead of the following column and thus had a small measure of privacy. She decided to use it in order to separate Ralph from his recriminations.

'There is no point in dwelling on it,' she said.

'On what?'

'The past.'

'Is that what I am doing?'

'Your face was not designed for deception.'

A little smile. 'Can you read it so easily?'

'Easily but not happily,' said Golde. 'There is no pleasure for me in travelling beside your distant memories.'

'They are not distant,' explained Ralph, making a sweeping gesture with his arm. 'When I gaze around, those memories are fresh and immediate. As if it all happened yesterday.'

'But it did not.'

'My brain tells me that, but my eyes contradict it.'

'Then shut them,' she said testily. 'If we all let the past drag us down, we might just as well not be alive. This is not the only place to feel the might of the Normans. My own county of Herefordshire suffered dreadfully at your hands.'

'Not to the same extent.'

'That is beside the point, Ralph.'

'Is it?' he said, taken aback by the astringency in her tone. 'Why do you upbraid me thus?'

'Because you deserve it. I respect your right to feel guilty about your part in what happened here all those years ago, but that does not mean you can burden me with your morbid recollections. We must shake off the past, Ralph.'

'How can I when it is all around me?'

'By exerting more will-power. As I have had to do.'

'You, Golde?'

'Yes, my lord.'

'I do not see how you come into this argument.'

'That is because you are too bound up in your own concerns,' she scolded. 'Have you forgotten what I am? And where I lived? I am the daughter of a Saxon thegn. I was born and brought up in a county that was overrun by Norman soldiers. Yet here I am, riding alongside one of those same invaders, instead of staying at home to revile him and his whole race.'

Ralph was stunned. 'Golde, what are you saying?'

'You are one of the conquerors and I am one of the victims. That is naked fact. If I let the events of the past dictate my life, then I would not allow you near me, still less welcome your embraces in my bed.'

'You swore that you loved me.'

'Why, so I do,' she said earnestly, 'and I foolishly hoped that you were likewise prompted by the heart.'

'I was, Golde! I still am!'

'Then why do you hurt my feelings so?'

He was perplexed. 'Have I done that?'

'Yes, my lord.'

'How?'

'By harping on about your uneasy conscience as if it is the only thing that matters. Put yourself in my position for a moment. Imagine that *you* are enduring the miseries of travel to be with the person you love. What would you think if that person became so wrapped up in her memories that you were completely ignored?' Her cheeks were aflame now. 'Why did you invite me on this journey, Ralph? To lie beside you at night and keep loneliness at bay? Is that my sole purpose?'

'No!'

'Then what am I *doing* here?'

He bit back a reply. Taking a deep breath, he tried to compose himself. No woman had ever chastised him so openly and it had caught him on the raw. At the same time, he came to see that he had given Golde just cause for her anger. He had been moody and preoccupied all morning. She had received little courtesy and even less consideration.

'You are right to chide me, my love,' he said.

'I hate myself for having to do it.'

'Blunt speech is what I deserved.'

'It made me sound like a fishwife.'

'I was too distracted by self-affairs,' he admitted. 'I can only beg your forgiveness.'

'It is yours,' she said, touching his arm.

'The events of last night are partly to blame. They left me tired and seething with frustration.'

She stifled a grin. 'I noticed.'

'We searched in vain for hours for those foul villains. I do not like to fail, Golde. It was very painful to have to call off the search.'

'You came back safely; that is the important thing.'

'It is not,' he argued. 'Finding those outlaws was far more important. Yet we could not. That grieves me. I lost five horses and all our provisions.'

'What about me?'

'You?'

'Yes, Ralph,' she said. 'You are thinking only of yourself again. All you lost in those packs were some supplies, but my apparel was also carried by the sumpter horses. Those men made off with my entire wardrobe.'

'Dear God! So they did.'

'What will they think of me in York if all I wear are these mean travelling clothes?'

'The loss will be repaired at once!' decided Ralph. 'The city will have tailors enough to dance to your whims. Order what you wish. My purse is at your command.' A new zest had come into his voice. 'Why do we amble when we should make speed? Onwards!'

Grabbing the reins of her palfrey, he kicked his horse into a brisk trot and pulled her along behind him. The whole company closed in on York in time to hear the Minster bell boom out for Nones.

Micklegate was the only point of entry from the south-east. Once inside the city walls, Ralph led the bulk of his party off towards the castle on the left, leaving Canon Hubert and Brother Simon to continue alone towards the bridge over the River Ouse. Both were relieved to be free of their escort, Hubert because he bore letters to the Archbishop of York and was thus assured of an audience with him, and Simon because the Minster precinct would offer him an escape from the proximity of a lascivious woman, the rough-tongued jocularity of the soldiers, and the foul-smelling sea of humanity which now washed around his ankles.

The others, meanwhile, were being greeted by the castellan. As they clattered into the courtyard, Aubrey Maminot, dressed in his finery and radiating delight, was waiting to embrace his old friend the moment he dismounted.

'Ralph!' he said warmly. 'Welcome to my home!'

'It is good to see you again, Aubrey.'

'We have been apart far too long, my friend. What is it? Seven, eight years?'

'Ten at least!'

'We'll drink away each one of them!' He looked up

hospitably at the rest of the party. 'Welcome, one and all! Treat my castle as your own. You shall lack nothing while you are here.'

He signalled to some waiting men-at-arms and they led the escort off to their quarters on the other side of the bailey. Aubrey was introduced to Gervase Bret and Tanchelm of Ghent and he clasped each in turn, but his most cordial salutation was reserved for Golde. He helped her down from her horse, kissed her hand, pressed her to call on him for anything which she needed, offered to give her a personal tour of the city, then kissed her hand again before turning to Ralph with a sly wink.

'I am so glad that you came to York!' he said.

'We are glad to be here,' said Ralph.

'I have a thousand things to tell you, but they can wait until a more fit time. You are weary from travel on a dusty road. Take your ease and have refreshment. Tonight, you will banquet in the hall and wipe away all memory of the tiresome journey from Winchester.' He spread his arms wide. 'We will set such a feast before you that you will not need to eat for a week. Dress in your brightest array and surrender to my hospitality.'

Golde exchanged a meaningful look with Ralph.

'We are most grateful for your kindness, Aubrey,' he said, 'and we will be delighted to sit at your table. But some of us may not be as gaily-attired as we might wish. Outlaws fell on us in the night and stole the sumpter horses and their packs. Much of our apparel vanished.'

Aubrey was shocked. 'Outlaws! Where?'

'We were staying at the manor house in Howden.'

'And they dared to attack you there?'

'There was no assault on us, my lord,' said Tanchelm, keen to establish the facts. 'The two men guarding the stables were overwhelmed by numbers and our animals were taken. It all happened so quickly that we had no chance to stop them.'

'Did you pursue them?' asked Aubrey.

'Diligently,' said Ralph, 'but we lost them in the darkness. I had not thought to shed any more blood on Yorkshire soil, but I would have done so last night had I caught the rogues. I would dearly love to know what brazen rascals had the effrontery to steal my sumpter horses from beneath my nose.'

'Then I will tell you, old friend.'

'You know?'

'I can hazard a guess. From what you say, the crime was well planned and swiftly executed.'

'Indeed it was.'

'Then we are talking about audacious thieves, who were undeterred by your armed escort and who knew that part of the county so well that they could find their way around it in the pitch dark.'

'They spared our guards,' reminded Tanchelm.

'That makes it certain.'

'I will not spare them when I catch them,' vowed Ralph. 'And I mean to track them down, no matter how long it takes me. Will you help me, Aubrey?'

'In every way I can. But it will not be easy.'

'Why not?'

'The man you seek is a notorious devil. He and his band have evaded me a dozen times or more. Chase them and they will outrun you. Confront them and they will outwit you. Ambush them and they will vanish into the earth like drops of rain.' He gave a bleak smile. 'You have come up against a cunning adversary this time, Ralph.'

'Tell me his name that I may call him to account.'

'It is one that I have cause to rue myself.'

'Who is the villain?'

'Olaf Evil Child.'

There was enough food to last them for days and they fell on it with relish. The cargo had been packed by experienced travellers, men who knew how to provision a long journey and who took account of such contingencies as an unexpected night camping under the stars, or the arrival at a lodging whose kitchens could not cope with the several appetites which descended on them. Bread, cheese and fruit were in abundance. Salted meat, salted fish and cold roasted chicken were also discovered in the horde.

One man cackled with delight as he found a flagon of wine, and he uncorked it at once to take a first guzzling swig, only to spew much of it out again as he learned that French wine was too weak a taste for someone reared on strong English ale. Another of the outlaws located a cache of honey cakes and chomped happily on them. It was a good haul and worth all the risks they had taken.

There were a dozen or more of them, a cheerful crew

dressed in rough garb. Their spears, swords, daggers and other weapons lay on the grass beside them. They had sought the cover of woodland to assuage their hunger and to examine their other spoils. Lookouts had been posted but each man was his own best sentry, eyes constantly scanning the trees and ears pricked to catch the first sound of danger.

Olaf Evil Child sat cross-legged in the middle of them as he searched through the last of the packs. He was a slim, wiry man in his thirties with beard and hair of a reddish tinge. His face had a rugged charm which belied his name and there was a benign twinkle in his eye. Seated beside him was an hirsute giant whose features were all but hidden behind a dark bushy beard. He popped a whole apple into his cavernous mouth, chewed noisily and spat out the pips.

'Have you found them?' he asked.

'No,' said Olaf. 'There's nothing but apparel here. They were probably in those satchels we saw them carrying. It was too much to ask that they'd leave them in the stables as well.' He put the pack aside. 'The horses are the real treasure from last night, Eric.'

'And the food,' said his companion, stuffing another apple into his mouth. 'Normans eat well.'

'So will we for a while.'

'And then what?'

A wistful expression came into Olaf's face. Hauling himself to his feet, he gave Eric a pat on the shoulder before crossing to speak to another of his followers. His orders were brief and explicit. The young man to whom he was speaking nodded as he listened. Olaf Evil Child talked in a quiet voice that yet carried great authority. None of them would ever dare to disobey him. Given his instructions, the young man went straight to his horse, leapt into the saddle and rode off in the direction of York.

A burst of laughter drew Olaf's attention back to Eric. The giant had rummaged through the clothing in the pack to pull out a woman's gown. Holding it up against himself, he lowered his eyelids, struck what he thought was a feminine posture and treated them to a winsome smile. His fellows roared their approval and shouted their advice.

'Put it on, Eric!'

'Over your head!'

'It will hide your ugly face!'

'You could pass for a woman in that gown.'

'A bearded woman!'

Eric responded to the guffaws with a gap-toothed grin.

'You may laugh,' he said, 'but this will buy me a night of pleasure. I know a woman who will be so glad to have this that she will let me lie with her.'

The boast produced a fresh crop of jeers but they were cut short by Olaf. Crossing to his friend, he took the gown from his hands and folded it neatly. 'Find another way to rub thighs with a woman,' he said.

'Why?' asked Eric, bemused.

'Because this gown would only betray us. Give this to some peasant girl and she will be the envy of her friends. They are bound to ask where such a fine garment came from. Word will reach York and they will come looking for her. What woman will not break under torture?'

Eric scratched his head. 'I never thought of that.'

'Pick her some flowers instead.'

'The gown would be a finer present.'

'Only if you want to get her locked in a dungeon.'

'You are right,' said the other, slowly working it out. 'It would be foolhardy. I see that now.'

'Think with your brain instead of with your pizzle.'

'Yes, Olaf.' Eric gave a sheepish smile as the others ridiculed him. Having folded the gown, Olaf put it carefully back with the rest of the wardrobe. He knew what he would do with it.

Aubrey Maminot was determined to erase the bad memories of the long journey made by his guests. The banquet which he set before them that evening, and the entertainment with which it was garnished, were both so lavish that they drove all other thoughts from the mind. Ralph Delchard, Gervase Bret, Tanchelm of Ghent and Golde were treated like visiting dignitaries and they succumbed willingly to the situation. Brother Simon was too terrified to accept his invitation to the feast, and Canon Hubert, weighing the interests of his stomach against the care of his soul, opted for the latter and sampled more moderate fare with the archdeacon at the Minster.

The hall had been swept, strewn with fresh rushes, hung with aromatic herbs and lighted with a veritable host of candles. When Ralph first led Golde into the glittering magnificence of the room they were astounded. He had now exchanged his hauberk for a tunic, mantle and cap, while she was wearing a chemise, gown and wimple borrowed from Aubrey's wife and altered to fit her by a sempstress. Knowing how primitive some castle interiors could be, Ralph was duly impressed by the lengths to which his friend had gone to make the hall both attractive and comfortable.

Golde's nostrils twitched slightly. 'What's that strange odour?' she whispered.

'Herbs.'

'There's something else. More acrid.'

Ralph sniffed. 'I can't smell it.'

Before she could pursue the matter, Aubrey fell on them and introduced them to the other guests before clapping his hands for the musicians. Harp, lute and viele combined in a pleasing melody that flew around the room like a flock of small birds. Bodin the steward emerged from the shadows to conduct everyone to a seat at the long table. Twenty of them in all took their places for a sumptuous repast, presided over by Aubrey and his wife, Herleve.

Inches taller than her husband, she was an elegant woman with a fading beauty that was held in check by the subtle use of cosmetics. A polite smile was painted on her lips and her manner was effortlessly gracious, but Ralph sensed a coldness in her that he did not like. Golde, anxious to thank her hostess for the loan of the apparel, made a number of attempts to engage Herleve in conversation but the latter could not be drawn. There was one moment, as Golde plucked gently at the woman's sleeve, when the mask of hospitality slipped slightly and Herleve shot her a look of mute disapproval.

Served with style, the food was rich and delicious. Bodin made sure that each course followed the other smoothly and without delay. He also supervised the entertainment so that there was always something fresh to watch or to hear. Minstrels sang, dancers disported themselves, jugglers displayed their skills, tumblers whirled through the air, and a conjurer performed tricks that baffled his spectators.

The most sensational performers were reserved until the end. On the command of his master, Bodin slipped quietly out of the hall to fetch them. Aubrey Maminot banged the table for quiet before turning to Ralph.

'You were not the only ones to be troubled by intruders in the night,' he said. 'We, too, had unwanted guests.'

'When?' asked Ralph.

'A few days ago. Two men scaled the castle walls. Fortunately, my guards were more alert than yours.'

'You captured the intruders?'

'One of them escaped, the other was dealt with in the way that he deserved.'

'And what was that?'

'He was eaten alive.'

The guests reacted with horror. Herleve turned away. Aubrey beamed. 'No man could sneak past my pets.'

'Pets?' echoed Gervase.

'Yes. It is time for you to meet them.'

A sweep of his arm directed their gaze to the end of the room where the huge oak door suddenly swung back on its hinges. There was a gasp of fear from the guests. Some of the women screamed and even the bravest of the men felt a shiver of apprehension. Ludovico brought them in. Straining on their leashes, two full-grown lions bared their fangs and ripped at the air with their claws, emitting such terrifying roars that the whole room reverberated.

Golde clung to Ralph's arm in trepidation, but he was more fascinated than afraid. While others shrunk back from the roaring animals, he noticed how great a control Ludovico had over them. The Keeper of the Beasts was not just exhibiting his charges, he was jerking on their chains alternately to prompt their snarls. When Ludovico used his strength to turn their fearsome heads towards him, he grinned at the lions and shouted something in Italian.

The roars stopped immediately. Instead of threatening with their claws, they lay on the floor and rolled over on their backs like a pair of playful kittens. Ludovico let go of their leashes and crouched down to stroke them. Aubrey skipped down the hall to join him.

'I had them as cubs,' he explained. 'When I journeyed to Rome, they were a gift to me from a friend. That is why I called them Romulus and Remus. The founders of the Eternal City grew up with wolves, but I prefer to consort with lions.'

To the amazement of his guests, Aubrey Maminot sat on the floor between the lions and put an arm around each of their necks. After rolling their heads and emitting a token snarl, they closed their eyes and purred with contentment.

'My pride and joy,' said Aubrey. 'The lions of York!'

Chapter Three

Their first full day in York was largely taken up with administrative duties. The list of cases to be examined was dauntingly long and the commissioners faced the prospect of endless sessions in the shire hall. Gervase Bret suggested a means of speeding up the legal process without significant threat to justice. Since many of the cases involved relatively small amounts of land, contested in each instance by only two claimants, he argued that they could be resolved summarily. If, therefore, the commissioners divided into two separate groups, one could deal with these minor disputes and leave the other free to handle the more complex cases.

Ralph Delchard was entirely in favour of the plan. He had, in fact, been primed by Gervase days in advance, but he pretended to be hearing the notion for the first time and he banged an imperious fist on the table in the shire hall.

'An excellent idea!' he announced. 'We'll act on it.'

'Yes,' agreed Tanchelm of Ghent. 'It will spread the load and save us all a great deal of time.'

Canon Hubert wagged a finger. 'Not so fast, my lords.

We must not make such a radical change in our *modus operandi* without a discussion of the implications.'

'This *is* that discussion,' said Ralph. 'And it is effectively over. Three of us vote in favour of this plan to expedite matters, and Brother Simon, I am sure, will also see its essential wisdom.'

'Indeed I do, my lord,' said Simon, before quailing under a glare from Hubert and qualifying his comment. 'Not that my opinion has any value here. I am but the humble scribe.'

Ralph smiled. 'That still leaves three to one, Hubert.'

The canon squirmed visibly for a few minutes. He hated the feeling of being outmanoeuvred and of suffering even the most miniscule loss of authority. Unable to prevent the new dispensation, he was nevertheless determined to haggle over its constituent elements.

'So be it, my lord,' he said. 'Gervase is our lawyer and I am the most skilful interrogator. It is thus appropriate for he and I to form the senior of the two teams and grapple with the intricate cases. You and my lord Tanchelm will, I am sure, be capable of dispensing justice where the more trifling issues are at stake.'

Ralph glowered at the bland insult and framed a barbed reply, but it was Gervase who answered for him.

'That may not be the best deployment of our strengths.'

'Then what is?' challenged Hubert.

'The most powerful advocate should sit with the least experienced,' said Gervase persuasively. 'If you and my lord Tanchelm join forces, he may follow where you lead.'

'Sound reasoning,' observed Tanchelm.

'Brother Simon would naturally act as your scribe,' continued Gervase, indicating the monk, 'giving you another seasoned mind at your beck and call.'

Touched by a rare compliment, Simon acknowledged it with a little nod and positively glowed with satisfaction. Canon Hubert, meanwhile, was scrutinising the partnership that was being offered to him. Tanchelm's lack of experience was a severe handicap but it did have one major benefit. Much more responsibility would be shifted to Hubert's shoulders, ensuring virtual control of events. He would lose Gervase's legal expertise, but he felt that his own thorough grounding in canon law would compensate for that loss, and at least he would not be sitting alongside the combative Ralph Delchard. Tanchelm of Ghent might turn out to be the ideal colleague.

'It is settled,' Hubert decided at length. 'We will handle all matters of consequence while you, my lord, offer judgement on cases too trivial to tax your limited abilities.'

'My abilities are *not* limited!' retorted Ralph.

'They are best suited to the more undemanding cases.'

'Those are your province, Canon Hubert. It would be unfair on my lord Tanchelm to expose him to the full rigour of legal debate when he has only just been recruited to our cause.'

'I endorse that wholeheartedly,' said Tanchelm. 'I am

not proud. I do not insist on sounding the deeper waters. Put me on the side of simplicity. It is where I belong.'

'But not where *I* belong!' insisted Hubert.

The argument continued for the best part of an hour before the canon finally gave way to the weight of numbers. As a concession to him, Ralph allowed them to have the use of the shire hall while he and Gervase would operate in the adjacent premises. Application would be made to the Archbishop for someone who could act as scribe during the proceedings conducted by the two friends. The reeve was brought in and given separate lists of witnesses to be summoned for the following day. When the debate finally broke up, considerable progress had been made.

Canon Hubert departed in a huff towards the Minster, with Brother Simon padding at his heels and savouring the remark about his seasoned mind. Tanchelm of Ghent elected to explore the city while he had the opportunity, leaving Ralph and Gervase to ride back to the castle alone. Their horses picked their way through the milling crowd.

'I do not like him,' opined Ralph.

'You and Canon Hubert will never be soulmates, I fear.'

'I talk of Tanchelm, that devious Fleming.'

'I do not find him devious,' said Gervase in surprise. 'He is the most open and straightforward of men. He has been nothing but a source of help since he joined us.'

'That is my main strike against him, Gervase. The

fellow is *too* helpful. Too ready to defer to us. Too damned obliging.'

'I'd call that a virtue rather than a vice.'

'So would I with anyone else, but this Tanchelm of Ghent . . .' He pursed his lips and shook his head. 'Somehow I cannot bring myself to trust him.'

'Why not?'

'I do not know. It is just a feeling I have.'

'Are you sure?' said Gervase, fishing politely. 'Could it not just be a case of pique?'

'Pique?'

'You were very annoyed last night when my lord Tanchelm tried to stop you riding off in pursuit of those outlaws. He was not obliging then.'

'No, Gervase. He was an infernal nuisance.'

'Who made a sensible point. It *was* a wild goose chase.'

'It need not have been if Tanchelm had not delayed me for those vital moments. We might have caught the rogues.'

Gervase was sceptical. 'Might you?'

'No,' said Ralph after a considered pause. 'We might not. It was an impulsive act. We were chasing moonbeams. Tanchelm gave wise counsel.' He inhaled deeply through his nose. 'Perhaps I am mistaken about him. You like him. So does Golde. So does Aubrey, though he is something of a friend to all the world. And even Canon Hubert has been won over by our Fleming. Maybe *that* is the objection I have. Tanchelm of Ghent is not a fellow Norman.'

'Nor am I,' reminded Gervase.

A hearty laugh. 'You? You are just a mongrel.'

'My father was a Breton, my mother a Saxon.'

'A mongrel of mongrels!'

'Do not let Golde hear you. She might take offence.'

'Justly so,' said Ralph with a fond smile. 'Golde has taught me to show more respect towards Saxons. She is a good influence on me, Gervase. I have learned tolerance. Henceforth, I'll pour no mockery on your dear mother.'

'That would be appreciated.'

'I'll save my contempt for your father.'

Gervase laughed. 'Bretons are used to being undervalued by their neighbours in Normandy. But I ask you this. What hope would you have had at Hastings without an army of Bretons to help you? Not to mention the Flemings. My father was a mercenary in the pay of the Duke. So was Tanchelm of Ghent.'

'I had forgotten that. Something in Tanchelm's favour at last. He is a soldier.' Ralph turned his mind to a more pressing concern. 'Enough of Bretons, Saxons and Flemings. All that I am really interested in at the moment is the Vikings.'

'Vikings?'

'One in particular. Olaf Evil Child.'

'Does that wound still smart so?'

'It opens afresh every time I think about that night. He stole our property, Gervase. I do not care how long it takes, but one thing I have promised myself: before I leave York, I will come face to face with Olaf Evil Child.'

'Can we be sure that he was indeed the thief?'

'Aubrey was convinced of it.'

'He could have been mistaken.'

'I doubt it,' said Ralph. 'He was reared as a soldier like me. He knows how to read the marks of an enemy. And he has lived in this city for many years now. If Aubrey tells me that I must search for Olaf Evil Child, then I will.'

'Our work here will leave you little time to do so.'

'I'll contrive it somehow.'

They were over the bridge now and trotting towards the castle. When Ralph looked up at its wooden palisade, another memory nudged him. He gave a quiet chuckle.

'Did you enjoy the banquet last night?' he asked.

'It was the best meal I have eaten in a year.'

'I'll wager you've never feasted with lions before. Romulus and Remus. What amazing beasts!'

'They were frightening, Ralph.'

'Yet as harmless as rabbits when Aubrey stroked them. I could not believe my eyes. If you or I had tried to fondle them, they'd have torn us to shreds.'

'Yes,' said Gervase uncomfortably. 'We'd have no more chance than that poor wretch who was mauled by them the other night. I have to admit that *he* occupies my thoughts much more than Olaf Evil Child.'

'That intruder who climbed into the castle?'

'I feel deeply sorry for him.'

'He paid the price for his boldness.'

'No man deserves to die in that hideous way.'

'I can think of one I'd gladly feed to Romulus and Remus!'

'No,' said Gervase. 'You can be hard, but you could

never be that cruel. You would not let two wild beasts patrol *your* home.'

'Too true. The stink would revolt me.'

'Why does such a kind man as my lord Aubrey take such a brutal delight in the way his lions savaged a human being? And who *was* the unfortunate victim?'

'Nobody seems to know.'

'Who was he?' puzzled Gervase. 'And what on earth was he doing in the castle at that time of night?'

Golde had a full day. True to his word, Aubrey Maminot found time to conduct her on a painstaking tour of the city. It was a fascinating experience. By comparison with York, her own home town of Hereford appeared small, cluttered and curiously provincial. Over seven times as many people lived in the northern capital and every one of them seemed to be out and about, turning every street and lane into a clamorous meeting place. York even smelled bigger, and the salty tang of its fish, unloaded from the boats on the Ouse and displayed in countless market stalls, invaded the nostrils at every turn in a way that Hereford could not match.

Yet there were similarities between the two cities, and Golde took due note of them. Both had been sacked and rebuilt more than once. While Hereford had suffered from the incursions of the Welsh, it was the Danes, Scots and native aristocracy of the north who had pillaged York. Castle and cathedral dominated the border community just as surely as that in the West Riding. The Normans put their faith as ever in a combination of high walls and religion. Both places, too, were polyglot, and the general pandemonium was fed by a variety of languages, dialects and accents. Riding beside her guide, Golde enjoyed the simple pleasure of listening to it all.

It was York Minster which impressed her most. Even in its unfinished state it was vast. Destroyed by Danes less than a decade earlier, it was being rebuilt on a different site at a completely different angle. Thomas of Bayeux, Archbishop of York, was determined to make the Minster an inspiring monument to the glory of God. Still swarming with craftsmen of all kinds, and marred by the unsightly presence of wooden scaffolding, the cathedral church of St Peter was over a hundred and twenty yards long with a nave that was fifteen yards across. Golde's jaw sagged as she stood in the apsed chancel and looked up at the distant roof.

Aubrey Maminot chortled at her stunned reaction. 'We do everything on a large scale in York,' he said.

'It is colossal, my lord!'

'Wait until it is finished.'

'That will never happen in my lifetime.'

'Oh, it will, it will.'

He was a patient guide with a fierce pride in the city, and Golde learned an immense amount from his comments and anecdotes. But the outing was not entirely devoted to the architectural wonders of York. Knowing how keenly she felt the loss of her wardrobe, Aubrey introduced her to a sequence of tailors and dressmakers until she found one who could meet her needs in the shortest possible time. When she returned to the castle with him, Golde was in a buoyant mood. She went straight up to the chamber she shared with Ralph Delchard and collected the apparel she had borrowed the previous evening.

She found Herleve in the solar, working on some embroidery in the company of a young gentlewoman.

'May I join you?'

'Please do.'

'I do not wish to interrupt, my lady.'

'We were all but finished here.' Herleve had the same polite expression she had worn at the banquet and the same air of gracious resignation. A glance dismissed her companion and she indicated the stool which had just been vacated. 'Do sit down,' she invited.

'Thank you,' said Golde, lowering herself down.

'Did my husband show you our city?'

'It is breathtaking.'

'I am glad that you like it.'

'We also managed to engage a dressmaker so I can return this with thanks.' She offered the clothing but Herleve's hands were both employed. 'Where shall I put it?'

'On the floor.'

'I am very grateful to you, my lady.' Golde placed the bundle gently beside the stool. 'It saved me in my hour of need.'

'You are most welcome.' Her needle started to move again and she did not look up. 'Did you enjoy the banquet?'

'It was delightful.'

'I did not care for some of the entertainment.'

'We adored it all. Your husband went to enormous trouble on our behalf. And considerable expense.'

'Yes, he is a generous host.'

'And you were a most generous hostess,' said Golde softly, but the compliment elicited no response. She waited a moment. 'My lady?' Again, no response. 'My lady.' Herleve raised her eyes. 'May I ask a question?'

'Well?'

'Have I offended you in some way?'

'No.'

'I feel that there is a coldness between us.'

'Do you?'

'There was a moment . . . last night . . .'

Herleve addressed herself to the embroidery once more. 'I am a rather private person,' she said in a neutral voice. 'My husband is very gregarious, as you have witnessed. Nothing pleases him more than to entertain guests in the most extravagant fashion. That is his nature. It is not mine.' She turned pale blue eyes on Golde. 'I prefer seclusion. That is why I am sometimes uneasy in company and may appear indifferent to our visitors. The truth is that I have no liking for idle conversation. The mindless banter of the table tires me. What I value is solitude. I have come to be most content in my own company.'

Golde felt obscurely rebuked. For a few moments, she watched Herleve intently, unable to decide if the woman was deliberately snubbing her or if she was overcome by a disabling shyness. Either way, it left Golde wishing that she had not come into the solar at all. She rose to leave.

'Thank you again, my lady.'

'I was glad that my wardrobe could help you.'

'So was I. But I'll trouble you no further.' With the merest curtsey, Golde backed out of the room.

The gentlewoman was waiting in the corridor and she slipped back into the solar immediately. Gathering up the apparel from the floor, she stood beside her mistress and waited until Herleve glanced up.

'Where shall I put this, my lady?'

'On the fire,' murmured the other. 'Burn it.'

'Where would I be likely to find him?' asked Ralph Delchard.

'I wish I could tell you.'

'How should I start looking?'

'Behind every tree.'

'Can you give me no more guidance than that, Aubrey?'

'None at all, old friend.'

'Someone must know where Olaf Evil Child is!'

'They have not passed on the intelligence to me.'

'A band of outlaws cannot roam the countryside and remain invisible. They must have been *seen*.'

'Of course,' said Aubrey Maminot. 'Dozens of people have sighted Olaf near their village or hamlet or manor, but they would never admit it to you or me.'

'Are they so afraid of him?'

'Afraid of him and resentful towards us.'

'That is understandable,' sighed Tanchelm of Ghent. 'North of the Humber we are still the vile usurpers. They will not lift a hand to help us. I daresay the other night's escapade is still being laughed about. We will be held up to ridicule.'

'Without question,' confirmed Aubrey. 'Olaf Evil Child will be seen as some sort of hero for tweaking your noses.'

Ralph bristled. 'That is what makes me so mad! The ridicule! Snigger at us, will he? I'll do more than tweak his Viking nose when I catch him.'

The three men were strolling around the bailey at the castle. Ralph and Tanchelm had just spoken to their respective men, giving them their orders for the morrow when some of them would be needed in attendance. Aubrey was now showing them the finer points of his defences, but their abiding interest was in the leader of the outlaws.

'Who exactly is this Olaf?' said Ralph.

Aubrey grimaced. 'One more lordless man in a county that already has too many of them.'

'Are you certain that is all he is?' asked Tanchelm.

'What do you mean?'

'It is rumoured that the Danes are about to launch another attack. That is one of the main reasons why King William set this whole Domesday Inquest in motion. So that he will have an accurate picture of the spread of wealth in England. In times of crisis, a king must know where his sources of strength and manpower are.'

'The Conqueror knows that by instinct,' said Aubrey.

'If an invasion did come, it would most probably start on the eastern coast not far from here.'

'So?'

'Could not Olaf Evil Child be playing a deeper game?' said Tanchelm thoughtfully. 'You know the man of course, and I do not, but . . . well, is it at all conceivable that he is in league with the Danes?'

'No, it is not.'

'Can you be certain?'

'Absolutely certain!' said Aubrey with emphasis.

'It does seem highly unlikely,' added Ralph. 'If Olaf is planning to assist a Danish invasion, why is he preying on travellers and stealing their horses?'

'Who knows?' said Tanchelm. 'To give them to a raiding party? Perhaps he has stolen other horses and holds them in readiness. Mounted warriors move much faster than long ships sailing upriver. They have an element of surprise.' His brow furrowed, then he shook his head dismissively. 'No, it is only a wild guess. Take no notice of it. My reasoning is too simple. Because Olaf Evil Child is descended from the Danish Vikings, I wondered if he might be scouting for his friends from across the water.'

'He has no friends,' said Aubrey scornfully. 'Except those who ride at his back. Olaf Evil Child is an outcast. He insists that he was dispossessed of land that was legally willed to him by his father. That is arrant nonsense. He has no legitimate claim. And he will never own a square inch of Yorkshire soil while I am here to stop him.'

'I am hopelessly wrong,' said Tanchelm, conceding his error with an apologetic shrug. 'He is obviously no agent for the Danes. Olaf is merely a man with a grudge.'

'A hundred of them!'

'Some of which concern you, I fancy,' said Ralph.

'Quite a few.'

'I, too, can bear a grudge.'

'Not as well as Olaf,' said Aubrey. 'He has been a thorn in my flesh for the best part of a year. I would not be in the least surprised if he attacked your party on the road because he knew that you would be my guests in York. It was yet another way of baiting Aubrey Maminot.' His lip curled. 'Sooner or later he will try it once too often, and then he will be mine.'

'Leave a piece of him for me,' said Ralph.

'No, old friend,' warned the other. 'Olaf Evil Child is already spoken for in this castle. If you catch him, he is yours. But if I snare him, he will be the next meal for Romulus and Remus.'

'They are remarkable pets, Aubrey.'

'England holds nothing else like them, Ralph.'

'Tell me this. How is it that two wild beasts, who can eat a man alive, are yet tame when you handle them? What sorcery do you practise?'

'No sorcery,' said Aubrey with a chuckle. 'Ludovico taught me the secret. Lions are like women. They need constant attention. Stroke them every day and they will purr like cats. Neglect them in any way and they will sharpen their claws in readiness to draw blood.'

'You want to *see* him?' asked the chaplain, aghast.

'Yes, please. If at all possible.'

'Have you any idea what state the body is in?'

'I know it was badly mauled.'

'That is too mild a description of what happened. The poor creature was literally torn limb from limb. I have looked on death in many weird forms, but I have never seen anything as grotesque as this.' Philip the Chaplain gave a shudder at the memory. 'I could not eat for two days after.'

Gervase Bret was persistent. Once his curiosity was aroused, he was not easily deflected from satisfying it. While Ralph and the others were down in the bailey, he had decided to call on the chaplain to see what further light could be cast on the incident which led to the gruesome death of an intruder. He was astonished to learn that the remains of the deceased were still in the tiny mortuary below the chapel.

'Why did you not bury the body?' he asked.

'In case somebody came forward to claim it. Not that my lord Aubrey would have released it, but he was anxious to know the man's identity and his reason for entering the castle in such a headstrong way. Word was spread throughout the city.'

'No one came forward?'

'Not a soul.'

'Fear of suffering a similar fate?'

'Or of being forced to view a loved one in that pitiful condition,' said Philip. 'Who can tell? The point is that decay has set in badly and the burial must take place first thing tomorrow or the mortuary will not hold in the stench.'

'You have odours enough to contend with here,' said Gervase. 'The lions' cage nearby is not exactly a perfumed arbour.'

'It will seem so after you have viewed the corpse.'

'Lead on.'

Philip the Chaplain was a short, podgy man of forty with a world-weary air. Whatever upsurge of faith had brought him into the priesthood had long since spent itself, and there was now a sense of duty rather than dedication about his manner. He was a caring man, but he had forgotten exactly why he should care and what his mission in life properly ought to be.

Taking a lighted candle from beside the altar, he opened a door and led Gervase down a narrow circular staircase. The chapel was heavily impregnated with the aroma of burning incense, and Gervase soon discovered why. Philip unlocked a heavy door which swung slowly back on its hinges, averting his head as he did so. The stink came out to hit them like a punch and Gervase recoiled. He coughed uncontrollably for minutes.

'Do you still wish to go in?' said Philip.

'Please.'

'Let us be quick about our business.'

'We will be.'

'It is the body on the left.'

Gervase had not realised that the morgue had another occupant. Two stone slabs stood side by side, with a tenant lying on each one. As the candle was held up to throw its light more widely, Gervase had no trouble picking out the correct remains. The body on the right was that of an old servant who had died peacefully in his sleep. The shroud clung tightly enough to describe a long angular frame with two large feet that pointed up towards heaven with the quiet certainty of a welcome.

On the other slab, the body did not lie so docilely at rest. It seemed to be half the size of its neighbour and was covered by a shroud that was soaked with blood. Herbs were strewn all around it but they could do little to sweeten its noisome reek. Hell itself might reject such a foul smell. Gervase looked up at the chaplain, but the latter had seen all that he wished to of the mangled remains. Eyes closed, he was reciting the Lord's Prayer to himself in an undertone.

'*Pater noster, qui es in caelis, sanctificetur nomen tuum, adveniat regnum tuum . . .*'

Bracing himself for the worst, Gervase took the shroud between his fingers and peeled it slowly back. As he saw a face that was half-eaten away his stomach began to churn, but he forced himself to go on. Romulus and Remus had been voracious diners. One arm had been ripped off and both legs had been chewed down to the bone. Part of the torso had been bitten open and the chest was one huge scarlet hole. It was a repulsive sight, but Gervase kept looking as he tried to reconstruct, in his mind's eye, something at least of the victim's appearance.

The man had been young, healthy and fair-haired, with a lean body agile enough to bring him up over the castle wall. Though smeared with gore, the surviving part of his face hinted at good looks which would surely be missed by a sweetheart or by a wife. He might be alone and deserted now, but the young man exuded a strong sense of belonging to a community. Gervase was overtaken by a sudden urge to find that community so that they could be informed of the fate of the nameless figure on the slab. Pity soon gave way to crippling queasiness. Gervase bent double and started to retch.

'Have you seen enough?' asked Philip the Chaplain.

It was less of an enquiry than a command to leave, and Gervase obeyed it without complaint. Pulling the shroud gently back over the cadaver, he lurched out of the mortuary and fell against the wall for support. When he had closed the door behind them, Philip practically had to carry his visitor up the stairs.

Back in the chapel, he snuffed out the candle with absent-minded skill. The incense enveloped them both and smothered the fetid stink of decay.

'Is there anything I can get you?' Philip said with offhand sympathy. Gervase shook his head. 'I did warn you.'

'I am glad I saw him – God rest his soul! He merits a Christian burial.'

'He will get one, Master Bret. Though I do not think that body will lie easy in its grave.'

'What was he *doing* here?' said Gervase.

'Trying to get into the keep.'

'For what purpose?'

'The murder of my lord Aubrey. That is what everyone is saying. It is not the first time someone has tried to kill him.' He rolled his head. 'For myself, I have doubts.'

'Why?'

'To begin with, an assassin would be better armed for his task. One dagger would not have got him anywhere near my lord Aubrey. And why try to strike when his victim was safely locked away in the most fortified part of the castle? It is suicide.'

'Did he know that the keep was guarded by lions?'

'Apparently not.'

'Then he clearly did not live in York. Their roars can be heard as far away as the Minster. Everybody in the city must know there are two wild beasts in here.'

'The victim did not.'

'We have learned something else about him then,' said Gervase. 'Little by little, I will rebuild that face and body of his until he is whole again. By that time, I dare swear, I will have found a name as well.'

'Why are you going to such trouble on his behalf?'

Gervase smiled wanly. 'Because nobody else will.'

It was late. Ralph Delchard and Golde lay naked in each other's arms, slowly getting their breath back after their exertions. Covered in perspiration, they remained locked together for several minutes. He kissed her tenderly on the lips before rolling over on to his back. She nestled into his glistening shoulder.

'Are you happy?' he whispered.

'Yes, Ralph. Are you?'

'I thought I just answered that question.'

She brushed her lips against his chin. 'You did.'

'Are you glad that you came to York?'

'I am glad to be with you,' she said.

'That is not what I asked.'

There was a pause. 'York is a beautiful city and I am delighted to have seen it, but . . .'

'Go on. I hear a note of reservation in your voice.'

'But . . .'

'Speak freely. There are no secrets between us.'

'I would rather lodge elsewhere,' she said.

'Elsewhere?' He was stunned. '*Why?*'

'Because I would be more comfortable.'

'No place in York has the comforts that this castle can offer. Aubrey has spent a fortune on the place and he is overjoyed to have us here. We could not ask for a more attentive and open-handed host.'

'Yet I still feel unwelcome.'

Ralph gasped. 'After all he has done for us?'

'My lord Aubrey has been kindness itself,' said Golde. 'The same, alas, may not be said of his wife.'

'Herleve has always been a little strange.'

'She disapproves of me, Ralph.'

'No, my love.'

'She does. She is so cold and distant with me that I might almost be one of the servants. I will not be looked down on by anybody. It is demeaning.'

'Take no notice of her.'

'Why is she so full of reproach towards me?'

'Reproach towards *us*,' he corrected. 'I have met Herleve a number of times and always got on well with her in the past. At the banquet, however, even I came in for a frosty glance or two.'

'What does she have against us?'

'We share a bed without first taking vows of marriage. Herleve is devout. She frowns on our behaviour. In her eyes, we are sinners.'

'And in *your* eyes?' Golde probed.

'Lovers.'

'Is that all?'

He fondled her hair. 'Is that not enough?'

'I begin to wonder.'

'Golde!'

'Censure from Canon Hubert and Brother Simon is one thing. They are holy men and could not, in all conscience, smile upon us. But when I meet rejection at the hands of your friends . . .'

'You are not rejected.'

'Look in her face. Watch her gestures.'

'Forget Herleve.'

'How can I when I am her guest?'

'We are the guests of Aubrey Maminot,' Ralph explained. 'He would never reject us. Herleve is a good woman but he should never have married her. Aubrey needed a more spirited creature to lie beside him. His wife is too bloodless. She has many virtues and is the soul of loyalty, but Herleve is more fit for the convent than for the marital couch.'

'And what of me, Ralph?'

'You?'

'I am fit for neither, it seems.'

'Not for the convent, surely!' he said with a chuckle. 'It is too late for that.' He became defensive. 'And too soon for the other.'

'Too soon?'

'I made no promises, Golde.'

'Nor did I seek to extract any from you.'

'I feel that you may be doing so now.'

'No,' she protested. 'I simply wish to know where we

stand and what the future holds for us.'

'I love you!' he affirmed. 'That says all.'

'Not quite.'

'I can make no further commitment as yet.'

There was a long pause. 'Then I'll not press you to do so,' she said at length. 'I simply ask you to remember that I have my pride and I have my feelings.'

'Where would you rather be at this moment?' he asked. 'In my arms or brewing your ale back in Hereford?'

'That is not a fair question.'

'Answer it anyway.'

By way of reply, she held him tight and kissed him fully on the lips. Ralph sought for the words to assuage her disquiet.

'Rise above Herleve's reproof,' he soothed. 'Ignore her. Pretend that she is not even here.'

'What am I to do for companionship?'

'You have me.'

'At night,' she said, pulling him closer, 'but not in the day. You warned me how busy you would be once you began the work that brought us here.'

'That is true. It occupies me completely.'

'Then I'll be locked up alone in here.'

'I'll ask Aubrey to devise entertainment for you. We'll surround you with so many pleasures that you will beg me to stay longer when our business is completed here.'

Since the night when intruders climbed in, additional guards had been assigned to patrol the walls of the castle. Torches burned in the courtyard below to throw patchy light on the various buildings, but there was little illumination beyond the palisade itself. When the moon was hidden behind a blanket of cloud, the guards found themselves staring into an impenetrable blackness. It was tedious work and they complained bitterly to each other, but they did not dare to leave their posts. They knew better than to provoke the ire of the castellan. The soul of benevolence to his guests, Aubrey Maminot could be less indulgent towards his soldiers. Those who failed him might find themselves on night duty at the castle in perpetuity.

'Did you hear anything?'

'No. Did you?'

'I'm not sure. Listen.' A pause. 'There it is again!'

'I heard nothing.'

'Listen!'

'I am listening.'

'Shut up! You'll miss it.'

'Miss what?'

'Listen!'

The hissed command silenced the young guard. He and his companion were patrolling the wall above the castle gate. It was a cold night and they stayed on the move to keep themselves warm. Now, however, they were motionless as they peered out into the darkness and strained their ears to catch any sound other than the murmuring conversations of their fellow guards and the occasional whinny of a horse in the stables.

The younger man soon tired of the exercise. 'There's nothing there.'

'There was,' argued his companion.

'What was it?'

'I don't know.'

'What did it sound like?'

'A noise, that's all. Fetch a torch.'

'It's gone now.'

'Fetch it!'

The younger man strode quickly along the wall to collect a torch that was burning in an iron holder. When he returned to the area of the gate, he held it high so that they could look over the palisade and down into the ditch. The light was too poor for them to pick out anything and they eventually gave up, returning the torch to its holder before continuing their patrol. There was nothing outside the castle. The older guard decided that his ears were playing tricks on him.

Dawn revised his judgement. As the first fingers of light began to pluck at the darkness, they caught a glimpse of something lying just outside the gate. It was quite still and seemed harmless, but they could take no chances. Alerting their fellows with a shout, they trotted down the steps to the gateway. A dozen guards came running with enough torches to turn night into a sunlit day.

More men arrived with weapons drawn, and they formed a line as the gates were unbolted and opened. Eager for action, the young guard was the first to venture out, using his spear to jab menacingly at the objects on the grass. Torchlight showed him that he was launching no brave attack on a potential enemy. All that his spearpoint had touched was one of three large bundles.

Olaf Evil Child had come calling.

Chapter Four

In order to get through the volume of work which confronted them, the two sets of commissioners made an early start that morning. The bell for Prime seemed scarcely to have died away before they were leaving their respective lodgings to make their way to their places of business. Canon Hubert led the delegation at the shire hall and occupied the central position at the table. Tanchelm of Ghent and Brother Simon were happy to sit in silence with him, the former so that he could learn through close observation, the latter so that he could record the proceedings on the sheets of parchment that lay before him.

The adjoining building was smaller, darker and decidedly less suitable. It was occasionally used as a meeting place for the city's four judges, who enjoyed custom beyond the normal privileges of a burgess, but its musty atmosphere suggested that it might also have done duty as a grain store. Ralph Delchard was plainly disgusted with its interior.

'I will not preside in a stable!'

'It will suffice,' said Gervase Bret.

'For horses, yes. For royal commissioners – no!'

'You were the one who offered the shire hall to our colleagues. It is too late to change your mind now.'

'The place is covered in dust.'

'According to the reeve, it has not been used for some time.'

'Fifty years or more, by the look of it.'

'We will manage somehow.'

'I'd sooner sit in judgement in the fish market.'

Two servants arrived and mumbled their apologies before cleaning the room as best and as quickly as they could. Ralph sneezed at the cloud of dust set up by the broom, but his howl of protest was cut short by the arrival of their scribe. Brother Francis was a big, solid man of middle years with a genial smile and a willing manner. Ralph could never bring himself to enjoy the company of a Benedictine monk, but the newcomer at least promised to be rather more forthcoming than Brother Simon.

Introductions were made and Francis beamed helpfully.

'How may I best serve you?' he asked.

'I want you to look, listen and set down anything that I tell you,' ordered Ralph. 'Bear in mind that what you write will have the force of a legal document. It must be clear and exact.'

'I understand, my lord.'

'You have brought all that you need?'

'Yes,' said Francis, tapping the leather satchel that hung from his shoulder. 'Everything is here. I am honoured to take part in matters of such weighty importance.'

'That makes a change. Brother Simon is always terrified when he sits beside us.'

'Brother Simon?'

'Our accustomed scribe,' said Gervase. 'A punctilious man. He sets high standards.'

Francis smiled. 'I will try my utmost to emulate him.'

Ralph gave him more detailed instructions and the monk plied him with a number of questions. While they were still deep in discussion, Gervase took charge of the servants and made them move the table, chair, stools and benches into their appropriate positions. The place was markedly cleaner when the two of them left. Even Ralph was agreeably surprised.

'It is now almost civilised,' he said, leading the way to the table. 'At least I will not cough to death.'

Lowering himself into the chair, he gestured for Gervase and Francis to sit on the stools either side of him. Both began to empty the contents of their satchels. The absence of Canon Hubert was a bonus to Ralph, though he would have preferred Brother Simon's experienced hand to that of their new scribe. Brother Francis was eager and respectful but he was as yet unproven.

Tanchelm's men-at-arms were on duty inside and outside the shire hall, but Ralph had brought ten from his own escort to give his deliberations a show of strength. Since the room was so cramped, only four of them were on duty inside it. Their companions acted as sentries in the street, keeping prying eyes at bay and marshalling the witnesses as they arrived. Inured to the sight of Norman soldiers, most of the citizens of York shuffled past without comment.

Gervase handed a document to Ralph, who glanced down at it to refresh his memory before issuing a curt command.

'Bring in the first witness! Her name is Sunnifa.'

'Yes, my lord,' said one of the soldiers. Ducking to avoid the lintel over the door, he went outside to discharge a duty that should have taken no more than thirty seconds. Instead, he was gone for a couple of minutes. Ralph grew impatient with the delay. When sounds of a violent argument reached his ears, his impatience spilled over into anger. Rising to his feet, he sent the three remaining men out after their colleague.

'Fetch the woman in at once!'

They obeyed instantly. Voices were raised in protest then the witness was more or less hustled in by two of the soldiers. She was a tall, graceful woman in her forties with a nobility in her bearing that even her unceremonious entrance could not entirely obscure. At her heels, arguing noisily and struggling with the other two soldiers, were a younger woman and a man in the garb of a parish priest. All three of them stood before the table and complained simultaneously.

Ralph's voice smothered them into a hurt silence.

'Enough of this caterwauling!' he yelled. 'We are servants of the King and we demand full respect!'

A flick of the hand sent his men back to their post at the rear of the room. The visitors studied him warily. Ralph lowered himself into his chair and deliberately made them wait before he was ready to speak.

'Now,' he said sternly, 'which of you is the person for whom I sent?'

'I am,' said Sunnifa, taking a step forward.

'Then who are these other people?'

'They are here to support my claim.'

'When I call for one witness, I do not need three.'

'But they are witnesses in their own right, my lord.'

'Let them wait outside.'

As the soldiers moved in once more, protest resumed in earnest. Sunnifa took another step forward. 'No, my lord,' she pleaded. 'They must stay.'

'Hear us out!' implored the priest.

'We demand it!' asserted the third member of the group. 'If Norman justice consists in laying rough hands upon a priest and a woman, then it is a despicable instrument and does not deserve our respect. I am Inga, daughter of Sunnifa, and I insist on remaining with my mother.' She indicated the man beside her. 'This is Brunn the Priest, who will confirm our testimony. All three of us must be heard together. We have come to report a heinous crime and will not leave this place until we have done so.'

Inga was fearless. There was such passion in her voice that the three men behind the table were stunned and the soldiers hesitated to take hold of her. Here was someone, nineteen years old at most, daring to challenge the authority of royal commissioners, and doing so not in the rudimentary Norman French employed by Sunnifa and by Brunn the Priest, but with a fluent control of the language of her masters. Inga was clearly an extraordinary young woman. Gervase was struck by the vehement loveliness of the face beneath the wimple and by the sharp intelligence in her eyes.

Ralph consulted the document before him once more. 'Seventeen witnesses have been called,' he said to Inga. 'Your name and that of Brunn are among them. The pair of you will have to wait your turn with the other fourteen.'

'The other fourteen are not here, my lord.'

'They must be. I issued a summons for each one myself.'

'It was ignored,' said Inga bluntly. 'Send for any of those witnesses and you will find that they are not here. They are too frightened to present their evidence. We are not. That is why we have made the long journey here.' She took a firm hold of her mother's hand. 'Now, my lord. May we stay to seek justice or will you have us thrown out?'

Ralph turned first to Gervase, who gave a gentle nod, and then to Brother Francis, who offered a philosophical smile. Little could be gained by separating the three witnesses and much by keeping them together. Inga was patently their spokesperson and her control of Norman French would be an undoubted asset. Ralph did not like to have his decisions questioned but, in Inga's case, he was prepared to make allowances for the rashness of youth. It had brought a pleasing colour to her cheeks.

Sunnifa did not have her daughter's throbbing energy and Brunn the Priest was an old man worn down by the cares of his ministry in a county which had suffered the most terrible afflictions. It was easy to see why they preferred to let Inga represent them. Ralph switched to a gruff courtesy.

'If you have travelled far,' he said, 'you will be weary. Please take a seat so that you may give your evidence in some degree of comfort.'

'Be careful!' warned Aubrey Maminot. 'Don't touch it!'

'Why not?' said Golde.

'It may be some sort of trap.'

'No, my lord. It's the pack which contains my apparel.'

'If it was left by Olaf Evil Child, it may well contain something else. I know him. He would not scruple to conceal a poisonous snake or a wildcat inside there. Open it without due caution and you may regret it.'

They were in the solar, where the three packs found outside the castle gates had now been taken. Thrilled to see that her clothes had been returned, Golde was being stopped from unpacking them by her host. He jabbed at the first bundle with his sword.

'Stay, my lord,' Golde said with concern. 'You may damage the fabric within.'

'It may already have been damaged beyond repair. I do not believe that Olaf would return any of your possessions without first mutilating them in some way. There is no telling what outrage we may find within.'

He prodded at the bundle with more conviction, moving around it in a circle to attack it from all angles. Putting the safety of her apparel first, Golde jumped in to stop him.

'Let me open it, my lord.'

'It is too dangerous.'

'I'll take that risk.' Golde undid the leather straps and began to sort through the contents of the pack, examining each garment with care before laying it aside. None of them was damaged in any way. She looked up at Aubrey.

'This Olaf has turned Good Samaritan.'

'Never!'

'He stole my attire, now he returns it unharmed.'

'It is a ruse, I tell you,' said Aubrey. 'One pack may be untouched but the others may still hold an ugly surprise. Olaf Evil Child does nothing without a purpose.'

'Could this not be a gesture of friendship?'

'Towards royal commissioners? Impossible! Besides, if he wishes to show amity, why has he not sent back the remainder of your cargo?'

'That contained food. He and his men needed that.'

'What about the horses that were stolen? There is no sign of them. With respect to you, they are worth far more than your wardrobe. Had Olaf restored the horses to you, even I would begin to think more favourably of him.'

'I am just grateful to have my attire back,' Golde said as she undid the straps on the next pack. 'My lord Ralph will be pleased to see that his is returned as well.'

'Open it with caution!' he advised.

'I sense no trap here.'

'I do.'

Aubrey stood over her with his sword still drawn,

but Golde was unworried. She emptied the second pack with brisk confidence and laid Ralph's attire beside her own. The third pack belonged to Gervase, and its contents, too, had been left unharmed. Three bundles of clothes and other possessions now lay on the floor of the solar. Aubrey walked around them with evident distrust.

'There *has* to be a trick involved,' he said.

'It does not lie here, my lord.'

'Why did he send all this back?'

'Because he has no use for it himself.'

'He has stolen sumpter horses from other travellers before now and they have had nothing handed back to them. Why make this gesture towards you?'

'I do not know.'

'More to the point,' said Aubrey, crossing to the window to glare down into the courtyard, 'how was he able to do so? Olaf Evil Child or some of his men gained entry to the city and stood at the very gates of my castle without being seen or heard. Someone will pay heavily for this!' He turned back to Golde and his manner softened. 'Forgive my anger. It is directed at the failings of my men. I am annoyed with them but glad for you. It is a relief to know that someone in this castle has gained from last night's escapade.'

'Indeed we have.'

'Good.' He pointed at the piles of clothing. 'I will send servants to move all this to your apartments.'

'Thank you, my lord.'

'I just wish that I could make sense of it all.'

'Sense?'

'Yes, Golde,' he said. 'A few days ago, someone climbed into my castle and met up with Romulus and Remus. I think the intruder was one of Olaf's men. Last night, packs from your sumpter horses are left outside my gate.' He shook his head in bafflement. 'It does not make sense. Why should Olaf Evil Child send an assassin to kill me one night and yet restore property to my guests shortly afterwards. I want to know what is going on here.'

Still bemused, Aubrey went out of the solar. Golde checked through her belongings again, noting with pleasure that her trinkets had also been returned. Her attention then turned to Ralph's apparel and she reached out to pick up his tunic. After stroking it lovingly, she folded it neatly and gave it a gentle kiss. It was only when she raised her eyes that she realised she was being watched.

Herleve stood in the doorway, her face impassive, her eyes cold. After a pause, she moved swiftly away.

Sunnifa lay claim to being the injured party, but it was her daughter who pleaded her case. Inga was a persuasive advocate with real skill in presenting an argument and an excellent grasp of detail. Nor was she at all deflected by the frequent interruptions from Ralph Delchard. She showed an ability to think on her feet which was surprising in one so young and so untrained. A lawyer himself, Gervase Bret was especially impressed. Inga had a true legal brain.

The dispute centred around the alleged annexations made by Nigel Arbarbonel, one of the leading barons in the North Riding. Land which had been bequeathed to Sunnifa by her late husband, Thorbrand, had been systematically taken away. The amount involved was substantial, running to almost eight hundred acres and, although some of this land was waste, the bulk of it was fertile enough to yield a crop. From being the wife of a relatively wealthy man, Sunnifa had shrunk to being a widow in straitened circumstances.

Gervase took over the cross-examination of Inga. He admired her courage in calling so powerful an opponent as Nigel Arbarbonel to account, but it was not his place to take sides. Convincing as she sounded in full flow, there were elements of her statement that needed to be probed.

'You make serious charges against my lord Nigel,' he said. 'But you offer little evidence to support them.'

'I have offered a great deal,' she retorted. 'I have explained how each part of my father's estate was seized from us over a period of time and why we have been unable to regain ownership. You have heard my mother's testimony and Father Brunn has also spoken under oath. Surely you do not doubt the word of a priest?'

'That is not the point at issue.'

'Then what is?'

'Documentary proof,' said Gervase. 'To justify your claim, there must be a will and title deeds to the property.'

She bridled. 'Do you think that we came here to *lie*?'

'Of course not.'

'And do you have any idea how many threats were

made against us when we dared even to raise this matter?'

'How could I?'

'We mustered fourteen other witnesses to speak on our behalf,' she continued. 'Each one of them was stopped from travelling to York. Some were bullied, some were beaten, one even had an eye put out when he tried to defy them.' She held up her palms. 'No. I do not have any documentary proof of this either, and if you ask of Hogni the Blacksmith he will tell you that his eye was blinded when sparks flew up from his fire – but I know the truth. My mother and Brunn the Priest know it also.'

Sunnifa and the old man nodded in agreement.

'These are heavy accusations . . .' said Gervase.

'I do not make them lightly.'

'The King's writ runs in the North just as effectively as in any other part of England. If we choose, we can compel witnesses to appear before us.'

'They would refuse to speak on our behalf.'

'Even under oath?'

'Hogni does not want to lose his other eye.'

'We have only your word that the first was put out as an act of malice,' said Ralph. 'I have heard good things of Nigel Arbarbonel. Men whose opinion I respect have praised him. He has also served his king by fighting bravely against the Scots. Do not make wild allegations about him unless you have the means to substantiate them.'

'Am I to produce the title deeds to Hogni's missing eye?' she said with sarcasm.

Ralph tensed. 'Show contempt and you will be ejected from here. That will not advantage your mother's position.'

'No, my lord,' said Inga, flashing a steely smile. 'And I apologise for my rudeness. I do not mean to offend you in any way. You are, after all, our only hope of retribution.'

'You would do well to bear that in mind.'

'Let us return to the question of documents,' said Gervase, taking over from Ralph once more. 'In the last resort, everything turns on that.'

Inga nodded. 'I agree. May I please ask a question?'

'If you wish.'

'The first team of commissioners visited Yorkshire earlier in the year. They were larger in number and did their work with great thoroughness.'

'So will we,' promised Ralph.

'When my lord Nigel was called before them, did he produce documents to show that he owned the land that once formed my father's estate?'

'No, he did not,' admitted Gervase.

'How do you know that?'

'The returns relating to this county were sent to the Exchequer in Winchester. I studied them with great care before we set out. I also had the good fortune to talk with one of the commissioners who visited York. No documents were offered by Nigel Arbarbonel as proof of ownership in this particular instance.'

'Then how was that property deemed to be his?'

'By word of mouth. He swore under oath that the carucates now under dispute belonged to him, and his sub-tenants swore likewise. The account book confirmed that they paid their rent to Nigel Arbarbonel. That was proof enough that he was the legitimate holder of the land in question. Nobody came forward to contest his claim.'

'For one good reason.'

'What was that?'

'We were not given the opportunity to do so.'

'You must have been,' said Gervase. 'That was the main function of the commissioners' visit. To establish who owned what and for how long they had held it.'

'We were deceived,' Inga said bitterly. 'When the summons came we thought we finally had a chance to get our rightful inheritance back again. But it was not to be.'

'Why not?'

'We were deliberately misled. By the time we got to York, the commissioners had completed their work here and moved on to Beverley.'

'I find that hard to believe.'

'It happened, I assure you.'

'The commissioners would never request you to appear at a place from which they were about to depart. That would be perverse. Who brought the summons?'

'He claimed to be the reeve's man.'

'Claimed?'

'We think he was an impostor.'

'On what grounds?'

'He gave us false information,' argued Inga. 'We were prevented from contesting my lord Nigel's claim.'

'Did you not take this up with the town reeve himself?'

'Naturally.'

'When had he sent his messenger?'

'Two days earlier.'

'And the man who came to you . . .?'

'The reeve did not recognise him from our description.'

Gervase sat back pensively. He was at least ready to consider the possibility that her version of events might be true. Ralph was not. He struck a note of jocular derision.

'One-eyed blacksmiths. Phantom messengers. Deep-laid plots to cheat you out of a mythical inheritance. How much more of this nonsense is there?'

'It is the truth,' Inga said indignantly.

'You tell a good story, I grant you that.'

'I am explaining what actually happened.'

'What you want us to *believe* actually happened,' Ralph corrected. 'But it will not hold water, I fear. Three of you are trying to discredit the testimony of Nigel Arbarbonel and several reliable witnesses. Against them, you carry little weight in the scales of justice.'

'We would carry much more if fourteen other voices had not been silenced. We are the victims of a conspiracy.'

'They all say that.'

Inga struggled to control herself, all too conscious of the fact that hot words might relieve her anger but they would certainly prejudice her case. Gervase could see her predicament. He adopted a more polite line of questioning.

'Let us return to your summons,' he said. 'You were given misleading information about the time when you could appear before the first commissioners. Is that what you claim?'

'Yes,' she said through gritted teeth.

'And the reeve did not send the man who came to you?'

'That is what he told us.'

'Then what of the messenger he *did* send?'

'Good question, Gervase,' said Ralph. 'I never thought of that.' He smiled at Inga. 'Well?'

'I do not know,' she confessed.

'Another crack opens up in your argument!'

'No, my lord!' she denied. 'I do not know because we did not stay in York while the reeve tried to ascertain how his summons went astray. My mother and I set off to Beverley in pursuit of the commissioners.'

'Did you catch up with them?' asked Gervase.

'We did, but it was too late. Their business in York was concluded and they were only dealing with claims relating to property in the East Riding. It was a crushing blow for us.' She winced at the memory then rallied slightly. 'But they did have the grace to let us state our complaint even if they could not look into it. We were told that a note of our protest would be included in the returns that were sent to Winchester.'

'That is how it came to our notice.'

'We are very thankful. It shows that our journey to Beverley was not in vain.'

'Did you not then return to York?'

'It would have taken us out of our way,' she said. 'We

took ourselves home by another route and still have no idea why the reeve's summons did not reach us when it should have.' She turned to Ralph. 'I urge you to look into it.'

'Do not try to tell us our job.'

'It is a request and not a demand.'

'We will handle this case in our own way.'

'Then I have nothing more to add.'

'That still leaves the vexed question of documents,' said Gervase. 'Your father must have been able to prove his right and title to that land.'

'He was,' she affirmed.

'Then where are those documents now?'

Inga turned to her mother. The speed of the argument had left the older woman confused and her daughter had to explain the situation in her own tongue. Sunnifa and Brunn grew increasingly anxious. Inga attempted to reassure them.

Gervase prompted her. 'Well?'

'The documents are in existence,' she said, 'but we do not have them in our possession at the moment.'

'Where are they?'

'We will bring them to you.'

'When?'

Sunnifa and Brunn looked forlorn, but Inga drew herself up to her full height. Her voice had a confident ring.

'Soon.'

Canon Hubert was quick to realise his error of judgement. Tanchelm of Ghent was by no means the silent observer he had anticipated. The Fleming became too interested in the cases before them to stand completely apart from the proceedings in the shire hall, and began to make comments of his own. Hubert clicked his tongue in disapproval at first but he came to see how pertinent Tanchelm's questions were, putting more than one witness in difficulty and eliciting valuable information which might otherwise have remained hidden. Since the canon's authority was in no way jeopardised by his colleague's interventions, he began to encourage them.

As another case was dispatched, he turned to Tanchelm. 'Thank you for your assistance, my lord.'

'It was your interrogation that was decisive.'

'I sensed that the fellow was lying.'

'And I took my lead from you, Canon Hubert,' said Tanchelm. 'That is why I pressed him so hard. Between us, we finally broke him.'

'Indeed we did. Though I do have a reservation.'

'Reservation?'

'Yes, my lord. At one point, you spoke to him in Danish.'

'That is the language he best understood.'

'But *I* did not understand it,' said Canon Hubert.

'No more did I,' added Brother Simon. 'I could record nothing of what was said between the two of you because I have no command of that tongue.'

'I learned it from my wife. Marry a Danish woman and she will do the same for you, Brother Simon.'

'Never!' gasped the monk, blanching at the notion. 'I prefer to remain ignorant of the language and isolated from females of every description. I embrace chastity.'

'It does you credit,' said Tanchelm without irony.

'Be more sparing in your use of Danish,' said Hubert pleasantly. 'That is all we ask, my lord.'

'I obey your instruction.'

'Thank you.'

Canon Hubert was content. He shuffled through the papers in front of him to see what their next case was. Dispensing summary justice was a source of great pleasure to him. He had the satisfaction of sitting in judgement on lesser mortals without having to get too embroiled in complex legal debate. Ralph Delchard's absence was a double blessing. It saved Hubert from the usual bickering with his fellow commissioner and enabled him to have the final word in each case. Piety and practicality informed his approach. A high moral framework and an almost saintly fair-mindedness were tempered by the need to move the business of the day along. Brother Simon was duly impressed.

'You have shown the wisdom of Solomon,' he said.

'I simply wield the sword of justice, Brother Simon.'

'With consummate skill.'

'The Lord guides my hand.'

'You are too modest, Canon Hubert,' said Tanchelm. 'Take pride in your own abilities. Without your knowledge of law and understanding of human nature, we would still be toiling through the first case that came before us. Thanks to your adroit handling of affairs, we have already settled half a dozen disputes. I will sing your praises to Ralph Delchard.'

'That will be most gratifying, my lord.'

'My own contribution has been small, I know, but it is good to feel that church and state can work so effectively side by side.'

'Unhappily, that is not always so,' said Hubert with a sidelong glance at the adjacent building. 'Some colleagues are not as amenable as yourself. However, we delay. Let us turn our attention to the next case. It concerns a dispute in the wapentake of Skyrack.'

Six of Tanchelm's soldiers stood on duty at the rear of the shire hall. Two of them were dispatched to bring in the people involved in the next case. Waiting for a fresh batch of witnesses, Hubert recalled the last who had stood before them. He turned to Tanchelm.

'What did you say to him, my lord?'

'To whom?"

'The man from Barkston Ash whom we examined even now. When you spoke in Danish, what did you ask him?'

Tanchelm of Ghent gave an enigmatic smile. 'Nothing of importance,' he said.

Intense discussion followed the departure of Inga, Sunnifa and Brunn the Priest. Their evidence had intrigued Gervase Bret but struck a different chord in Ralph Delchard. While the former believed that they had told the truth, the latter suspected that their stories were largely confected, especially as they could produce no written proof of their claims. Nigel Arbarbonel himself had still to be questioned, and they would reserve their judgement until that examination had been completed, but their respective sympathies were already tipping in opposite directions.

Brother Francis preserved a tactful silence. Completely detached, his sole aim was to fulfil his duties as a scribe in a satisfactory way. Ralph and Gervase were more than pleased with him. When they read through his record of what had so far transpired, they could see a penetrating mind behind the neat calligraphy. Brother Francis had missed nothing of significance in Inga's impassioned testimony.

Before continuing, the commissioners elected to take a break for refreshment. Ralph went out with Brother Francis, and the men-at-arms also vacated the room. Gervase remained behind to clear up his papers and put them back into the satchel. When he was ready to leave, he was astonished to see Inga standing just inside the door.

There was a long pause. Some of her earlier confidence seemed to have drained away and there was a hint of apprehension in her eyes. For the first time, Gervase saw how vulnerable she really was. His sympathy welled up.

'May I please speak with you?' she asked softly.

'Not if it concerns the dispute under consideration.'

'But there is something you must know.'

'You should have divulged it under oath when you had the opportunity.'

'And risk the scorn of your colleague?' she said with asperity. 'You listened to what we said. He simply attacked our evidence.'

'My lord Ralph is a just man,' said Gervase firmly. 'You will not find a more honest and impartial judge. It is his job to sift every allegation with care just as it is mine to support him. We may have a different approach but we seek the same end: to establish the true facts of every claim and to rectify any illegalities.'

'What are you telling me?'

'Do not try to advance your cause by seeking me out alone so that you may in some way influence me.'

Inga was hurt. 'Is that what you think I am doing?'

'Why else have you come?'

'To explain.'

'This is not the time and place for explanation.'

'A few moments is all that I crave.'

He shrugged his reluctance. 'I must decline.'

'Was I so wrong about you?' she said, coming across to him. 'All I seek is a fair hearing but you believe I am here to exert influence. *How?* Am I supposed to give you money? Or did you expect me to offer myself?'

Gervase was jolted. Without meaning to, he had clearly insulted her. His cheeks burned with embarrassment and his guilt deepened when he saw the first tear in her eye. He stepped around the table to stand next to her. Striking a note of appeasement he spoke to her in Saxon. 'I am deeply sorry if I have offended you,' he said. 'It was not intentional.'

Inga blinked at him. Surprised by the apology, she was even more surprised to hear it offered in the language of the common people. She scrutinised him with new interest.

'I had a Saxon mother,' he explained. 'When you

talked to your own mother and to your priest, I understood what you were saying. I feel that you should know that.'

'Thank you.'

'Not that you said anything which compromised you in this dispute. And I was certainly not eavesdropping in the hope of catching you out.'

They were only a couple of feet apart now and Gervase became more fully aware of her charms. When they had faced each other earlier across the table, she had been a bold advocate in search of justice. Inga was now a handsome woman with the bloom of youth on her. Gervase felt strangely drawn to her and had to school himself to remember his judicial role. She, too, sensed an affinity. As they gazed at each other, they shared a momentary tenderness that neither of them dared acknowledge.

Inga lowered her head while she gathered her thoughts. 'Toki,' she said at length. 'His name is Toki.'

'Whose name?'

'He has the evidence that you demand.'

'The relevant documents?'

'Toki has been gathering proof on our behalf.'

'He is not listed among the witnesses,' said Gervase.

'No,' she said. 'He works through us. His job was to provide us with the documents in this case.'

'Then where are they?'

'We have no idea.'

'Why not?'

'Toki has vanished. There has been no trace of him for days. Something dreadful must have happened. He knew how important it was for us to present a strong case while you are in York. Toki would never deliberately let us down.'

Gervase did not need to ask what relationship she had with Toki. The softness in her voice and the wistful look in her eye told the same story. Toki was her beloved and she was shattered by his disappearance. Gervase had the uneasy feeling that he might know where the absent friend was.

'What was Toki like?' he asked.

'The most caring and honest man in the world.'

'Can you describe him to me?'

'Tall, fair and lean with a kind face.'

'And a beard?'

'Yes, Toki wore a fine beard.'

'Was he strong and lithe?'

'Very strong and as lithe as a cat. Toki knew how to defend himself in any situation. He would not easily be struck down.' Quiet despair seized her. 'Where can he be?'

'*Misereatur vestri omnipotens Deus et dismissis peccatis vestris, perducat vos at vitem aeternam* . . .'

Philip the Chaplain conducted the burial service with brusque solemnity. Nobody was there to mourn the deceased. The mangled remains of an unknown man were lowered into the ground and the chaplain tossed a handful of earth on to the coffin as his chant continued. When the signal came, the gravedigger stepped in quickly with his spade to suffocate the foul smell which rose up from inside the wooden box.

As he turned away, Philip heaved a sigh of relief. A burdensome responsibility had been lifted from his shoulders and an excrescence had been removed from his mortuary. He found it difficult to view the corpse as a human being. Romulus and Remus had left so little of the body that he had virtually consigned no more than a pile of bones to the earth. His relief was overtaken by a sudden remorse and he turned to look back. The gravedigger was still busy.

Philip the Chaplain thought of the dismembered corpse which had lain on his slab in an attitude of torment. Pity surged.

'Who *are* you?' he asked.

It never occurred to him that Toki would soon answer the question from the grave.

Chapter Five

Olaf Evil Child chewed his way through the roasted capon and washed it down with a cup of strong ale. He and his men were camped near a stream so that the horses could be watered. There was abundant cover from the trees and bushes, but sentries were posted as a matter of course. Olaf had also sent out scouts to comb a wider area in search of prey or potential danger.

The giant figure of Eric dropped down beside him.

'Why did you do it?' he asked.

'Do what?'

'Return those packs to the castle.'

'The visitors needed them and we did not.'

'Then why did we steal them in the first place?'

'For this,' said Olaf, holding up the carcass of his capon before throwing it into the undergrowth. 'We wanted their provisions and not their clothing. It will do no harm to let them see we can be bountiful.'

'But you took such a risk, going into York like that.'

'It was worth it, Eric.'

'Was it?'

'Of course.'

'How?'

'Imagine the look on my lord Aubrey's face when he opened the castle gates to find that we had walked right up to his fortress in the night. He would have been enraged. His guards will have been roundly swinged for not spotting us.'

'We know how to make use of darkness.'

'And of the river.'

Eric pondered. 'Is that why we went?' he said, still not comprehending. 'To enrage my lord Aubrey once more?'

'No,' said Olaf. 'We tried to win their good opinion.'

'Who?'

'The guests at the castle.'

'Ah.' More rumination followed. 'Why?'

'It does not matter.'

'I want to know.'

'All will become clear in time. With luck.' The huge face beside him puckered with bewilderment. Olaf gave his friend a good-humoured slap on the thigh. 'Do not puzzle over it, Eric. You are a fine warrior but a poor philosopher. Stick to fighting. Leave the thinking to me.'

'But I need to see what we are fighting *for*.'

'Ourselves. Our future.'

Eric brightened. 'Will there be women?'

'Dozens of them,' teased Olaf.

'It gets lonely out here at night.'

'Our time will come.'

'When?'

'Wait and see.'

The sound of approaching hoofbeats brought both men to their feet and they drew their swords from force of habit. The rest of the camp were also on the alert. When a familiar figure came riding into the camp, they all relaxed and sheathed their weapons. The newcomer reined in his mount and dropped to the ground before limping across to Olaf Evil Child.

'Riders!' he reported. 'Heading for York.'

'How many?'

'Twenty or more.'

'Did you recognise them?'

'They were too far off. You told me to bring warning of any travellers on that road. I galloped straight here.'

'You did well,' said Olaf, giving him a grateful pat. 'Let us take a closer look at them. Mount up!'

Within seconds, every man was in his saddle. Led by their scout, they set off in the direction from which he had just come. It was not a long journey. When they reached the top of a wooded slope, they dismounted and crept through the undergrowth. Hooves were soon clacking on the track below them. Olaf Evil Child was the first to push back a branch and take stock of the travellers.

There were two dozen of them in all, Norman soldiers in their distinctive armour, riding their destriers at a steady canter over the last mile to York. At their head was a tall, slim man who sat upright in the saddle exuding an air of authority. His face was hidden from the onlookers but Olaf knew his identity at once. He spat out the name with hatred.

'Nigel Arbarbonel!'

* * *

Romulus and Remus roared with anticipation as the key was inserted into the lock of their cage. It was feeding time and they were hungry. Ludovico made them wait, talking to them as he entered the cage and ordering them to lie down before he gave them any of the meat he was carrying in a large wooden bowl. The lions snarled in protest but their keeper would not yield up their meal until his orders were obeyed. Ludovico stood over them until both Romulus and Remus lay down on the floor, their ears pricked and their tails flicking to and fro.

When the animals were quiescent, the Italian threw a glance at his master. Aubrey Maminot let himself into the cage and crossed to take the first hunk of meat from the bowl. When he placed it in front of Romulus, the lion pounced on it with eager teeth. Remus was soon also tearing apart the carcass of a lamb. Keeping them supplied with fresh meat on a daily basis was an expense that Aubrey was glad to meet. His beloved lions were a high priority in the account book of the castle. Since they were so dependent for their welfare on Ludovico, Aubrey made sure that the Keeper of the Beasts was well paid for his services.

'Do you still miss Rome?' he asked.

'Only in winter,' said Ludovico. 'York is so much colder than Italy.'

'We have ways to keep you warm.'

The Italian grinned. 'Your women are hot-blooded. They are lionesses in bed. I enjoy taming them.'

'You have a gift with wild animals, Ludovico.'

'I simply teach them that I am their master.'

Romulus and Remus were still eating noisily. The door of their cage had been locked as a precaution. Only Aubrey and Ludovico were allowed inside it when the lions were in residence. During the night, when the animals were let out to patrol the ditch at the base of the mound, servants cleaned their cage and strewed the floor with fresh rushes. Only Ludovico knew how to make his charges return to their prison each morning, but Aubrey was working hard to increase his own power over his pets.

'Leave me alone with them,' he said.

'They are a little restless today.'

'I am not afraid, Ludovico.'

'Let me stand where they can see me.'

'No,' said Aubrey. 'I will be fine.'

The Italian nodded and let himself out of the cage before locking it behind him. When he tried to linger, he was waved away by Aubrey. Alone at last with his lions, the castellan felt happy and confident. They would not harm him. He reached into the bowl and tossed more meat to each of them. Romulus and Remus gave lazy roars of gratitude. Aubrey chuckled as a sense of power coursed through him. They were his.

Nigel Arbarbonel strode into the room with the assurance of a man about to meet old friends rather than the caution of a witness about to be questioned by royal commissioners. He ducked beneath a low beam before drawing himself up again to smile at Ralph Delchard and Gervase Bret. Having dealt with so many hostile witnesses in the past, they were caught off guard by his affability. His swarthy face was striking rather than handsome, but there was no denying his charm.

'Nigel Arbarbonel!' he announced. 'Welcome to the dank city of York, gentlemen. How may I help you?'

'By sitting down for a start,' said Ralph. 'Before you knock your head, as I have already done more than once. This room was not built for people as tall as you and me.'

Nigel laughed as he tossed back his mantle and lowered himself to the bench. Ralph performed the introductions then pointed to a leather satchel on the table.

'Your reeve kindly delivered this to us.'

'It contains all the documents you may need to see,' said Nigel helpfully. 'I thought it best to send them in advance so that you would have time to study them before my arrival.'

'That was most considerate.'

'Did you find everything in order?'

'You must ask that of Gervase. He alone has read them.'

Nigel turned to him. 'Were you satisfied, Master Bret?'

'Up to a point, my lord.'

'Oh?'

'The documents submitted establish you without question as the legitimate holder of most of your property, but the land which forms the basis of this enquiry – in the wapentakes of Bulmer, Halikeld and Manshowe – have no title deeds attached to them.'

'I explained that to your predecessors.'

'We have a record of that explanation, my lord.'

'Then you will know that countless witnesses came forward to swear that I was their overlord.' His smile broadened. 'The name of Arbarbonel is well known in the north. My reputation stretches across the county. Aubrey Maminot is your host, is he not? Send for him and he will vouch for my integrity.'

'That is precisely why we may not send for him,' said Ralph sternly. 'My lord Aubrey is a personal friend. It was only because he is not a subject of investigation that I felt able to accept his hospitality. Because we must be strictly impartial at all times, we are only sent to places where we are not known so that bias or favouritism will not ever arise.'

'That is as it should be,' said Nigel easily. 'It is the one sure way to guarantee a fair trial. When Aubrey Maminot had a banquet in your honour, he took care not to invite me lest that be seen as a means of courting you on my behalf. Had we met in such convivial circumstances, you might not now be able to exercise your impartiality quite so freely.'

'I am glad that we understand each other on that.'

'Completely, my lord.'

Ralph was satisfied with his polite acceptance of the situation, but Gervase was more wary. Having failed to use the name of Aubrey Maminot to his advantage, Nigel Arbarbonel had given the impression that he would never seek favour of any kind. A man who could contradict himself so smoothly and so convincingly needed to be watched.

Nigel swung his attention back to Gervase again. 'Bulmer, Halikeld and Manshowe, you say?'

'Yes, my lord.'

'Then I know who contests the property.'

'Sunnifa appeared before us earlier today.'

'Poor, distracted creature! If she were not such a nuisance to me, I could almost feel sorry for the woman.'

'It was her daughter who presented the claim.'

'Inga is an even greater nuisance,' said Nigel with a slow smile, 'but I have more time for her. You have met the lady and will understand why. She is fighting for what she conceives to be the inheritance from her father. I respect her for that. But when Thorbrand died, she was young and unaware of what really happened to the property. Inga is too impetuous. With no real evidence at her disposal, she attacks me with claims based on distant memories of her father.'

'Those memories are not so distant to Sunnifa,' noted Gervase. 'Nor to Brunn the Priest.'

'Brunn is a good man. But old. And very tired.'

'He spoke fondly of Thorbrand.'

'I would expect no less.'

'Brunn was at his bedside when he died. He attested that Thorbrand bequeathed his property to his wife.'

'That is how it may have seemed at the time.'

'What do you mean, my lord?'

'Only this,' said Nigel quietly. 'To watch a loved one die is always painful. It plays cruelly on the emotions. Things get distorted. Sunnifa was grief-stricken when she lost her husband. She is still in mourning. That clouds her judgement badly.'

'What of Brunn the Priest? Is his judgement clouded?'

'He is an honest man who has served his flock to the best of his abilities for many years. But time and the northern climate have taken their toll, as you have seen. Brunn wanders. His mind is no longer reliable.'

'Inga did not wander. Her mind was crystal clear.'

'But she takes her lead from Sunnifa and the priest.'

'We are going around in circles,' said Ralph with impatience. 'Instead of trying to discredit those who oppose you here, my lord, simply tell us how Thorbrand's property came into your possession.'

'With pleasure. It was by deed of gift.'

'Gift?'

'Thorbrand had cause to be deeply grateful to me.'

'Why was that, my lord?' asked Gervase.

'Because I protected him and his family.' He gave a tolerant smile. 'You are no soldier, Master Bret, and you have no notion of the problems that beset us here. We are in constant danger of attack from the Scots. It is vital to have a strong bulwark against them. That is why the King granted such huge amounts of land in the north of the county to his two most trusted friends.'

'It is true,' confirmed Ralph. 'The King's own half-brother, Robert, Count of Mortain, holds vast estates along with Alan the Red of Brittany. Between them, they form a solid band across the north of the county.'

'My land lies directly south of them,' said Nigel. 'If they are a first line of defence, I am a palisade behind them. Thorbrand understood this only too well because his land was twice overrun before I drove out the raiders. They had cunningly penetrated the gaps. Thorbrand came to see that a second continuous line of defence was needed and that could only be formed if he willed his land to me and enabled my holdings to be linked together in a wide strip.'

Gervase was doubtful. 'He *willed* the land to you?'

'On his deathbed.'

'Brunn heard no mention of this.'

'Other witnesses sat in that room with him. They will support me to the letter.'

'Is there no written proof of this?'

'Unhappily, no,' said Nigel. 'Thorbrand renounced his will in his last hours on earth and bequeathed most of his property to me. His family were not left unprovided for but their inheritance was somewhat reduced.'

'It was cut to shreds, my lord.'

'Of necessity.'

'He consigned his own wife and daughter to a life of comparative poverty? That verges on the incredible.'

'Not if you had undergone the rigours that he did,' said the other earnestly. 'Thorbrand suffered badly at the hands of raiding parties because he had no means of defending himself. That is why he turned to me. And why he put the safety of his wife and daughter before anything else. He went to his grave knowing that they would be well protected even if their means were more modest.'

'And *are* they well protected, my lord?'

'Yes!' he said proudly. 'They are shielded by the arm of Nigel Arbarbonel.'

'They pay a high price for that honour,' observed Gervase as he glanced at the document before him. 'Since the land came into your possession, the rent from it has risen appreciably.'

'There has been a slight increase, I fear.'

'Thorbrand was a less demanding landlord.'

'He did not have to maintain any defences.'

'The rent has more than trebled since he died.'

'Is that relevant?' asked Nigel pleasantly. 'You are here to determine who owns that land and not how much rent it yields. That amount is already on record and your predecessors raised no objection to it. Why should you?'

Gervase traded a glance with Ralph. It took no more than a split second but a signal had passed between them. They knew how to deal with their suave witness.

Nigel Arbarbonel was enjoying himself. Polite, plausible and supremely confident of his position, he answered every question with an obliging readiness. His word would always outweigh that of his detractors. The first commissioners were a more powerful and formidable team, yet he had survived their examination without any discomfort. He decided that their successors would be even less troublesome. His policy of willing co-operation would confound them.

Gervase Bret forced him to revise that opinion.

'That is all,' he said dismissively. 'I have no more questions.' He turned to Ralph. 'My lord?'

'I have nothing more to add,' said Ralph.

Nigel smiled hopefully. 'You have finished with me?'

'For the moment,' said Gervase.

'And it is all settled?'

'Far from it, my lord.'

'But you have heard my evidence.'

'Indeed we have, and it has been most interesting. But it does not resolve the matter. On the contrary, it directs our enquiries to a wider field than we foresaw.'

'I want this whole business settled here and now.'

'There is too much evidence still to collect.'

'From whom?'

'You will find that out when we next send for you.'

'It is a long ride to York from my castle.'

'Then stay in the city until we need you,' suggested Ralph with a grin. 'We are as anxious as you to reach a verdict in this dispute, but we cannot do so until we have considered every possible aspect.'

Indignation stirred. 'Do you doubt my word?'

'Not in the least. What you have told us may well turn out to be the truth. We would just like to make sure that it is the whole truth.'

'One last thing, my lord,' said Gervase casually.

'Yes?'

'Thorbrand, I believe, lived in the wapentake of Bulmer.'

'That is so. Close to Dalby.'

'How long would it take to get there from York?'

'Four or five hours at most on a fast horse.'

'The town reeve's man rode hard, we are told.'

'To Dalby?'

'Yes, my lord,' said Gervase. 'To summon Thorbrand's widow to make her claim before our predecessors. The messenger did not arrive in time. He left here on the appointed day, he claims, yet the summons did not reach Dalby until over forty-eight hours later. Does that not strike you as odd?'

Nigel shrugged. 'Perhaps he went astray.'

'He insists that he did not.'

'Then I am as baffled as you by this mystery.'

'Only one solution offers itself, my lord.'

'And what is that?'

'The man who took the summons from York was not the same person who arrived in Dalby over two days later. The reeve's messenger handed over the duty to somebody else.'

'Why on earth should he do that?'

'To ensure that vital evidence never reached York.'

'That same evidence has reached it now,' said Nigel as he rose to his feet. 'Was it really so vital? Do the ramblings of a widow and an old priest really have any credence? You say that Inga presented the case against me, but did she provide any documents to back it up? Unlike you, the first commissioners were not inclined to suffer fools gladly. They would have exposed this vital evidence as the tissue of lies that it is.'

'We will be in touch,' said Ralph grimly.

'I await your call.' Nigel Arbarbonel turned away and headed for the door. Feeling that he had put the commissioners firmly in their place, he could not resist a parting shot. 'Have you really come all this way to discuss the riding habits of the reeve's man?' he said, swinging round. 'There may yet be another explanation of why it took him so long to deliver his summons to Dalby. Perhaps he lost his way or fell among thieves.

Perhaps he was chased off course by wild bears.' He grinned amiably. 'Or perhaps his horse simply cast a shoe.'

'Hogni the Blacksmith would have replaced it for him,' said Gervase evenly. 'He could see with both eyes then.'

The grin remained on their visitor's face as he went out. Gervase was disappointed. Though he and Ralph had applied pressure on the witness, it did not have the desired effect. Nigel Arbarbonel was too composed and well-defended to give anything away.

Frustration made Gervase click his tongue. 'I am sure that he is lying,' he said.

'So am I,' said Ralph, 'but how do we prove it?'

'By gathering more evidence.'

'Where?'

'In the land under dispute, if need be. It may be the only way to grapple with the true facts of the case.'

Ralph shook his head. 'Time is against us, Gervase. This is only the first of a number of claims into which we must look. If we ride out to view the property in question each time, we will be stuck in Yorkshire for months!'

'This dispute merits special attention.'

'Because of Inga?'

'No, Ralph.'

'I think that you are falling in love with the girl.'

'That is absurd.'

'Is it? If I did not have my dear Golde beside me, I would be tempted myself. Inga certainly merits special attention.'

'I am only concerned with her testimony,' said Gervase. 'And with that of my lord Nigel. Why did he confront us in person when he might so easily have let his reeve speak on his behalf? Why did he wish to have the dispute resolved so quickly? Why try to woo us with a show of assistance?'

'I do not know,' conceded Ralph. 'I do not trust him, but no more do I trust Inga and her mother. They made some wild accusations. Nigel Arbarbonel does not resemble in any way the ugly portrait they drew of him.'

'We shall see.'

'What next?'

'We need to pick our way more carefully through this sheaf of documents from my lord Nigel. There is something I have missed here, I feel certain.'

'I leave that task to you, Gervase. I would not know what to look for and my Latin would be woefully unequal to the demands made upon it. And when you have finished . . .?'

'I need to speak with Inga once more.'

'Ah!' teased Ralph. 'So she *has* touched off a spark in you.'

'It is not like that,' said Gervase. 'She is a witness in a dispute and nothing more. But there is something that I must tell her.' Ralph's rich chuckle threw him even more on the defensive. 'I must remind her that the burden of proof lies on her mother. If they are to win the dispute, they must produce the documents that they claim to have.'

'Otherwise, Nigel Arbarbonel retains that land.'

'Quite so.'

A discreet cough turned their heads towards Brother Francis. He had been so quiet and unobtrusive that they had completely forgotten he was there.

'Will you require my services again today?' he asked.

'Not for some time,' said Ralph.

'Then I will withdraw, my lord.'

'Please do, Brother Francis. You have earned a rest.'

The monk beamed. 'It has been an education to me.'

'You bore up well in the presence of women. Brother Simon would have been reduced to a quivering wreck. He prefers the safety of the cloister.'

'It has its compensations, my lord.' He padded towards the door. 'You know where to reach me. Farewell.'

Golde was finding life at the castle increasingly irksome. There was nowhere in the building where she could feel completely at ease. If she went to the solar, she was met by the unwelcoming smile of Herleve. If she strolled in the courtyard, she was the target of lustful comments from the soldiers. If she stayed in her apartment, she was bored. When she ventured down to peer through the lions' cage, she only sent Romulus and Remus into a frenzy of snarling.

Her growing discomfort made her ask herself what exactly she was doing at the castle. She loved Ralph enough to follow him anywhere, but events had forced her to view their relationship through the eyes of others. The romantic glow in which she had abandoned her home in Hereford had faded to a dim flicker in York. Proud to be his lover, she resented being seen as

Ralph's mistress. When she looked into the unforgiving face of Herleve, she was made to feel that she was no more than his whore. It was humiliating.

Golde was distressed. Leaving her house, her occupation and her sister had not been done on impulse. She had given her decision great thought. Her Christian upbringing had taxed her conscience sorely, and her strong ties with Hereford provided further resistance. Yet she had left. When Ralph asked her to go with him, making no promise of marriage, or indeed of anything else, Golde had accepted his invitation because it contained both rescue and hope for her. They were delightfully happy when alone together, but a dark shadow was now falling across that happiness. As she sat brooding in her apartment, Golde began to wonder if their love would be resilient enough to survive what might well be a lengthy stay in York.

Unable to relax, she adjourned to the one place in the castle which offered peace and seclusion. The chapel was empty. Its very coldness was a source of refreshment to her. Kneeling at the altar rail, she offered up a silent prayer and asked for guidance. No answer came but her mind slowly began to clear. She was able to consider her situation in a more honest and objective light. What was her moral duty? What were her true feelings for the man with whom she shared her life? Where did her future lie? She remained on her knees for a long time. Golde was still trying to reconcile conflicting values when a figure crept up behind her.

Ralph had returned briefly to the castle. Finding her

in the chapel, he was struck by her attitude of submission and by the deep concentration on her face. Without saying a word, he moved forward to kneel beside her and took her hand gently between his own. Golde did not need to open her eyes. She knew that it was him and drew immense strength from his proximity. Ralph, too, was touched. A wayward Christian, he yet sensed the true power of spiritual commitment in the tiny chapel. He also felt closer than ever before to Golde.

Whatever disapproval they might meet, whatever sneers they might hear, whatever obstacles they encountered, they would not be separated from each other. That certainty now united them. In their hearts and, at that precise moment, in the sight of the Almighty, they were conjoined as firmly as any man and wife. Golde's doubts fled. She would withstand anything to be with Ralph Delchard. Reading her thoughts, he squeezed her hand softly in reciprocation.

They remained side by side in perfect union. It was a scene at once so solemn and so joyful that even the watching Herleve was moved. She stole quietly away.

Tanchelm of Ghent more than proved his worth in the shire hall that afternoon. Not only did he ask searching questions of evasive witnesses, he also acted as an intermediary between Canon Hubert and those who could only understand the Saxon tongue. Gervase Bret's customary role of interpreter was taken over by Tanchelm whose command of languages was impressive. He was even able to converse freely in Latin with his two colleagues.

Brother Simon was suffused with admiration for the new commissioner and Hubert came to rely more and more on the timely interventions of the Fleming. Only one small doubt lingered in the canon's mind. He wondered why Tanchelm was so keen to question certain witnesses, and he had the occasional feeling that their answers were not translated back to him in full. While functioning as a commissioner, Tanchelm of Ghent seemed to be conducting a supplementary enquiry of his own.

As another dispute was resolved, Hubert turned to him. 'You have missed your vocation, my lord,' he said.

'Have I?'

'Instead of being a soldier, you should have taken to the law. You are a born interrogator.'

'I could never match your expertise, Canon Hubert.'

'Thank you,' said the other, basking in the flattery but not allowing it to deflect him. 'Why did you ask that last witness about Olaf Evil Child?'

Tanchelm feigned surprise. 'Did I do so?'

'More than once. My knowledge of Saxon is fragmentary but I did recognise that name. You used it four times yet it was not included in your translation.'

'That is because it was not germane to the dispute in hand,' explained Tanchelm. 'When I mentioned Olaf Evil Child, I did so out of idle curiosity. The man is a fascinating blend of outlaw and benefactor. What other robber would steal our sumpter horses then return part of their cargo to us? He interests me.'

'What did the witness say of him?'

'He had to guard his words for fear of giving offence.

Everyone in York knows that we were set on by Olaf and his band. The witness could hardly praise an outlaw in front of his victims.'

'Did you sense a hidden approval of the rogue?'

'It was more of a reverence, Canon Hubert. The man to whom we have just restored four carucates of land was unfairly deprived of them. Olaf Evil Child, he told me, was likewise dispossessed when his land was annexed. While most people tried to regain their property by legal process, Olaf had the courage to take up arms and fight back. That has made him something of a hero.'

'Only to ignorant fools. Crime is never heroic.'

'I would agree with you there.'

'Olaf is a coward and a thief.'

'He could be defended against the charge of cowardice but he is certainly guilty of theft. But then,' said Tanchelm, indicating the papers before him, 'so it seems are a number of outwardly respectable magnates. Who is the more reprehensible thief, Canon Hubert? A man who steals five horses or one who seizes upon five hundred acres of someone else's land?'

Gervase Bret pored for a long time over the documents relating to the property of Nigel Arbarbonel. A clear pattern emerged. By a series of annexations, the Norman lord had slowly connected his scattered holdings into a solid unit. Militarily it might have some purpose, but it must also have left much hardship in its wake as tenants found themselves paying increased rent for land they had once owned. Yet everything seemed to have been done legally and to the satisfaction of the first commissioners, who had effectively ratified his multiple acquisitions. It was only over the transfer of Thorbrand's holdings that a question still hovered.

A tap on the door went unheard. It was only when a louder rap was delivered that Gervase raised his head.

'Come in!' he called.

Inga let herself into the room. Gervase sat up with a jolt, surprised at how pleased he was to see her again. It was a few moments before he even noticed that she was not alone. Brunn the Priest had followed her in. Gervase felt a resentment at his presence but he could see why it was necessary. With the priest beside her, Inga was absolved of all charges of trying to exert undue influence on a royal commissioner.

Gervase stood up and walked across to them. Inga was watchful but Brunn volunteered a weary smile. The priest spoke in Saxon.

'We have not come to importune you,' he said.

'I appreciate that.'

'Something of a personal nature is vexing Inga.'

Gervase looked into her face and saw the anguish. She was deeply troubled. Turning for help to someone whom she regarded as a natural enemy was an added source of pain. In her eyes, Gervase was a figure of authority from whom she could expect no sympathy, yet he might hold information that was crucial to her peace of mind.

'When we spoke earlier,' she said, 'I mentioned a friend.'

Gervase nodded. 'His name was Toki.'

'You behaved strangely when I talked of him.'

'Did I?'

'Toki is not only an important figure in this dispute, he is very dear to me.'

'That became obvious. He was a fortunate man.'

'*Was?*'

One word gave a glimpse of the truth. Gervase braced himself to impart the bad news. Inga tensed and Brunn reached out a hand to support her. They feared the worst. Gervase ran his tongue across his lips before speaking.

'You came back because you had the feeling that I might know what had happened to your friend.'

'Yes,' she said. 'There was something about the way you looked at me when I described Toki to you. Have you seen him?'

'I think so.'

'When? Where?'

'It might be wiser if you sat down,' he advised.

'Tell me!' she demanded. 'I must know the truth.'

'I am not certain that I know it myself, Inga. For your sake I hope that I am mistaken. But I fear that I may have met Toki. Your description tallied with . . . what I saw.'

'Go on.'

'I believe that your friend may be dead.'

Inga reeled and Brunn had to steady her. When she recovered, she gave a faint nod to show that she wanted the details. Gervase felt uneasy at having to pass on such dreadful tidings but they could not be kept from her.

'Earlier this week,' he said, 'someone climbed into the castle belonging to Aubrey Maminot. The soldiers on duty that night were lax but the intruder could not evade the other guards who lay in wait.'

'Other guards?' she whispered.

'My lord Aubrey keeps two lions at the castle.'

Inga was rocked. As the full horror was borne in upon her she emitted a cry of despair and began to sway to and fro. To lose her beloved was tragedy enough. The thought that he had been savagely torn to pieces was unendurable.

'No!' she howled, flinging herself at Gervase and trying to beat him with her fists. 'It's not true, it's not true!'

Her rage was short-lived and she collapsed into his arms. With Brunn's help, Gervase carried her to the bench and sat her down. It was minutes before she recovered enough to realise where she was. When she saw that Gervase was supporting her, she pushed him away with contempt. There was a note of profound betrayal in her voice.

'You *knew*,' she accused him. 'You knew all the time.'

'I did not, Inga. I swear it.'

'You led me on to describe Toki so that you could be sure that it was him.'

'No,' said Gervase. 'On the night when he climbed into the castle, we were miles away from here. Nobody in York had any idea who the intruder was. How could a stranger like myself guess his identity?' He knelt beside her. 'It was only when you talked about the disappearance of Toki that I began to wonder if he might be the unfortunate victim.'

'Master Bret speaks honestly,' decided Brunn. 'Do not blame him. This was none of his doing.'

'He is involved now,' she said angrily, 'and he will use this against us to bring us down.'

'Why should I do that?' asked Gervase.

'Because you are a friend of my lord Aubrey. When you tell him that it was Toki who broke into his castle, he will come searching for us to exact punishment.'

'Full punishment has already been exacted by Romulus and Remus,' said Gervase ruefully. 'Besides, I do not intend to reveal Toki's identity to anyone as yet, so there is no question of retaliation against you. I will do everything in my power to save you from being pursued.'

'Will you?' she said in wonderment.

'I give you my word.'

'Why should you protect us?'

'Because I choose to, Inga. I am involved in another way here. I saw Toki's remains laid out in the morgue. No man should go to his grave in such a hideous condition without someone to grieve at his passing.'

'Toki will have grief enough now,' she murmured.

'Why did he climb into the castle that night?'

'I do not know.'

'What could he possibly have been after?'

'I cannot tell you,' she said with a hopeless shrug. 'Toki and I were very close, but there were things that he did not even tell me. Now I see why.'

Gervase did not press her further. Inga patently had no notion of the motives which had led a man to risk his life by scaling a castle wall in York. She was still trying to cope with the enormity of his loss. Toki had not just been beloved; he was instrumental in gathering the evidence with which to confute Nigel Arbarbonel. Without that, Inga and her mother would have little chance.

'Where is he?' she asked.

'Toki was buried this morning.'

'May I see the place?'

'Of course.'

'Will they be watching the grave to see who visits it?'

'I think not.'

'How can I be sure?'

'I will take you there myself.'

'Why are you being so kind to me?'

Gervase could find no answer.

Chapter Six

With an armed escort to clear a way through the crowd for them, Canon Hubert and Brother Simon walked towards York Minster with a sense of profound satisfaction. It had been a productive day. Many disputes had been settled and much land, albeit in small amounts, had been reassigned to its rightful owners. Some people had been foolish enough to try to give false evidence, but Hubert exposed them ruthlessly with the help of Tanchelm of Ghent. The two men had complementary virtues. As a team, they were shrewd, effective and totally impervious to corruption. Canon Hubert was increasingly grateful that he had accepted the Fleming as his judicial partner.

Another decision was also most pleasing in retrospect.

'I was right to insist on lodging apart from the others,' said Hubert. 'We belong on consecrated ground.'

Brother Simon shivered. 'To stay at the castle would have been an ordeal.'

'I could never have tolerated those lions.'

'The female presence would have been more disturbing to me, Canon Hubert. At least the lions are male.'

'But wild and ferocious, by all accounts.'

'It is in their nature. They have no control over their brutish inclination. A civilised man should.'

'You speak of my lord Ralph?'

'I think you know my feelings on that subject.'

'I share them, Brother Simon.'

'Then I will say no more.'

'Please do. Give vent to your thoughts.'

'I am not sure that it is my place to do so. I mean no disrespect to my lord Ralph. In many ways he is worthy of admiration.' Simon drew in his breath. 'In this instance, he most certainly is not.'

'I have endeavoured to make that clear to him.'

'What was his answer, Canon Hubert?'

'Modesty forbids me from repeating such foul language.'

'The lady is not his wife!' hissed Simon in alarm. 'Yet he consorts openly with her. Since we ride with them, we will be seen as condoning their sinful behaviour. But I most assuredly do not condone it.'

'No more do I. It offends me to the marrow.'

'The woman is . . . the woman is . . .'

'Do not be afraid to say the word, Brother Simon.'

'His concubine!'

'Quite so,' said Hubert. 'She travels with him for one purpose only, and that is to offer him delights of the flesh more proper to the state of holy matrimony, and then only in pursuit of lawful procreation.'

'It is shameful to look on such concupiscence.'

'Turn your gaze inward. Contemplate a pure soul.'

'I call the advice of Peter Damiani to my aid.'

'A wise teacher.'

'His words are ever a comfort. "Who, therefore, as a monk, hastens to attain perfection, let him confine himself within the walls of a cloister, let him love spiritual quiet, let him have a horror of running about in the world, as he would of immersing himself in a pool of blood." When I see my lord Ralph and the lady together, I see a pool of blood beckoning to me.'

'Peter Damiani had more to say,' reminded Hubert. 'And it is very relevant to us. "For the world is more and more every day polluted by the contaminations of so many crimes that the holy mind is corrupted by the merest consideration of it." Forced to look on sin, we are stained by its foulness ourselves.'

'I fear that we are!'

The discussion brought them close to the Minster but a bulky figure in a black cowl was now blocking their way. Recognising Brother Francis, they paused to exchange greetings. He smiled benignly at them.

'Are your deliberations concluded for the day?'

'They are,' said Hubert complacently. 'What of our fellow commissioners? Do they no longer require a scribe?'

'I have just been sent for once more.'

'Then we will not delay you, Brother Francis.'

'It is interesting work,' said the other, 'but I would much rather break bread with you in the refectory. I have no taste for secular matters.'

'We have just been saying the same,' boomed Hubert

with easy pomposity. 'Brother Simon and I venerate the monastic ideal – sobriety, humility, patience, obedience, chastity and charity.'

'And the greatest of these is chastity,' added Simon.

'We are all of one mind,' said Francis.

After polite farewells they parted company. Canon Hubert and Brother Simon moved nearer to their God with measured tread. Neither of them saw the contented smile on the face of Brother Francis as he strode with enthusiasm towards another session with the commissioners. When he turned the corner, he positively skipped along the street.

Gervase Bret was in a quandary. How much should he tell Ralph Delchard and how much keep from him? They were close friends as well as colleagues, and he ordinarily confided everything in him. Now it was different. Ralph had a right to know the name of the man who was devoured by the two lions, but Gervase could not divulge it without betraying Inga. He had given her his word. At that moment, for reasons he only vaguely understood, his promise to her took precedence over his obligation to Ralph.

There was an allied fear. If he disclosed the identity of the intruder to Ralph, the latter would feel duty bound to pass it on to Aubrey Maminot. He could hardly enjoy his friend's hospitality while keeping such a valuable piece of information from him. Once in possession of the name of Toki, the castellan would set in train an investigation that would surely lead to Inga and her mother. Though the women knew nothing of Toki's visit to the castle, they would come under grave suspicion and be hounded by Aubrey. Their credibility would be destroyed and their dispute with Nigel Arbarbonel would crumble.

Gervase was not bound to his host by any ties of friendship. Grateful for the accommodation, he had seen enough of the genial Aubrey to be wary of arousing his ire. Romulus and Remus were a lethal pair of pets. A man who took such pleasure in the way they had eaten a human being alive should not be unleashed on two defenceless women. Gervase resolved to keep his own counsel. There were many things he needed to find out about Toki before he passed on the name to anybody.

His meditations were curtailed by the arrival of Ralph Delchard, who marched into the room with four of his men-at-arms. Brother Francis came close on their heels and took his place behind the table. Gervase began to leaf once more through the documents supplied by Nigel Arbarbonel.

Ralph was in a characteristically jocular mood. As he took his seat between the two men, he leaned over to whisper in Gervase's ear.

'Where is she?'

'Who?' said Gervase.

'You know quite well. Where have you hidden her?'

'Inga is no longer here, Ralph.'

'But she was?'

'Very briefly.'

'It only takes a moment for love to blossom.'

'Brunn the Priest was with her,' said Gervase, trying

to sound calm. 'They came for advice.'

'As long as they did not try to bribe you.'

'There was no question of that. I told them that I could not violate my independence by discussing their case. What I did stress – as I told you I would – was the need for documentary evidence. I warned them that they did not have unlimited time in which to produce it.'

'And that was all?'

'That was all.'

Ralph became serious. 'I don't need to tell you of the dangers of being influenced by pleas from any witnesses.'

'No,' said Gervase. 'You don't.'

He met Ralph's gaze without flinching. His friend soon relaxed again and punched him playfully on the shoulder. He pretended to search under the table.

'I still think you have her hidden away somewhere.' He looked over at Brother Francis. 'She's not lurking under your skirt, by any chance?'

'Who, my lord?'

'The young woman we met earlier.'

'Heavens, no!' said the monk with a worldly chortle. 'That is no place for a woman, young or old. I renounced the flesh when I took the cowl.'

'Have you no regrets about such a rash decision?'

'None, my lord.'

'None?'

Brother Francis sat back with a quiet smile. 'None at all.'

'So be it,' said Ralph, anxious to set the wheels of justice in motion once more. 'Let us address our minds to the dispute in hand. Whom do we examine next, Gervase?'

'Tenants of my lord Nigel.'

'I am ready. Fetch the first one in!'

Golde stood at the window of her apartment and looked out at the city below. Night was falling but the moon was a kindly lantern. When she gazed across the river, she saw a larger and more forbidding castle on the eastern bank, surrounded by a moat which had been created when the Foss was dammed to form the King's Fishpool. Houses, meadows and orchards had disappeared to make way for the defensive ring of water around the fortress. It was a fearsome sight, yet the castle of Aubrey Maminot somehow had more character and menace to it. When Golde heard the telltale roar from below, she knew why. Romulus and Remus were in residence.

A tap on the door drew her away from the window. Expecting a servant, she was taken aback when Herleve stepped into the room. The visitor was strangely hesitant.

'May I please come in?' she asked.

'Of course,' said Golde. 'This is your home.'

'It is where I live. That much is true.'

Herleve looked as stately as ever, but her coldness had gone and the polite expression had changed to a wan smile. She glanced around the room before lowering herself into the chair which was offered to her. Golde sat on a stool opposite her, waiting for her visitor to speak first and feeling slightly invaded.

Eyes downcast, Herleve held her hands in her lap as she chose her words with care.

'I have come to apologise to you, Golde.'

'Why, my lady?'

'For my behaviour towards you.'

'That requires no apology.'

'I have been unforgivably rude to you.'

'That is not true, my lady.'

'Yes, it is,' said Herleve, looking up at her. 'When I should have welcomed you, I was cool and distant. Instead of making your stay here a pleasurable one, I have shown you nothing but disdain. I am very sorry.'

Golde could see the effort it had cost her to make such an admission. Herleve's face was tense, her eyes were haunted and her fingers were knotted tightly together. Golde was moved. She felt drawn to a woman whose frailty she was now glimpsing for the first time.

'Thank you, my lady,' she said, 'but you have nothing with which to reproach yourself.'

'Oh, I do, Golde. I do.'

'It is I who should apologise for offending you.'

'That is nonsense.'

'You did not choose to invite me here.'

'My husband's guests are mine also.'

'I was forced upon you.'

'Rules of hospitality must be observed,' said Herleve. 'I should have been warmer towards you. And more generous. I should have remembered what I knew of Ralph Delchard.'

'Ralph?'

'It is many years since we last met, but he is not a man one easily forgets. His wife was alive then. Elinor. She was very beautiful and he gloried in her. Ralph Delchard was a good, kind, loving husband.'

'He has often talked to me of Elinor.'

'A man does not change his character. I should have trusted him. I was wrong to believe that someone like Ralph would dare to come here with . . . with . . .'

'His whore?'

'I am ashamed that the thought even crossed my mind.'

'It hurt me, my lady. I must own that.'

'All the more so because it was cruelly unfair.' She reached out to take Golde's hands in hers. 'I watched you in the solar when you folded his tunic. You were so tender with it. So loving. That was not the behaviour of a . . .'

'I am his, my lady. Whatever name you call me.'

'You are his and he is yours,' said Herleve with a fleeting envy. 'I saw you earlier in the chapel, kneeling beside each other in prayer. That was no man and his mistress. I was filled with such remorse at the evil thoughts I had had about you.'

'They were not evil, my lady. They were natural.'

'I was too hasty in my judgement.'

'We are not married. It cannot be denied.'

'You are, Golde. Almost. You and Ralph Delchard have something just as binding and meaningful as a marriage.'

'I like to believe that.'

'Do not let it go.' Herleve squeezed her hands before

getting to her feet. 'I have one other confession to make.'

'It is not necessary, my lady.'

'Yes, it is.' She bit her lip. 'You recall that dress which I loaned you on your first night here?'

'Very well.'

'I had it thrown on a fire.'

Golde was jolted as she realised just how low an opinion her hostess had held of her. The dress was destroyed because Herleve felt that it was contaminated. Golde struggled hard to make light of the matter.

'Yorkshire is a strange place,' she said. 'Olaf Evil Child steals my apparel then gives it back to me. You loan me a dress then have it burned. Why do you deal so perversely with your wardrobe in this county?'

They shared a laugh but it did not reach Herleve's eyes. She seemed to be on the point of saying something else, but the words would not come. Golde waited in vain. After a long pause, Herleve leaned forward to kiss her softly on the cheek before going out of the room. The visit had yielded one real benefit. They were friends.

'Where else have you fought?' asked Aubrey Maminot.

'Wherever my sword was hired,' said Tanchelm of Ghent. 'It was a hard life but it taught me my trade and earned me a little piece of Lincolnshire in which to grow old. I may not have anything like your wealth and position, but I will die a contented man.'

'How many of us can say that?' wondered Ralph Delchard.

'I can,' boasted Aubrey with a chuckle. 'Life has been extremely kind to me.'

'You have earned your good fortune,' said Tanchelm. 'They hold you in high esteem hereabouts. Everyone in York speaks well of Aubrey Maminot.'

'Then some of them are arrant liars!'

They were in the hall at the castle. The three men were sitting over their cups of wine at the table. Gervase had retired to bed and left them to it. Aubrey had drunk far too much and Tanchelm far too little. Ralph had reached the point where the thought of Golde, waiting for him in bed, was infinitely more appealing than the banter of his drinking companions. He began to rehearse his excuse for leaving.

'Only one man spoke ill of you,' said Tanchelm.

Aubrey giggled. 'Who was the rogue? I'll have him flogged at daybreak.'

'You'll have to catch him first.'

'Who was he?'

'Olaf Evil Child!'

'What! You talked with Olaf?'

Aubrey was about to explode with rage when he realised that his guest was teasing him. Tanchelm had not seen the outlaw at all. Aubrey joined in the laughter.

'You fooled me for a moment,' he said, reaching for the flagon. 'More wine, Ralph?'

'No, Aubrey,' said the other, standing up. 'I have had enough. My legs want to take me to the bedchamber.'

'Not only your legs, I think!'

'Good night, old friend.' Ralph slapped him on the

back, then nodded to Tanchelm. 'We will confer in the morning.'

'Sleep well.'

As Ralph lurched off, Aubrey looked fondly after him. 'He is fortunate indeed. With a woman like Golde in his bed, any man would sleep well.'

'They seem well matched.'

'Well matched and well mated. I am so glad for Ralph. When his wife died, I never thought he would find the woman to replace her.' He poured wine for both of them. 'In Golde, I dare to hope, he finally has.'

'You fought beside him in the old days, I hear.'

'Yes,' said Aubrey. 'We came here with King William himself. I stayed but Ralph went back in disgust. He was not happy with the way we despoiled this county.'

'Were you?'

'I am a soldier. I obeyed my king.'

'And since then? Have you seen my lord Ralph often?'

'No more than once or twice. But we hear news of each other from time to time. His memory has always stayed bright in my mind. My wife, Herleve, has happy recollections of him as well. We were delighted to learn that Ralph was coming to York.'

'Has he changed much since you last met?'

'Not in the slightest. He is a soldier still.'

'Yet he tells me that he yearns for a quiet life on his estates in Hampshire.'

'Do not believe it!' said Aubrey with a grin. 'Ralph Delchard will always go in search of action. I am the same. It is in our blood. That is the main reason I remained here in York. It is a fine city, but it is also a dangerous place in which to live. I thrive on that danger.'

'So I see.'

'My wife, alas, does not find Yorkshire so attractive.'

'I gathered that,' said Tanchelm. 'At the banquet which you so kindly held in our honour, she told me that she has never felt wholly safe here. Especially when you are away.'

'But I rarely leave York.'

'That was not the impression she gave.'

'Herleve exaggerates,' said the other airily. 'You know how women are. I have to visit my estates in the East Riding occasionally and may spend a night or two away from here, but that is all. My wife really has no cause to fear. When I am absent, she has the finest guards in York to protect her.'

'Romulus and Remus.'

'They would fright an entire army.'

'Yet they are like babes in your arms.'

'Yes,' said Aubrey, swallowing his wine. 'To everyone else, the lions are instruments of death, as that intruder found out the other night.'

'And to you?'

'My children!'

Outside in the darkness, Romulus and Remus roared in acknowledgement. Aubrey gave a paternal chuckle.

Brother Francis was already seated at the table in readiness when Gervase Bret arrived next morning. The monk gave him a warm smile of welcome.

'You must have risen early, Master Bret.'

'Not as early as you, I think.'

'No,' said Francis cheerfully. 'While you were still caught up in your dreams, I was attending Matins and Lauds. It is an inspiring way to start the day. Canon Hubert and Brother Simon joined us in worship.'

'At the Minster?'

'Of course. Though I am attached to the abbey, I spend much time with the secular canons at the Minster. Our abbey is still in a rather primitive state, I fear. We will continue to lean heavily on the goodwill of Archbishop Thomas until our own buildings are fit to receive us.'

'And when will that be, Brother Francis?'

'Who knows?' said the monk sadly. 'Work on the Minster must naturally take first place. Archbishop Thomas has been exceedingly generous with his own wealth and his example has brought money flooding in from many sources. The Abbey of St Mary has not been so fortunate.' Optimism revived his smile. 'But we have kind benefactors as well. It is only a matter of time before the abbey plays a full part in the spiritual life of York.'

'I would like to view the site, Brother Francis.'

'Then you shall.'

'I know there is not much to see as yet, but the project interests me. Could I trespass on you when I have more time?'

'Please do,' said the monk with genuine delight. 'I will happily show you all that you wish to see. This is a quite unlooked for pleasure. When royal commissioners arrive here on secular business, I do not expect two of them to express such curiosity in our abbey.'

'Two of us?'

'I showed your colleague around but yesterday.'

Gervase was astonished. 'My lord Ralph?'

'No,' said Francis tolerantly. 'My lord Ralph is not as predisposed towards the Church as you and your other colleague seem to be. My companion last evening was my lord Tanchelm.'

'Indeed?'

'A most inquisitive visitor. I must have talked with him an hour or more. He wanted to know everything.'

'My questions may be more superficial.'

'I will be just as willing to answer them.'

'Thank you.'

A testing day lay ahead. Gervase took his place at the table and sorted through the documents in his satchel. He was not surprised that Tanchelm of Ghent had visited the Abbey of St Mary. What puzzled him was that his colleague had made absolutely no mention of the fact.

Nigel Arbarbonel was annoyed at having to spend the night in York. Business which was concluded during the visit of the first commissioners now appeared to be unresolved. It was galling to find that the past was not as completely behind him as he had assumed. Bolstered by the knowledge that he had nothing to fear, he determined to be helpful and even-tempered in the presence of his examiners. They were acting with royal warrant and that had to be respected. At the same time, he would not let them intimidate him in any way. There were limits even to his good humour.

Making virtue of a necessity, he paid a number of calls on friends in the city to exchange pleasantries and conduct business. That morning he was summoned before the commissioners again. As he rode through the streets with his men-at-arms, he caught sight of three figures emerging from their lodging. He could not resist accosting them.

'Good morrow!' he said with a courteous wave.

Sunnifa was startled to see him towering over her on his destrier. She stepped back and gave him a cautious nod. Brunn the Priest muttered a welcome. Inga merely stared up at him with defiance. He addressed his remarks to her.

'It is a long journey home,' he observed. 'You had best start out now to be sure of getting back before nightfall.'

'We have to give evidence about the theft of our land.'

'Hearsay evidence,' he mocked. 'It counts for nothing.'

'We will stay in York until we get justice.'

'Then you may be here for eternity, Inga. You have no case to offer and the commissioners must find in my favour.' He pointed in the direction of Monkgate. 'There lies your way. Take it while you may. You never know what perils lurk beside it if you delay here.'

'You are a brave man, my lord Nigel,' said Inga, glaring up at him. 'Threatening two unarmed women and a priest. That takes the courage of a true soldier!'

He smiled disarmingly. 'What I give is no threat. It is

sage advice. The countryside around York is infested with outlaws. The commissioners themselves were robbed on their way here.' He leaned closer to her. 'I will be pleased to offer you the protection of my men as you ride back.'

'No, thank you!' she said with scorn.

'You are tenants of mine. I wish to help you.'

'Then restore the holdings you stole from my father.'

'This argument belongs in front of the commissioners,' he said. 'When they have made their decision, I hope that you and your mother have the grace to abide by it.' He flashed a grin. 'And do not forget my offer.'

'Offer?'

'Yes, Inga. It still stands. You do not need to spend the rest of your days in that hovel where you live.' He gave her a polite leer. 'There is always a place for you in my household.'

'I would sooner die, my lord!'

Laughing happily, he rode off down the street.

Sunnifa was anxious. 'Do not provoke him, Inga.'

'I will not let any man insult me!'

'My lord Nigel is a cruel enemy,' warned Brunn. 'Fight him with legal argument, not with intemperate language. We have seen to what depths he will sink to achieve his ends.'

'We need Toki here,' said Sunnifa. 'He would advise us. Toki would know what to do.'

'He would furnish us with the proof we require,' said the priest. 'My lord Nigel holds the reins in this dispute. Our word alone is not strong enough to knock him from the saddle. Only Toki could do that. And we do not have him.'

'No,' said Inga sadly. 'We never will.'

Ralph Delchard subjected him to far more robust questioning that morning. Something about Nigel Arbarbonel's manner irritated him and he could not decide if it was the easy charm, the studied helpfulness or the deep complacence which lay behind both. Ralph worked hard to unsettle him, hurling a continuous stream of questions at him and wagging an admonitory finger for effect. Prompted by Gervase, he took the witness on a tour of his holdings, demanding to know how and when each came into his possession, and seizing on minor points in the title deeds to try to fluster him.

Nigel Arbarbonel was unscathed by the assault. His smile remained intact and his voice calm and unhurried. He behaved with the subdued arrogance of someone who knows that his position is quite unassailable. When Ralph finally paused to get his breath back, the witness smirked.

'How much longer must we play this game, my lord?'

'Game?' said Ralph.

'Asking me questions which are already answered by the documents that lie beside you and which are quite outside the scope of this enquiry.'

'It is for us to say what is and what is not relevant.'

'Of course,' conceded the other. 'But when you summon me here to discuss some disputed land in the wapentakes of Bulmer, Halikeld and Manshowe, why waste time arguing about my property in Allerton and Langbargh?'

'It all has a bearing on the case.'

'Let us turn to the disputed holdings,' said Gervase Bret. 'We are still concerned about the manner in which they were transferred to you.'

'Deed of gift is a legal process, is it not?'

'Yes, my lord.'

'Then what is the cause for concern?'

'Thorbrand's state of mind at the close of his life. Sunnifa and Brunn the Priest told us that he was very fevered and faded rapidly.'

'That is true.'

'He kept saying how anxious he was to safeguard the future of his wife and daughter.'

'Any husband and father would feel the same.'

'At the very end, when the fever tightened its grip on him and the herbal compound no longer kept out the pain, Thorbrand could do little more than babble incoherently.'

'I anticipate your question, Master Bret.'

'Do you?'

'Yes,' said Nigel. 'You wish to know how it was that a man who cared so much for his family, and who was racked by a terrible disease, nevertheless had the wisdom to revoke his will at the eleventh hour in favour of me.'

'That is precisely what I wish to know, my lord.'

'Ask of the witnesses at his deathbed.'

'I prefer to hear your explanation,' said Gervase.

'Then you shall. Fever is a capricious tormentor. It

will bring a man to his knees then allow him moments of calm and clarity before setting about him again with vicious intensity. It was during such a period of remission – when Thorbrand came briefly to his senses – that he voiced a decision he had long contemplated.'

'To surrender his land to you.'

'To ensure that his wife and daughter enjoyed my protection. That is why he willed his holdings to me. I am the trustee of their safety.'

'That is not how they see it, my lord.'

'They will. In time.' He became restless. 'Need we sit here speculating endlessly on the death of a good man? You are a lawyer, Master Bret, and I do not need to remind you of the legal position here. That land is in my possession. If someone wishes to wrest it from me, they have to provide conclusive proof of ownership. Am I correct?'

'Yes,' admitted Gervase.

'Can they provide such proof?'

'They believe so.'

'Then they are deluding themselves,' he said softly. 'And so are you.'

It was a long, tiring and singularly unrewarding day. Hours of questioning Nigel Arbarbonel ended in stalemate. Another extended session with Inga, Sunnifa and Brunn was equally depressing. All that they could do was to talk nostalgically about the time when Thorbrand was alive and to rehearse their grievances against their landlord. No documents were forthcoming to give their complaints any legal impetus. The commissioners had to turn them away yet again without the recompense they sought.

'We need more time!' pleaded Inga.

'I wish that we could offer it to you,' said Gervase. 'But this dispute has already eaten up two days.'

'Another twenty-four hours. That is all we ask.'

'You ask in vain,' said Ralph peremptorily. 'Enough is enough. My colleague and I will review this case and give our judgement first thing in the morning.'

'Then we have lost!' sighed Sunnifa.

'They could not be so heartless,' said Brunn.

'Is there *no* way we can persuade you?' implored Inga.

'This session has ended,' said Ralph, signalling to a guard to escort them out. 'Come back tomorrow to learn our decision. We will weigh all the evidence with scrupulous care. Be assured of that.'

Sunnifa and Brunn went out with an air of resignation but Inga paused in the doorway to look back at Gervase. She searched his face for a hint of encouragement but she could not find it. Gervase writhed in discomfort. Desperate to help her and to relieve her sorrows, he was quite unable to do so. It made him feel weak and inadequate.

Inga made a last attempt to win them over.

'What of the reeve's messenger?' she challenged. 'The one who misled us so that we were unable to appear before the first commissioners. Did you not look closely into that?'

'We did,' said Gervase. 'The reeve swears that he sent his man days earlier to fetch you.'

'Why did the summons take so long to reach us?'

'We do not know.'

'Then it is your duty to find out.'

'We know full well what our duty is,' said Ralph, stung by her accusatory tone. 'What happened in the past is of no account to us. If you were prevented from giving testimony before our predecessors, that is to be regretted – but nobody has stopped you from appearing before this tribunal. The evidence you would have presented to them you have instead given to us. We will consider it with all due care.'

Inga looked wounded. Disappointment clouded her eyes. When a soldier put a hand on her arm, she did not resist. He assisted her gently through the door.

'I am glad to see her go,' said Ralph, sighing with relief. 'She does not help her mother's case by showing contempt in that way. Inga is too headstrong.'

'We must make allowances for youthful zeal.'

'Not when it gets out of control.'

'My concern is with Nigel Arbarbonel,' said Gervase. 'Given his position, I am surprised that *he* has not been more assertive with us. All the advantages lie with him, yet he behaves with utmost civility. I wonder why.' He gathered up his papers. 'And there is another thing which worries me.'

'What is that?'

'My lord Nigel parried your questions so adroitly.'

'I tried hard to break him,' said Ralph, 'but I failed. He always seemed to be one jump ahead of me.'

'Yes, it was almost as if he knew what was coming.'

The Minster bell interrupted their conversation.

'Vespers,' said Brother Francis, rising to his feet. 'If you have finished with me for the day . . .'

'We have,' said Ralph.

'Thank you again for your help,' added Gervase.

'I kept a record, as instructed,' said the monk, pointing to the papers on the table. 'I think you will find it both accurate and legible. Pray excuse me,' he continued, moving to the door. 'Another duty calls. I would not be late.'

They waved him off, then made to leave themselves. Gervase glanced through the record of the proceedings before slipping it into his own satchel.

'We are blessed in Brother Francis,' he said. 'His mind is quick and his hand is sure. I did not think we would find as conscientious a scribe as Brother Simon.'

'No,' agreed Ralph. 'I never thought to hear myself speak well of a monk – for they are mostly sanctimonious eunuchs in flight from the world – but Brother Francis has been an asset to us. It is good to have a scribe who does not turn scarlet in the presence of a woman.'

'Brother Simon has many virtues.'

'That is my complaint against him, Gervase. Too many virtues but not a single vice to lend them some colour. Life is there to be *lived.*'

They came out into the street to find the sentries waiting for them, but there was no sign of Tanchelm's men-at-arms. Ralph turned to one of his soldiers.

'Have the other commissioners departed?' he said.

'Yes, my lord,' replied the man. 'Canon Hubert left

with Brother Simon some minutes ago. They headed for the Minster with a small escort. Their work is concluded for the day.'

'What of my lord Tanchelm?'

'He came out to dismiss his men and went back into the shire hall alone.'

'He is still here?'

'Yes, my lord.'

'Good,' said Ralph. 'I need to speak with him on several matters. He can ride back to the castle with us.'

'I would appreciate a word with him myself,' said Gervase. 'It concerns his visit to the Abbey of St Mary.'

He followed Ralph into the shire hall and entered a long room with a low ceiling and narrow windows that admitted poor light. Tall candles were set at intervals on the table to give further illumination, but their flames had been extinguished and smoke was still curling up from their wicks. Ralph and Gervase stopped with surprise in the middle of the room. There was no sign of Tanchelm of Ghent.

'Where can he be?' asked Ralph. 'There is only one door and he could not have left without being seen by my men.'

'Then he must still be here.'

It did not take long to find him. When Gervase crossed to the table at which the commissioners had sat, he saw that one of the stools had been knocked over. Tanchelm of Ghent lay on his back in the shadows behind it. His mouth was agape and his bulging eyes stared sightlessly up at the ceiling. Gervase rushed to kneel beside him but found no signs of life. Tanchelm of Ghent would now have his name inscribed in another Domesday Book.

Chapter Seven

Ralph Delchard moved swiftly to join his friend beside the body. They examined it with care and soon found the cause of death. Tanchelm of Ghent had sat in judgement bare-headed. An ugly red weal encircled his unprotected neck. Someone had choked the life out of him with brute force.

'He was attacked from behind,' decided Ralph. 'He must have been sitting at the table when the assailant struck.'

'It was the work of a powerful man,' noted Gervase. 'My lord Tanchelm was fit and strong. He would have fought an attacker. Even with surprise on his side, the man would have needed strength to subdue him.'

'Strength and skill, Gervase. He was proficient at his trade. Tanchelm was killed by a practised assassin.'

'But how did he get into the room?'

'And how leave it unseen?'

They stood up and looked around. At the rear of the room, some yards behind the table, was a small window high up in the wall. Its shutters were closed but not bolted. When Ralph went to stare up at it, his foot kicked something on the floor. He picked up some fragments of plaster and held them in his palm. When he reached up with his other hand, he could just touch the sill of the window.

'He came and went this way, Gervase,' he said.

'Then he must have been very agile.'

'One leap would have brought him within striking distance of the table. Tanchelm had no chance.' He grabbed the chair and set it against the wall. 'Let's see what is beyond.'

Standing on the chair, he was able to peer out at the narrow alley which ran at the rear of the shire hall to connect two larger thoroughfares. A few people were hurrying along it with baskets over their arms. Ralph jumped down and bellowed for his men. Hearing the urgency in his voice, all ten of them came running at once with their hands on their swords. They fanned out in the middle of the room.

'Foul murder,' said Ralph, pointing to the corpse. 'My lord Tanchelm has been killed. The assassin, we believe, came and went by that window.'

The men were shocked. Only five minutes earlier, they had seen Tanchelm alive and well. It seemed impossible that he could have been murdered while they stood outside in the street. Ralph whipped them into action with his commands. Two of them were sent to guard the door and to admit nobody without his express permission. Two more were dispatched in the direction of York Minster to alert Canon Hubert and Brother Simon. Four men were ordered to hasten around to the alley at the rear of the building to search for clues before looking for possible witnesses to the entry or departure of the assassin. One man rode off to raise the alarm at the castle and to return with members of Tanchelm's own escort who had been on duty outside the shire hall throughout the day.

Only the captain of Ralph's guard remained behind.

'The north has not been friendly to us, Fulco.'

'No, my lord.'

'We are robbed on the way here and now one of our number has been slain. What horror can we next expect?'

'I do not know, my lord.'

'When exactly did you last see my lord Tanchelm?'

'When he came out of here to dismiss his men.'

'And when was that?'

'Shortly before you and Master Bret emerged.'

'How close were you standing to him?'

'I was no more than five yards away, my lord. I had been talking to one of his men-at-arms. When my lord Tanchelm appeared, I saw and heard him very clearly.'

'What did he say?'

'He sent four of his men to escort Canon Hubert and Brother Simon to the Minster.'

'And the remainder?'

'They were told to return to the castle.'

'Why?'

'My lord Tanchelm had no further need of them. Somebody was meeting him at the shire hall, he said, and he would make his own way back in due course.'

'Did he name the person he was meeting?'

'No, my lord.'

'What happened next?'

'His men withdrew and he came back in here.'

'And nobody came in after him?'

'No, my lord.'

'Are you quite certain, Fulco? Could not someone have slipped in when you were chatting among yourselves?'

Fulco was adamant. 'Nobody entered through that door save my lord Tanchelm himself. We know better than to let our attention wander. We could see this building at all times. A mouse could not have got in without being observed.'

'It is not mice that we are after,' said Ralph darkly. 'But rats. Of the two-legged variety. This county seems to have a superfluity of them. We will do some assiduous rat-catching before we quit this place.'

'Yes, my lord.'

'Stay at the door with your men. If a meeting was arranged here, someone will turn up to see my lord Tanchelm. Do not tell him what has happened, Fulco. Conduct him in.'

'I will, my lord.' The soldier nodded and went off to take up his post. Gervase, meanwhile, had been conducting a more thorough search of the body and of the area surrounding it. He stood up.

'We are not looking for a thief,' he said.

'How do you know?'

'His purse is full but untouched. Whoever killed him did not do so for money.'

'Then what *was* his motive, Gervase?'

'Fear.'

'But he was the mildest and most pleasant of men. How could anyone be afraid of Tanchelm of Ghent?'

'Look at his papers, Ralph. There is our clue.'

Scattered across the table were the various charters which had been in Tanchelm's satchel. Some were torn, some were deliberately mutilated; all had been tampered with in some way.

'I'll wager some were taken,' said Gervase. 'That is why they were afraid of him. My lord Tanchelm found out something that they did not wish him to know.'

The commotion outside the shire hall drew a small crowd. Soldiers came from the castle, monks hurried from the Minster and the sheriff's deputy hastened to the scene. Passers-by were being questioned by Ralph's men-at-arms and the purpose soon became clear. Someone lay murdered within the building. Excited by rumour, those who swelled the knot of onlookers speculated on who had died and by what means. No details were released, no guesswork confirmed.

It was an hour before the body was brought out. Laid on a bier and covered by a large blanket, it was carried by six of Tanchelm's men and lifted into the back of a cart. As it trundled off in the direction of the castle, some followed but most lingered to discuss and surmise. The presence of so many soldiers attested the importance of the murder victim. Several hopeful suggestions were made about his identity.

In the fever of speculation, only one man remained silent. He kept to the back of the crowd and made sure that a swift departure was always possible. With his cap pulled down to conceal part of his face, he wore nondescript apparel and carried a staff. When soldiers started to disperse the crowd, he was the first to leave. Unlike the others, he did not need to ask who the murdered man was.

Olaf Evil Child stole quietly into the shadows.

Canon Hubert had many faults, and Ralph Delchard never tired of enumerating them, but even he was impressed by the way that his colleague reacted to the crisis. Snatched from Vespers and brought back to the shire hall, Brother Simon all but collapsed at the sight of the dead body. Hubert was quick to console him. With a blend of quiet dignity and paternal concern, he took Simon in his arms and rocked him gently to and fro, singing to him in Latin and soothing his troubled spirit. By the time the deputy sheriff arrived, the canon and the scribe were kneeling side by side on the hard floor, chanting the Lord's prayer in unison.

Ralph was grateful. The last thing he needed on his hands while he was trying to set an official investigation in motion was an hysterical monk, weeping and wailing. With Brother Simon quiescent, Ralph was able to give his statement to the deputy sheriff and pass on what evidence he felt that they had detected. Gervase Bret, too, gave a statement relating to the discovery of the corpse. The murder of a royal official was no small matter and all the resources at the sheriff's command would be brought to bear on the pursuit of the killer. The sheriff himself, absent from York on business, would be sent for so that he could lead the investigation.

The removal of the body of Tanchelm of Ghent served to restore Brother Simon's stability. He was still shocked and consumed with grief but he no longer burst into floods of tears. Left alone with Ralph, Gervase and Hubert, he was relatively calm. The canon himself maintained a rock-like equanimity throughout.

Ralph, too, showed that he had a compassionate side.

'Why not sit on the bench, Brother Simon?' he said.

'Thank you, my lord.'

'I can see that this tragedy has hit you hard.'

'It has destroyed me. He was such a good man.'

Hubert helped him up and the two of them sat on the bench. Gervase settled on a stool but Ralph stayed on his feet so that he could pace up and down during the conversation. The candles had now been lighted again and bright pools of yellow dappled the floor. Ralph bent solicitously over the monk.

'How do you feel now, Brother Simon?' he asked.

'A little better, my lord.'

'Able to answer some questions?'

'I believe so.'

'Good. I will come to you in a moment.' He turned to Canon Hubert. 'At what time did you leave the shire hall?'

'As the bell for Vespers was ringing,' said Hubert.

'And was my lord Tanchelm alone in the room?'

'Completely.'

'What of the men-at-arms on duty here?'

'They acted as our escort.'

'Did he say anything as you parted from him?"

'Nothing beyond a farewell.'

'No mention of a meeting?'

'None.'

'No name of a friend?'

Hubert shook his head. 'But that does not mean some meeting had not been arranged. My lord Tanchelm was a strange compound. Open in many ways, he was very private in others. Last evening, for instance, he paid a visit to the Abbey of St Mary's without even raising the matter with us. We would never have known about it had Brother Francis not let slip the details after Compline.'

'And there were other meetings about which we were not informed,' said Simon. 'My lord Tanchelm was ubiquitous.'

'I put it down to his fascination with this city,' continued Hubert. 'When he ceased to be a commissioner, he became a curious traveller intent on seeing all the sights of York.'

'How did you find him when he sat beside you?' said Ralph.

'Extremely able.'

'Brother Simon?'

'Astute and fair-minded,' said the monk.

'Did he upset any of the witnesses?'

'All the time,' said Hubert, 'but that is what we are here for, my lord. You will not get the truth out of people unless you press down on them, and that is bound to lead to antagonism. My lord Tanchelm aroused his share of that.'

'Anyone in particular?'

'Not that I recall.'

'One man threw foul abuse at Canon Hubert,' said Simon, 'but I do not remember harsh words against my lord Tanchelm. Scowls and muttering, yes, but no threats of any kind.'

'Why do you ask?' said Hubert.

'Gervase believes that the murder may be linked to one of the disputes that has come before you.'

'It is only a theory,' explained Gervase. 'I have this feeling that the killer is either a vengeful litigant who took offence when judgement was given against him, or a ruthless landowner who is trying to disable the commission because he fears that we may dispossess him.'

'The first possibility can straightway be ruled out,' said Hubert fussily. 'I was senior to my lord Tanchelm and it was from my lips that the judicial pronouncements were made. If anyone had resented a verdict sufficiently to contemplate murder, then I would certainly have been the victim.'

'Do not say that, Canon Hubert!' cried Simon.

'It is the plain truth.'

'I could not bear the thought of losing you.'

'Nor will you, Brother Simon.'

'If you are at risk, none of our lives is safe!'

'Calm down, calm down,' said Ralph. 'You are not in the slightest danger. Armed guards will attend you at all times.'

Simon jumped up. 'My lord Tanchelm had ten armed guards and yet he was killed under their very noses.'

'Sit down,' said Hubert, reinforcing his advice with a

sharp tug on Simon's cowl. 'This is needless panic.'

Simon was contrite and nodded apologetically. Gervase had been re-examining his hypothesis in the light of Hubert's comments. The canon's argument was compelling.

'You are right,' he said to Hubert. 'This is no litigant with whom you have already dealt. It is most likely a witness yet to enter the fray. Someone who has been summoned by you to the shire hall and not requested to present himself before us next door. He knew which of the two tribunals to attack.'

'Ours!' whispered Simon, eyes shut in terror.

'Do you agree, Canon Hubert?' asked Gervase.

'It lies within the bounds of possibility.'

'I think it is highly probable,' said Ralph. 'And it is the only real signpost we have. My men found no trail by which to follow the killer. People were stopped in the street by the score but not one could – or would – give any information of value.'

'My lord Tanchelm's papers were searched,' added Gervase. 'Some may have been stolen. That points to one of your claimants. What was the biggest case due to come before you in here tomorrow, Canon Hubert?'

'It relates to land in the wapentake of Burghshire.'

'Can you recall the name of the disputants?'

'I fear not. A hundred names have come in and out of my head since we have been in the city. Do not ask me to pluck some more out of the air.'

'I remember a name,' piped Brother Simon.

'What is it?' asked Gervase.

'It stuck in my mind because it conjured up a clear

picture of what the fellow must have looked like. He had holdings of some consequence in Burghshire when he died.'

'Who did?' said Ralph. 'Give us his name.'

'Sweinn Redbeard.'

'And he used to own this land, you say?'

'Yes, my lord. It should have devolved to his son.'

'And who might that be?'

'Someone that nobody could forget.'

'Go on.'

Brother Simon savoured a rare moment when he felt he had an advantage over his superiors. It earned him a respect from all three of them that he never normally enjoyed. His time perusing the documents relating to the claims had not been wasted. It elevated his importance for once.

'Well?' prompted Gervase.

'Who is the son of this Sweinn Redbeard?' said Ralph.

'Tell us, man!' urged Canon Hubert.

'Very well,' said Simon. 'It is Olaf Evil Child.'

Aubrey Maminot was dumbfounded when he heard the news about the murder. He had spent the day visiting one of his berewics to the west of York and only returned to the city in the evening. No sooner had he ridden into his castle with his men than the captain of the guard ran up to him to pass on the tidings. Aubrey was stunned but he recovered with speed as fury built inside him. Tanchelm of Ghent was a guest at his home. Any misfortune which befell the Fleming was a reflection on his host. Aubrey was beside himself.

'I should have been here to guard him!' he yelled.

'His own men were given that duty, my lord.'

'A guest of mine murdered! I will not believe it.'

'Unhappily, it is true.'

'Has my lord sheriff been informed?'

'His deputy has taken charge while he is away. The sheriff himself has been recalled with urgency.'

'I should hope so! What steps have been taken?'

'I do not know, my lord.'

'Is the killer's identity known?'

'Not yet.'

'God's blood!' snarled Aubrey. 'Then why have the gates been left open for him to escape? Every exit should have been sealed so that the villain was penned up inside York. Then we could have searched every inch of it until we rooted him out. The deputy sheriff is an imbecile.'

'You will have to take that up with him in person.'

'I shall, I shall!'

Aubrey let his horse feel his spurs and cantered out of the castle. Five minutes later he was in earnest discussion with the deputy sheriff, hearing what little progress had been made and offering a unlimited number of his own men to assist in the hunt for the killer. When he returned to his own castle once more, he was still so incensed at what had happened that he left the feeding of his lions to Ludovico for once. His guests were his prior concern.

'I blame myself, Ralph. It was unforgivable.'

'You were not responsible for his safety,' said Ralph.

'I feel that I was. I let him down cruelly.'

'No, Aubrey.'

'He was the victim of a cunning villain,' said Gervase. 'What safer place could there have been than the shire hall when armed men were within call? An attack would never be expected there. That is why he was taken unawares.'

Aubrey sighed. 'Shameful, shameful!'

It was late evening and the three of them were seated alone in the hall. Two flagons of wine had already been emptied. Even Gervase, habitually quite abstemious, felt the need of several drinks. The wine began to make him feel sleepy but Ralph and Aubrey slid into a maudlin mood.

'The irony of it!' said Ralph. 'Just as I was beginning to *like* the man, he gets himself killed.' He raised his cup. 'I drink to the memory of Tanchelm of Ghent!'

'Tanchelm!' echoed Aubrey.

'May he rest in peace!' said Gervase.

They sipped their drinks and Aubrey became wistful.

'Poor fellow!' he said. 'He and I sat in this very hall last night and caroused for hours. Tanchelm was a fine man. I tell you now, I do not like many Flemings and that may be accounted a prejudice in me, but he was different. He was an old soldier and that goes deep with me. But Tanchelm was something more. He was an educated man, a well-travelled man, and yet withal a humble man.' He gave a chuckle. 'Nobody could say that of Aubrey Maminot. Humility is a vice to me. But I did not see it as a flaw in Tanchelm's character.'

'I just wish that I had known him better,' said Ralph.

'So do I.'

'He was a deep man,' observed Gervase. 'I think that we knew him as well as he would let us.'

'What will happen to him now?' asked Aubrey.

'The body has been examined by all who need to see it,' said Ralph. 'It has now been released by the deputy sheriff. At first light, I am having it sent back to Lincolnshire. His wife will be distraught at the news of his death. We do not want to add to her misery by keeping the body here.'

'That is very considerate, Ralph.'

'We may need to borrow one of your carts, Aubrey.'

'Feel free to take anything you wish.'

'Thank you.'

'How will his wife be informed?'

'Riders have already been sent out. This is grim intelligence but she has a right to hear it as soon as is possible. On our return journey, I plan to visit his home and explain in more detail the circumstances of his death.'

'By that time we'll have hanged his killer.'

'I hope so, Aubrey.'

Gervase was becoming drowsy. He excused himself from the table and tottered off to bed, pausing first at the chapel to offer up a prayer for the soul of Tanchelm of Ghent.

Ralph and Aubrey continued to drink and reminisce.

'This has dealt a bitter blow to your work,' said the castellan. 'That must have been the intention.'

'It has stopped us in our tracks,' said Ralph. 'We will suspend our tribunal until this murder is solved.'

'Very wise.'

'It is the least we can do for Tanchelm. Finding his killer is far more important than settling property disputes. They can wait. Our colleague's death must be answered.'

'And when the villain is caught and punished . . .?'

'We will begin again,' sighed Ralph. 'With only one tribunal, alas. I cannot ask Canon Hubert to operate on his own, however much he might yearn for such autocracy. He and Brother Simon will renew their partnership with Gervase and myself. Our progress will be slower but we will get through our assignment in time.'

'The longer you stay, the more delighted I shall be.'

'Your hospitality is like the rays of the sun, Aubrey.'

'I feel that it is somewhat in eclipse.'

'Gervase and I could not have a finer lodging. And Golde told me only this morning how she has started to settle into the castle. You have three very contented guests.'

'Yes,' said Aubrey gloomily. 'But you are forgetting something, old friend. I had four.'

Philip the Chaplain had looked on death many times in his career. There had been a period when the castle had a garrison of over four hundred, and Aubrey Maminot's famed generosity meant that there were usually plenty of guests staying there as well. In an establishment of that size, there was a steady flow of fatalities. Soldiers might be killed in skirmishes, fever might carry off the weaker vessels, and old age would reap its own ineluctable harvest. Childbirth was another ready source of death.

The chaplain was accustomed to the sight of terrible wounds on the bodies of soldiers, and it had taken Romulus and Remus to autograph a corpse in a way that actually made him feel squeamish. Tanchelm of Ghent posed no such threat. As he lay on the slab in the mortuary, his eyes now closed by Philip's delicate fingers, the Fleming looked so calm and healthy that he might have been sleeping. Only his gruesome necklace hinted at a violent demise.

It would not be an onerous duty. The chaplain chose to do it himself rather than delegate it to an assistant. All he had to do was to strip, wash and prepare the body for a journey to its last resting place. He stood the two lighted candles in the most advantageous position and set to work, according the body all the respect due to the departed. As he rolled Tanchelm on to his side to remove his tunic, his hand encountered something that made him stop. A pocket seemed to have been sewn on the inside of the garment. Philip the Chaplain was intrigued.

Golde clung to him more tightly than ever in the darkness.

'It might have been you, Ralph!'

'No, my love.'

'If someone can kill my lord Tanchelm, he could just as easily have attacked you.'

'That is not true, Golde.'

'You are bound to have enemies in York.'

'We have hardly any friends here,' he admitted. 'We are royal commissioners with duties relating to the gathering of taxes. Unpopularity is assured. Especially in a city that already has good reason to hate Norman overlordship.'

'What if you are the next target?'

'I will not be.'

'How do you know?'

'Instinct.'

'Promise me that you will take care.'

'Do not fret.'

'Promise me, Ralph.'

He kissed her on the lips and stroked her hair.

'I will,' he said. 'But it is an unnecessary promise. I always take great care, Golde. When you have borne arms as long as I have, it becomes second nature.'

'My lord Tanchelm was a soldier also.'

'But caught off guard. That would never happen to me.'

She nestled into him for comfort and he ran a hand gently up and down her naked back. Anxiety made her tense and unresponsive. He tried to put her mind at rest.

'I am here, my love. I am safe. I am yours.'

'When you next venture out, you will be in danger.'

'No, Golde.'

'Take me with you. Let me be another pair of eyes.'

'That is the last thing I will do. I warned you before we set out that my work is paramount. It is something in which you can never be involved. You would make a charming sentry, my love, but you would also be a severe distraction to me. Besides, I do not need more eyes to watch over me.'

'I think you do.'

He chuckled quietly. 'You are worse than Aubrey. He offered to put fifty men at my disposal. I told him that there was only one kind of escort I would even consider.'

'And what was that?'

'Romulus and Remus.'

'The lions?'

'Yes, Golde. Imagine me walking through York with those two, like dogs on a leash. Nobody would dare to come near me.' He nibbled at her ear lobe. 'Not even you.'

'Yes, I would.'

'Do lions not frighten you?'

'I live with one.'

He kissed her with sudden passion and hugged her close. They lay entwined for several minutes in contented silence. When he spoke, it was in an affectionate whisper.

'Are you glad that you came here with me?'

'Very glad.'

'In spite of what has happened?'

'Yes, Ralph.'

'I must warn you that we may have to stay in York rather longer than we had planned.'

'I will be patient.'

'You were so uncomfortable in the castle at first.'

'I am more reconciled now.'

'Why is that?'

'Herleve has spoken with me. We have become friends.'

'I knew that you would melt that reserve of hers in time.'

'You helped, Ralph.'

'Me? How?'

'It does not matter,' she said with a yawn.

'But I want to know.'

'We are both tired. Let us get some sleep.'

'Not until you tell me about Herleve.'

'There is nothing to tell.'

'Why are you being so evasive?'

'Ralph . . .'

'Tell me what she said.'

'I do not want to make you angry.'

'Angry? Why should I be angry?'

'You will see.' Golde took a deep breath before she plunged on. 'Herleve saw us together in the chapel. That was what changed her mind about me, Ralph. And about us. She came to apologise for treating me with such indifference. When she saw me arrive at the castle in your train, she thought that I was nothing more than your paramour.'

'She called you *that*?' he growled.

'I knew that you would be angry.'

'It is an insult to both of us.'

'Hear me out and you will soon forgive her.'

'I'll not let anyone say that of you, Golde.'

'She misunderstood. Herleve saw two people sharing a bed without the blessing of the Church. She is a deeply religious woman. It was an affront to her.'

'But she changed her mind, you say?'

'Yes, Ralph. She saw how much we loved each other.

And when she found us kneeling together in the chapel . . .'

'Well?'

'Herleve said that we looked like man and wife.'

There was a long pause. His anger had evanesced into a reflective sadness.

She ran a palm across his chest. 'What are you thinking?' she asked.

'I had a wife once. Elinor was my whole world.'

'Herleve spoke fondly of her.'

'We were kindred spirits in every way. I never thought to find such love again. No man deserves that amount of good fortune. Least of all me.'

'And have you found that love again?' she murmured.

'I think so.'

'That gladdens me.'

'Golde . . .'

'No,' she said, stopping his lips with a kiss. 'Say no more. It is enough. The rest can wait.'

Gervase Bret was unable to sleep. Though his body was tired and his energy sapped by the wine, his mind remained active. The corpse which lay on the floor of the shire hall was such a vivid memory that it would not let him rest. Four commissioners had been sent to Yorkshire to deal with the large number of irregularities which had surfaced in the returns for the county. Why had Tanchelm of Ghent been singled out from the others? What special knowledge did he have which made him a threat while he lived? How had the killer known exactly when and where to find him alone?

Whom had Tanchelm arranged to meet?

These and other questions tormented him. Persuaded that Tanchelm's papers might yield the answers, he studied them by the light of his candle, putting them back in sequence and trying to establish why some documents had been rent apart while others were merely sullied. He was just beginning to impose some order on the confusion before him when he heard a footstep outside his door. He reached for his dagger.

'Who's there?' he called.

'It is me,' said Philip the Chaplain.

'So late?'

'I saw the light under your door.'

'What did you want?'

'I have something for you.'

Gervase put his dagger aside and unbolted the door. When his visitor had been admitted, he closed it again. Philip looked slightly apprehensive.

'I was hoping you would still be awake.'

'Why?'

'This could not wait until morning,' said Philip. 'I thought to go to my lord Ralph's apartment but I decided that you might be a more appropriate person.'

'Appropriate?'

'I was laying out the body of Tanchelm of Ghent. It occasioned me some sadness. I have spoken with him a few times since he has been staying here and found him to be a devout and serious man.' A smile crinkled his cheek. 'That is unusual among the soldiers I normally meet. The chapel is not a part of the castle that has regular visitors.'

'Go on.'

'I was in the mortuary, removing his apparel so that I could wash and prepare the body for tomorrow.'

'And . . .?'

'I found something concealed in his tunic.'

'What was it?'

'You must see for yourself, Master Bret.'

The chaplain handed over the letter clasped in his hand. He seemed relieved to get rid of it and shifted his feet uneasily. Gervase looked down at the missive.

'Did you read it?'

'I gave it the merest glance,' said Philip defensively. 'That was enough to tell me that it belonged more properly in your keeping. My lord Tanchelm was a colleague of yours. His personal effects will travel back with him to Lincolnshire but this letter, I think, must remain here with you.'

'Why?'

'Read it and you will understand.'

'Very well,' agreed Gervase. 'You said a moment ago that I was a more appropriate person.'

'Yes, Master Bret.'

'In what way?'

'I can trust you.'

'My lord Ralph is also trustworthy, I can assure you.'

'That may be,' said the chaplain, 'but he would never grant me the favour that I must ask of you.'

'Favour?'

'Say nothing of my part in this. You have the letter. Nobody needs to know how it came into your possession. I would not be involved in this in any way.'

'I respect that wish.'

'Thank you, Master Bret. I knew that you would. My lord Ralph might not. The pull of loyalty might prove too strong for him. He is a friend of my lord Aubrey, and might feel obliged to confide in him. That would embarrass me.'

'Your name will be kept out of this.'

The chaplain gave a nervous smile of gratitude and left the room. Gervase found his behaviour quite baffling and sought an explanation in the letter. Crouching beside the candle, he unfolded it to read it through. When he saw the seal properly for the first time, his mind raced. The words on the obverse side were extremely familiar to him.

HOC NORMANNORUM WILLEMLUM NOSCE PATRONEM SI.

It was a personal letter from King William himself.

Romulus and Remus were in a mutinous state next morning. Having been liberated from their cage for the night, they showed little enthusiasm for returning to it, and not even Ludovico's harsh commands could quell them at first. They roared their defiance then paced around the perimeter of the ditch with calm unconcern. When Ludovico came right down to them, they even dared to run away from him. He was livid.

Aubrey Maminot watched with exasperation. He was anxious to see his pets incarcerated again so that the body of Tanchelm of Ghent could be carried down the steps from the keep. As long as the animals were loose, nobody could leave the building. With a combination of threat and blandishment, the Keeper of the Beasts eventually managed to coax Remus back into the cage, but his brother remained at large. It was only when Ludovico approached him with his whip that Romulus finally succumbed. He bounded up the incline to join Remus and to snarl for food.

Ludovico waved to his master. Aubrey went off to apologise to his guests. Minutes later, Tanchelm was brought out in a wooden casket and carried down to the courtyard before being placed in a cart. Philip the Chaplain led the little procession in its wake. Ralph Delchard, Golde, Gervase Bret, Aubrey and Herleve had risen early to see the body leave. Canon Hubert and Brother Simon had come from the Minister to add their blessing. Brother Francis also wanted to share a valedictory moment with Tanchelm.

When the casket was tied in position and covered with a thick cloth, the chaplain led the tiny congregation in a small prayer. The cart then rolled out of the castle to begin its sad journey to Lincolnshire. Tanchelm's horse was towed along behind it. Still numbed by the murder, his men-at-arms fell in behind the body of their erstwhile master. It was clear from their stricken faces that they had held him in the highest regard.

Shedding remorse, Aubrey thought only of retribution. 'Now we can begin the hunt for the killer!' he said.

'It will not be easy,' sighed Ralph.

'He is out there somewhere. We will find him.'

Aubrey went off to marshal his men. The chaplain took the two women back into the keep and Canon

Hubert led his companions quickly out of the castle. Gervase was left alone with Ralph. It was the first chance they had had to speak alone that morning and Gervase seized it at once.

'We have been looking in the wrong direction,' he said.

'What do you mean?'

'My lord Tanchelm's death was nothing to do with his office as a commissioner. That was a false trail.'

'How do you know?'

'Intelligence has come into my hands which points us along another path altogether. A letter was found upon the body. It was sent by King William himself.'

'To Tanchelm?'

'Yes, Ralph,' he said. 'He was formally instructed to sit in commission with us and to discharge that duty with zeal. But it was only a cloak for his real purpose in coming to York.'

Ralph frowned. 'Real purpose?'

'My lord Tanchelm was a spy.'

'The whole city is buzzing with the news.'

'We have kept close to our lodging and only stirred from it this morning. When was this murder?'

'Yesterday evening. One of the commissioners was killed.'

'Dear God!' she exclaimed. 'Not Master Bret!'

'No, Inga,' said Nigel. 'Not him. Nor, alas, was it Ralph Delchard. I could willingly have spared either of them.'

'Then who was it?'

'Tanchelm of Ghent. A member of the other tribunal. He sat in commission in the shire hall and that is where he was murdered.'

'By whose hand?'

'They do not know, and they have curtailed their business until they find out. That could take a long time.'

'How long?'

'Days at least. Weeks, even.'

'And we have to wait for judgement until *then*?'

'Go home, Inga,' he urged, sheathing his sword. 'You wait here in vain. They have more important concerns than your mother's false claims to my land. When the commissioners resume their work again they will have forgotten all about you. Go home.'

'Not until a settlement is reached.'

'It *has* been reached. And I am riding back to my estate to celebrate.' He pointed a finger. 'You and your mother were very stupid to come here. I will not forget.'

Tugging on the reins, he turned his horse and trotted off in the opposite direction. Inga was demoralised. She was shaken by the news about the murder and even more so by the consequences of it. Nigel Arbarbonel was quitting York with alacrity. As far as he was concerned, the dispute was over. He had won.

Ralph Delchard read the letter with surprise and irritation.

> William, by grace of God king of the English and duke of the Normans, sends greetings to Tanchelm of Ghent and the assurance of friendship.
>
> I order you to accompany and assist my tribunal, going into Yorkshire to look into abuses that have been revealed in the Exchequer returns for that county in relation to the Great Survey of my kingdom. Render what service you may to the following, my commissioners, Ralph Delchard, Gervase Bret and Canon Hubert of Winchester, sitting with them as an equal partner in their judgements.
>
> I further order you to conceal your true purpose, the gathering of most secret intelligence concerning the safety of my kingdom, which we lately discussed at London . . .

By the time he finished, Ralph's temper was up. 'Why did he not tell us?' he demanded.

'My lord Tanchelm is expressly ordered not to.'

'I do not mean *him*, Gervase. I talk of the King himself. He spoke to me in person before we set out from Winchester. Why did he not have the grace to tell me that we would be carrying a spy in our cargo?'

'Because he chose not to, Ralph.'

'I had a right to know. I could have helped Tanchelm. Hell and damnation! I could have shielded the fellow from attack.' He waved the parchment in the air. 'This is not a letter – it is a death warrant!'

'Only because someone divined his deeper reason for coming to the north. What does that suggest to you?'

'Tanchelm grew careless.'

'Quite the opposite, Ralph. He was achieving success.'

'Is that what you call success?' said Ralph with scorn, thrusting the letter into his hands. 'Getting himself throttled to death in the shire hall? Talk sense, Gervase.'

'I will when you calm down enough to hear me.'

They were in Gervase's apartment at the castle and Ralph was pacing restlessly up and down like the lions in their cage. The contents of the letter had dealt a serious blow to his self-esteem. Dispatched from Winchester on the King's business, he now learned that he had been deliberately misled in a way that might have put the whole commission in jeopardy. If Tanchelm had been unmasked as a spy, the whole team could well have been suspected of being in league with him. Ralph dropped down on to the stool and punched a fist into the palm of his other hand.

'I deserved better than this!' he said. 'I have done King William much good service. He owed me the truth. I should have *known* about Tanchelm.'

'But you did,' reminded Gervase.

'What?'

'You did – in your heart. Have you forgotten? You had

doubts about my lord Tanchelm from the start. Canon Hubert was fooled by him, so was Brother Simon, so, I confess, was I at first. But not you, Ralph. You sensed that something was amiss.'

'Yes, yes, I did.'

'And that suspicion never fully left you.'

'True,' said Ralph, partially mollified. 'I could never quite believe in him. I *did* know that he was beguiling us. But it would still have been a courtesy to have been told.'

'No, Ralph. We must be honest with ourselves.'

'What do you mean?'

'My lord Tanchelm was trained for this work. You and I are not. Think how well he played his part and how effective he was when he sat in commission with Canon Hubert. Could *we* have carried the burden of a double life so easily?'

'I could, Gervase.'

'Well, I could not,' admitted the other. 'And I am glad that King William did not lay it upon my shoulders by taking me into his confidence. We have problems enough to contend with in our work here without taking on the responsibilities that my lord Tanchelm had. And the grave danger that they incurred.'

Ralph sat brooding for a long time before rising again. 'You are right,' he said. 'This was not for us.'

'Had all passed off smoothly, we would never have known the truth and never needed to know.'

'But it did not pass off smoothly, Gervase.'

'Alas, no.'

'That is why the word "success" jarred on my ear.'

'Let me explain why I used it just now. I think that my lord Tanchelm was skilled at his profession. The King would not otherwise have chosen him for so difficult a mission.'

'I accept that.'

'You know this county far better than I, Ralph. It has always been highly volatile, has it not?'

'It still is. Look at my friend Aubrey. He has been here for years, yet he has to hide behind castle walls and protect himself with wild animals.'

'What does he fear?'

'Revolt from within or invasion from without, Gervase.'

'Then that is what my lord Tanchelm came in search of,' said Gervase. 'Signs of stirring among the old nobility of the north. Or rustlings from the Scots or the Danes. I believe that he was successful enough to find out something of real importance. Why else would they have needed to kill him?'

Ralph became pensive. Moving to the window, he looked out over the city. He ran a hand slowly across his chin. 'What did he find out, Gervase?'

'I have no idea.'

'How, then, will we track down his killer?'

'By learning what he discovered.'

Ralph nodded firmly, then turned to face Gervase once more. 'Where did you get that letter?' he asked.

'It was given to me.'

'By whom?'

'A friend.'

'Friends have names.'

'This one prefers to remain anonymous.'

'Secrets between *us*, Gervase?'

'I gave him my solemn word.'

A long pause. 'So be it.'

'I must now ask you to give me *your* word, Ralph.'

'What about?'

'This letter,' said Gervase, holding it up between his fingers. 'Nobody must know its contents.'

'Nobody will – except Aubrey, of course.'

'*Nobody*. Including our host.'

'Why not?'

'Because the letter has already cost one life. The fewer people who know about it, the less chance there is of it causing another death.' He held the missive over the candle flame. 'I need your promise, Ralph.'

'You have it.'

Gervase dropped the letter on to the floor and watched it burn. As the parchment curled in upon itself, the writing was blacked out and the seal began to melt. He waited until it was burned through before grinding it beneath his heel.

'It is gone,' he said. 'There was no letter.'

'Would that Tanchelm had done the same with it!'

'He was not betrayed that way, Ralph. But by his own diligence. He got too close. That is what brought him down.'

'But why keep the letter at all?'

'For our benefit.'

Ralph started. 'Tanchelm deceives us and it is for our benefit? What kind of logic is that?'

'The letter had a double purpose.'

'I cannot even see a single one.'

'You had your reservations about him,' said Gervase. 'You found him too obliging. Supposing you had caught him out and demanded the truth from him. With his back to the wall – but only then, only as a last resort – he would have shown you his credentials.'

'The letter from the King.'

'Yes, Ralph.'

'I see. But you mentioned a double purpose.'

'Credentials and warning.'

'Of course,' said Ralph admiringly. 'That letter was kept in case anything untoward happened to him. It would explain why and point us towards his killer.' He grinned at his friend. 'You should have been a spy yourself, Gervase.'

'I have just become one. So have you.'

The sound of approaching footsteps made them react swiftly. Ralph moved quickly to the door while Gervase obliterated the last of the charred remains with his foot. As the footsteps halted, Ralph pulled open the door to reveal a startled young servant.

'What do you want?' said Ralph sharply.

'I have a message for Master Bret.'

'He stands beside me. Deliver it.'

'Yes, my lord.' The boy swallowed hard before turning to Gervase. 'A visitor waits for you at the gate.'

'A visitor?'

'A young woman. Most anxious to speak with you.'

'Did she give her name?'

'Inga.'

Gervase saw the twinkle of mischief in Ralph's eye. 'I will come at once,' he said.

Herleve was profoundly upset by the murder of their guest. Even after she saw the body sent home to Lincolnshire, she found it hard to accept that Tanchelm of Ghent had really been killed. It was an outrage too great to assimilate.

'I do not believe it,' she said quietly.

'My lady?'

'I do not believe that he is gone. I hear his voice, I see him sitting beside me. My lord Tanchelm is still here.'

'In some sense, he always will be.'

Golde was perched on a chair in the solar, keeping Herleve company and trying to help her confront the horror of what had occurred. The latter spoke movingly.

'He was such a gentle person,' remembered Herleve. 'He listened to me as no man has ever listened before. He was *interested* in me, Golde. We talked and talked.'

'I found him a most pleasant companion.'

'Soldierly in bearing, courteous in manner.'

'That sums him up perfectly.'

'There have been few such men in my life.'

Herleve drifted off into a private reverie which Golde did not try to interrupt. The older woman had a faraway smile on her face. Golde had a moment to consult her own memories of Tanchelm and to feel a deep pang of regret at his death. Her real sympathy went out to the wife and family who would be waiting at home for the return of his corpse. Theirs was the true grief.

Herleve gave a shudder and came out of her day-dream. 'He is dead,' she said levelly. 'I must not deny it.'

'No, my lady.'

'Who could have wanted to kill such a kind man?'

'I do not know.'

'Death is so indiscriminate.' The faraway smile came back. 'I liked him. He took me seriously.'

'Everyone does that, my lady,' said Golde.

'No, Golde. They only pretend to do so. I can read it in their eyes. Most people only humour me. That is why I keep my own counsel most of the time, as I told you. But my lord Tanchelm was different. He *cared*.'

'What did you talk about with him?'

'Anything and everything. He wanted to know what kind of life I led here in the castle, who came, who went, what it was like in the depths of winter. And Yorkshire. He was intrigued by the countryside around here.' She pursed her lips. 'Most men can only talk about themselves and their ambitions. Not him. He said so little about himself.'

'That was his hallmark, my lady.'

'Self-effacement.'

'We rode from Lincoln to York in his company, but I cannot say that I knew him all that much better when we arrived. He never pushed himself forward.'

'Find me another man like that.'

'They are not plentiful, my lady.'

'I would settle for one.' Herleve put her head to one side and scrutinised Golde. 'Are you content to be here?'

'Now that we are friends, I am.'

'Good.'

'I did appreciate what you said to me.'

'Will you sit with me for a while?'

'As long as you wish, my lady.'

'Thank you. I feel the need to talk.'

'I am your audience.'

'You will find me ready to listen as well. Tell me about Ralph Delchard. Tell me how you came to meet.'

'It is a lengthy tale.'

Herleve smiled. 'I insist on hearing it in full.'

The grave was no more than a mound of earth on which a raven was strutting as they walked up. The last remains of the nameless intruder had been buried in the courtyard closest to the castle. Aubrey Maminot had wanted to toss the body into the cesspit at first, but his conscience had guided him back towards a token Christianity. Romulus and Remus had already acted on their master's behalf. No further humiliation of the body was required.

The raven began pecking at the earth. When it saw them coming, it flapped its wings and took to the air.

'Is this it?' said Inga softly.

'I believe so.'

'Are you not sure?'

'It is exactly as Philip the Chaplain described,' said Gervase, looking around to check his bearings. 'There is no mistake, Inga. Your friend lies here.'

'Thank you.'

'Would you like me to leave you alone?'

'No. Please stay.'

'I never knew Toki. I feel out of place.'

'I will not keep you long.' Inga knelt down beside the grave and smoothed the earth with her bare hands. Her eyes closed as she offered up a silent prayer. After a few moments, she flung herself full length on the ground as if trying to embrace Toki. She made no sound but lay there quite motionless. When she finally began to get up, Gervase put out a hand to help her.

'Thank you, Master Bret.'

'I kept my word.'

'Yes.'

Holding back tears, she turned away and walked towards the gate. Gervase was glad when they were back in the lane at the side of the church. He did not wish to be seen at the graveside with Inga in case awkward questions were asked. Aubrey Maminot was still seeking the name of the intruder.

Inga was lost in her thoughts for several minutes. When she realised that he was still beside her, she reached out a hand to touch him with gratitude.

'Now you can understand,' she said.

'Understand?'

'What it is like to lose a friend. Toki has been snatched from me, and you too have suffered a loss.'

'Yes,' he said. 'We will miss my lord Tanchelm. He died a harsh death. That makes it harder to bear.'

'I know. I think of Toki and those lions.'

'Do not dwell on it, Inga.'

'I will not. It hurts me so.' She straightened up and tried to master her emotions, but there was still a deep sadness in her voice. 'When will we hear the judgement in our dispute?'

'When the tribunal reconvenes.'

'Have you come to a decision yet?'

'You know that I cannot tell you that.'

'Is it worth waiting in York?'

'That is up to you.'

'My lord Nigel has already left,' she said bitterly. 'He told me the argument has been settled in his favour and that he is done with your interference.'

'We may need to enlighten him on that score.'

'Is there *nothing* you can tell me, Master Bret?'

'No, Inga.'

'Must our suffering go on?'

'I am sorry,' he said gently, 'but the murder of our companion has changed everything. Our work is in abeyance until that crime has been solved. My lord Tanchelm was here with us on the King's business. We will not rest until his killer has been brought to justice.'

'And what of Toki's killers?' she demanded. 'Will they be brought to justice? He was murdered just as surely as your colleague, but will there be any retribution?'

'I fear not.'

'Those lions should be destroyed.'

'Inga . . .'

'They are monsters!'

Torn between fury and despair, she began to sob fitfully. Gervase took her in his arms to comfort her and she slowly calmed. When she looked up at him, he saw the anguish in her face and realised for the first time the true hopelessness of her position. Inga's future was bleak and Gervase was anxious to relieve her pain in some way. She had lost her beloved and her father's property. If her mother's claim was rejected by the commissioners, she and Inga might well face unpleasant repercussions. Gervase distrusted Nigel Arbarbonel. Behind the studied charm lay more sinister qualities. When the commissioners left, Inga and her mother would be at the mercy of their landlord.

Inga broke away from him and looked back towards the grave.

'What was he doing in the castle that night?' Gervase asked.

'I wish I knew.'

'Have you made no effort to find out?'

'We have done little else since we have been in York.'

'There were two of them,' he recalled. 'Toki climbed into the castle with an accomplice. The guards said that they saw someone running away. If we can trace that man, he may be able to tell you what really happened.'

'I have tried.'

'You know who he is?'

'I think so.'

'What is his name?'

Inga hesitated. 'I cannot tell you.'

'Why not?'

'It does not concern you.'

'But I may be able to help you find him.'

'How do I know you will not pass the name on?'

'Have I passed on the name of Toki?'

'No, you did not.'

'And did I keep my promise to bring you here?'

'Yes,' she said, casting her last doubts aside. 'You have been true to your word. The accomplice was Ragnar Longfoot.'

'Ragnar?'

'He was Toki's best friend. They went everywhere together. If someone else climbed into the castle, it must have been Ragnar Longfoot.'

'Have you learned nothing about him?'

'Only that he vanished the same night as Toki.'

'Does he not have a family?'

'They are as anxious to trace him as I am.'

'What sort of man is this Ragnar Longfoot?'

'Good, honest, reliable, but weak-willed. He was older than Toki but always let him take the lead. Ragnar will always follow a stronger man. That is why I believe that the rumours may be true.'

'Rumours?'

'They are all that I have been able to pick up.'

'And what do they tell you?'

'Ragnar has run off to join the strongest leader of all.'

'And who is that?'

'Olaf Evil Child.'

They had pitched camp in the Forest of Galtres. Ragnar Longfoot sat on the ground and stared into the embers of the fire. It had been almost a week now, but the agony would not go away. His conscience was a scourge. As he gazed down, a breath of wind came to ignite the embers again. In their sudden glow, he saw the face of a dear friend, looking up at him with smouldering accusation. Ragnar shut his eyes to block out the sight.

A consoling hand fell on his shoulder. 'You were not to blame,' said Olaf Evil Child.

'I was. I should have stayed.'

'No, Ragnar.'

'I ran away. I deserted Toki.'

'You had no choice. It was too late to save him.'

'I should have *helped*, Olaf.'

'How? By getting yourself captured? What purpose would that have served? Aubrey Maminot would only have fed you to the lions as well. You were right to flee.'

'I was a coward.'

'Climbing into the castle took a lot of courage.'

'I only followed Toki. I fed off his courage.'

'He would not have gone without you.'

'Yes,' said Ragnar, rallied by the thought. 'That is true. Toki needed me. I did help.' His guilt returned. 'But I betrayed him at the end.'

'You did not,' argued Olaf. 'He was betrayed by his own boldness. Toki did not look ahead. He was too hasty. Did he not realise the danger that lay in wait?'

'No.'

'You must have known about the lions.'

'We had heard they were there – who has not? – but we did not expect them to be let out at night.' Ragnar trembled. 'Toki learned the truth too late. I shall never forget the sound of his cries. And all I could do was *run*.'

'You had to, my friend.'

'I took to my heels like a frightened rat.'

'You survived, Ragnar.'

'But Toki did not.'

'He took his chance and failed,' said Olaf, crouching beside the other. 'You live to fight another day. That is the way to serve his memory. By striving to achieve what Toki was after. By continuing the battle.'

Ragnar stared down at the fire again. The embers had lost their glow and the face had turned to white ash. He gritted his teeth and turned back to Olaf Evil Child. 'You are right, Olaf. I must fight on.'

'With us?'

'With you.'

'This is where he must have got in,' said Ralph Delchard. 'And made his escape by the same means.'

'In and out in a matter of minutes.'

'With a man's life snuffed out in the process.'

'Why were the shutters unlocked?' said Aubrey Maminot. 'They are usually kept bolted from the inside. Anyone might lurk here otherwise, to eavesdrop on what is being said in the room. The murderer must have slipped into the building earlier to release the bolt on the shutters.'

'Unless he had a confederate who did that office.'

'That, too, is a possibility.'

The two men were standing in the lane at the rear of the shire hall. Like many other buildings in the city it had a sunken floor. What was a high window on the back wall of the interior was only at chest height when viewed from outside. Entry would not have been difficult. The alley was no more than a muddied track, and hundreds of feet had churned it up since the time of the murder. A search for clues was fruitless.

Men-at-arms had been stationed at either end of the alley by the deputy sheriff, to question people who used it on a regular basis and ask if they had witnessed anything suspicious taking place around the time of Vespers on the previous day. Aubrey was sceptical about their chances of learning anything.

'They were too late and too lenient,' he said. 'The time to ask questions was directly after the event and the way to do it was with threats and fists. These people will never give their help willingly.'

'Someone must have seen him.'

'They did, Ralph. This alley is in constant use. Several people saw him clamber in through that window. But you will not get them to admit it. We are Normans.'

'Tanchelm was not.'

'He served the King. That is all they need to know. We may mourn a friend but the rest of the city will be rejoicing. We are an island in a sea of hatred.'

Ralph was rueful. 'I helped to create that hatred.'

'So did I,' said Aubrey, 'and I have no regrets. We had to crush the north and we did it in the only way that would have a lasting effect.'

'Yes, Aubrey. We saw some of those lasting effects on the way here. They were not inspiring sights.'

'You are getting soft, old friend. Live in York and you would soon change. There is no room for softness here.'

'I will be harsh enough when we catch our villain.'

'Then let's about it,' said Aubrey. 'I need to speak to

the deputy sheriff again to put a burr under his backside.'

'I would like to take another look inside.'

'We will meet back at the castle.'

While Aubrey marched off with six men-at-arms, Ralph walked around to the front of the shire hall. People were still showing a ghoulish interest in it as they walked past, and small clusters formed as speculation thrived afresh. Accompanied by two of his men, Ralph unlocked the front door and stepped into the hall. It was bare and cold. All the shutters were locked now, but shafts of light crept around them to stripe the floor and lend it a ghostly quality.

When he looked at the table, Ralph could envisage the scene clearly: the stern, judicial figure of Canon Hubert seated between the urbane Tanchelm of Ghent and the scribbling meekness of Brother Simon. All three had worked well together, and neither of the ecclesiastics would ever know that their good-natured companion was using them to mask his other activities in the city. Ralph crossed to the stool on which Tanchelm had sat. It had been replaced behind the table now, and he lowered himself on to it.

The two men-at-arms were puzzled when he started to read some invisible documents in front of him. When he turned over a non-existent page, they exchanged a look of disbelief. Neither was prepared for what came next. Ralph put his hands to his neck, struggled with an unseen assailant and fell backwards. As the stool rolled on to the floor, the two soldiers ran to the assistance of their master.

'I am fine,' he said, grinning up at them.

He got back to his feet and righted the stool before taking a final look up at the window. Satisfied at last, he went out again with his men at his heels. Ralph strode around to the alley at the back and walked its full length. Soldiers at the far end were questioning a man and his wife about their movements the previous evening. Ralph caught sight of the deputy sheriff nearby and decided that he would communicate his own sense of urgency to the investigation.

Before he reached him, however, someone else captured his attention and brought him to a halt. Further along the street, huddled into a doorway to ensure some privacy, were two men locked in animated conversation. Given what he knew of them, he was surprised that they were even acquainted with each other – yet Aubrey Maminot was talking familiarly with Brother Francis.

'The Abbey of St Mary?' said Golde. 'I did not see it, my lady.'

'It lies outside the city wall to the north-west.'

'Your husband did mention it when he conducted me around York. It is still in its early stages, I believe.'

'Yes, Golde.'

'There is no shortage of work for stonemasons.'

'We will keep them busy for many years to come,' said Herleve proudly. 'It will be a majestic sight when it is finished, with its own fortified precinct. Nothing will ever challenge the Minster in magnificence, of course, but the abbey will fulfil a significant role.'

'It is fortunate to have such patrons as yourself.'

'It is my prime interest, Golde,' said the older woman. 'And my husband's one indulgence of me.'

'Indulgence?'

Herleve lowered her head. She and Golde were still alone in the solar, talking quietly, allowing their friendship to roll forward at its own gentle pace. Golde had learned not to press her hostess for answers or she would retreat into herself as she was doing now. It was only when she felt relaxed that she would volunteer information about herself.

'Where will you live?' asked Herleve.

'Ralph will decide that.'

'His estates are in Hampshire, are they not?'

'They are, my lady, but he has spent precious little time there this year. The King's business compels him to travel, and I have cause to be grateful. That is how we met.'

'When he came to visit Hereford with his colleagues?'

'Yes, my lady.'

'And how did they welcome you?'

'Gervase has been wonderful to me. He says that I help to calm Ralph down and is delighted for both of us.'

'What of the others?'

Golde grimaced. 'Canon Hubert disapproves,' she sighed. 'He has said nothing to my face and has always been quite pleasant to me, but I feel the weight of his censure. It is inevitable; we cannot expect him to understand. Still less can we ask for understanding from Brother Simon.'

'Your scribe, whom I met this morning?'

'Women are an abomination to him, my lady.'

'I wondered why he was startled by my approach.'

'He worships celibacy.'

'It has much to commend it,' said Herleve wistfully. A smile brightened her face. 'Ralph is blessed in you.'

'And I in him.'

'You are the one to make sacrifices, Golde. You gave up everything to ride at his side. Even your respectability.'

'That was the easiest sacrifice.'

'And yet you grieve at its loss. Any woman would.'

A taut pause. 'Yes, my lady. In some sort, I do.'

'Well, you need fear no more disapproval from me. I like to think I am a true Christian, and that has taught me the value of tolerance. When I was cold towards you . . .' Her voice faded and she seemed to be in mild distress.

'Let us put that behind us, my lady,' suggested Golde.

'But I need to explain.'

'Your friendship is explanation enough.'

'I owe you the truth, Golde.'

'Not if it causes you sadness.'

'I have learned to bear that.' She lifted her chin and locked her hands in her lap. 'It is difficult for me, Golde. I have never talked to anyone about this, not even in the privacy of confession. I hope I can talk to you.'

'I am listening, my lady.'

'When you first came here I was very unkind and resentful. That was not your fault, Golde. Before I knew anything about you, I made a harsh judgement. There was a reason for that.'

'I appreciate how it must have seemed.'

'This is nothing to do with you and Ralph Delchard,' said the other woman quietly. 'It is to do with my husband and myself. We have not been happy. Whatever it was that Aubrey wanted in a wife, I have been unable to supply.'

'I am sure that is not true, my lady.'

'It is, Golde.'

'But he talks so fondly of you.'

'Yes,' sighed Herleve. 'He talks fondly of me to everyone because that is his way. He never speaks thus to me. I have let him down. I never gave him the children he wanted or the love he needed. Aubrey has many good qualities, but he also has wants, Golde, like any other man. I have never been able to satisfy those wants.' Her eyelids flickered. 'He was bound to look elsewhere.'

'I see.'

'That is why I was so cold towards you. I thought you were simply another one. It never crossed my mind that you and Ralph could be . . . as you are. I thought you were *her*.'

'Who?'

Herleve sat up with as much dignity as she could.

'My husband's mistress.'

Aubrey Maminot lay sprawled on the bed while she ran a hand languidly through his hair. He was still panting and perspiring freely. Her youth excited him and her passion seemed boundless. Each time he visited her they seemed to reach new heights of pleasure and invention. Aubrey had found something he did not believe existed: a woman who never disappointed him, a love that never staled.

He rolled over to cradle her in his arm, running his finger down her nose and on to her lips. She kissed it.

'Are you happy, my love?' he asked.

'Very happy.'

'And were you pleased with my present?'

'Delighted!'

'Do you mean that?'

'It is the nicest gift you have ever given me.'

She reached out with her hand for the garment that lay beside the bed. Clipped on to it was the gold brooch in the shape of a lion. She brought it up to her face so that she could rub the animal against her cheek.

'I love him,' she said.

'Does he have a name?'

'Of course. I call him Aubrey.'

He was thrilled. 'He is named after me?'

'No,' she said. 'He *is* you.'

'In what sense?'

'You are my real lion!'

Aubrey laughed and embraced her with renewed ardour.

Chapter Nine

Brother Simon would be the first to admit it: he was spiritually and constitutionally unsuited to the rigours of the workaday world. A simple journey through the streets of York was an assault on his sensibilities. The pungent smells made him swoon and the swirling activity all around him unsettled his stomach. The swooping birds frightened him and the packs of roaming dogs seem to elect him for special persecution. But it was the sight and sound of countless females which really edged him towards hysteria. Fishwives screeched, washerwomen cackled, ancient dames traded gossip, and every mother in the city seemed to be engaged in haggling aloud in the market.

With the supportive bulk of Canon Hubert beside him, he would have withstood it all had there not been the horrendous event in the shire hall. Tanchelm of Ghent had been murdered not ten feet from the place where Simon had earlier sat at the table. The monk felt the hand of death brush the side of his face. It reduced him to gibbering incoherence. York was a crucible of evil. He fled from its tumult into the Minster.

Canon Hubert was more resilient. While his companion yearned only for solitude, he was ready to brave the turmoil of the streets in the interests of justice. Tanchelm had been a friend and a colleague, and Hubert wanted to do all he could to assist the hunt for his killer.

Having spent more time with the victim than most people, he felt that he knew him better and might therefore contribute details that would elude anyone else. An hour exploring a pile of documents convinced him that he had pertinent information to offer. Mounting his donkey, he wobbled off to the castle once more.

Ralph Delchard was less than ecstatic to see him. 'This is no place for you, Canon Hubert.'

'But we must have conference.'

'Our business here is postponed until we have tracked down a murderer. He occupies all our attention.'

'I have come to help you to that end.'

'It is soldier's work.'

'My lord . . .'

'Leave it to us.'

They were in the courtyard. Ralph had just returned to the castle when Hubert had arrived at a bouncing trot. The canon was an unnecessary distraction. Ralph was pursuing enquiries independent of the investigation led by the deputy sheriff, and he needed time alone to think and to plan. With a blunt farewell he turned on his heel, but Hubert would not be shaken off so easily. His bulbous heels took the donkey scurrying in a circle to obstruct Ralph's path.

'Hear me out, my lord,' he said. 'I beg you!'

'Move aside.'

'I am as desperate as you to catch the murderer.'

'Then return to the Minster and pray for our success. We will need all the assistance we can coax from above.'

'But I have a *name* for you.'

'A name?' Ralph was checked. 'Of the killer?'

'I would not go that far without further proof,' said Hubert, 'but one name might lead to another. It is at least worth considering.'

'As you wish,' said Ralph impatiently.

'May we not go somewhere more private?'

'The courtyard will do.'

'But someone may overhear us.'

'Only your donkey. Now, what is this name you brandish?'

Hubert dismounted and moved in closer to Ralph. 'Yesterday,' he said in a confidential whisper, 'you asked what disputes we were about to consider. One of them, you thought, might have a bearing on my lord Tanchelm's death.'

'That was Gervase's belief. He no longer holds it.'

'Why not?'

'That is immaterial.'

'Is there some fresh evidence about which I should hear?'

'No,' said Ralph, anxious to detach himself. 'You know all. Now, what is this name?'

'The man has holdings in the wapentake of Burghshire. Several of them once belonged to Sweinn Redbeard.'

'I remember. The father of Olaf Evil Child.'

'The competing claims did not come before our predecessors here because neither Olaf nor his rival was able to appear before the commission.'

'The contest is void,' said Ralph. 'Olaf cannot come to York this time either. If he dares to show his face in the city he will be arrested as an outlaw.'

'My lord Tanchelm felt otherwise.'

'On what grounds?'

'That Olaf Evil Child had a strong case to offer.'

'A horse thief given the benefits of law?'

'I protested strongly on that account.'

'What was the answer?'

'My lord Tanchelm felt that Olaf at least had the right to be heard and that his other crimes came not within our purview.'

'This is madness!'

'So I represented to him.'

'He'd never get Olaf Evil Child near the shire hall.'

'My lord Tanchelm swore that he would.'

'How?' wondered Ralph. 'How could he succeed where Aubrey Maminot and a hundred men have failed? They have been searching for Olaf for months. Did Tanchelm really believe he could entice the rogue here?'

'Yes, my lord. You forget something.'

'What is that?'

'He had a Danish wife.'

'So?'

'Olaf has Danish forbears.'

Ralph fell silent. Rash dismissal of Tanchelm's intentions might prove to be folly. The man had worked in strange and subtle ways. If he was going to such lengths to lure Olaf Evil Child to the city, it might be for reasons unconnected with the disputed property. Ralph was glad he had been forced to listen to Canon Hubert. His perennial adversary might have stumbled on some valuable intelligence.

'You have still not told me the name.'

'No, my lord,' said Hubert. 'I felt I had to acquaint you with the circumstances before I did so.'

'That was wise.'

'Olaf's claim is that he was ousted from his land.'

'By whom?'

'Robert Brossard.'

Ralph shrugged. 'I have never heard the name before.'

'Nor I. It was my lord Tanchelm who discovered the coincidence. He said that you and Gervase mentioned him several times when you discussed a case of your own.'

'Mentioned whom?'

'The half-brother of Robert Brossard.'

'And who might that be?'

'Nigel Arbarbonel.'

Whooping with delight, Nigel Arbarbonel rode his horse at a gallop towards the hill with his men-at-arms behind him like a giant swallowtail. He had left York with a feeling of exhilaration that had not abated. Everything had worked out to his satisfaction. His estates had been preserved, his enemies routed and the tribunal confounded. His position in the county would henceforth be invincible. He was once more a law unto himself.

When he reached the crest of the hill, he reined in his mount and looked down at the vale ahead. Sitting at its heart was a large house with a thatched roof. A cluster of outbuildings stood nearby. The place looked deserted but it had a solidity and sense of purpose which gave it a lustre.

Nigel Arbarbonel spoke to the man beside him. 'The house of Thorbrand,' he sneered.

'Well placed and well built, my lord.'

'It offends my eye.'

'You thought to live there yourself at one time.'

'No,' corrected Nigel with a smirk, 'I thought to stay there for a night or two when the fancy took me. But the lady would not have me as her lodger so I drove her and her mother out to meaner habitation. The house disgusts me now.'

'What will you do with it, my lord?'

'Destroy it!'

'Why?'

'Because it reminds them,' he said. 'It brings back memories of the time when Thorbrand owned and farmed this whole vale. Those days are gone for good and they must be taught that. As long as that house stands, they will hope.' He gestured to some of his men. 'Burn it!'

Four of them immediately cantered down into the vale. Nigel Arbarbonel watched with malignant pleasure as the first plume of smoke began to rise.

'They will see it as they ride past,' he said.

'When will that be, my lord?'

'When they tire of waiting in York for a victory that will not come. The commissioners will not resume their business until they have solved a murder. And they will never do that.' A knowing grin appeared. 'Never!'

'What else did she say about him?' asked Gervase Bret.

'How courteous and attentive he was,' said Golde. 'My lord Tanchelm talked with her for hours. More to the point, he listened to Herleve.'

'I am sure he did,' murmured Ralph Delchard.

'That was what impressed her most.'

Golde had been a revelation. She was in the solar with the two of them, recounting her conversation with their hostess though omitting any reference to the problems within Herleve's marriage. What Ralph and Gervase really wanted to hear was any detail about Tanchelm of Ghent. Golde talked at length on the subject and they came to see how guileful Tanchelm had been in his dealings with Herleve. He had had a genuine respect for the lady, but that did not prevent him from gathering information with great dexterity from her while appearing to offer a sympathetic ear.

'Where is she now?' asked Ralph.

'With the chaplain. He is taking confession.'

'What sins does she have to confess? She has led a blameless life and is an example to us all.'

'Herleve feels the need to be shriven,' said Golde.

'You perform that office for me, my love.'

'Hardly!'

'You cleanse my soul.'

Golde smiled before excusing herself. She could see that they wished to be alone to discuss the murder enquiry and she left the solar without realising how much she had just contributed to their investigation.

Ralph was uneasy. 'We should have told her.'

'No,' said Gervase. 'Golde must not know.'

'I felt so cruel at having to deceive her.'

'The deception is necessary, I fear. If she learns the truth, she will be drawn into a game that she is not really qualified to play. It will place an immense strain on her and that might well show.'

'Yes,' said Ralph. 'You are perhaps right.'

'I know I am,' said Gervase with a modest smile. 'Did I see you below in the courtyard with Canon Hubert earlier?'

'You did. For once we had a useful conversation.'

'What was its content?'

Ralph related the whole story and his friend listened with rapt attention. By the time the tale was over, Gervase had come to a decision. He slapped a palm on to his knee.

'I must go to see him!'

'Who?'

'Olaf Evil Child.'

'Whatever for?'

'Because he is a crucial figure in all this, Ralph.'

'Yes. Olaf stole our sumpter horses!'

'He may yet help to solve a more serious crime.'

'How?'

'I do not know. But I must meet him.'

'Are you insane?'

'Probably.'

'You cannot treat with an outlaw.'

'My lord Tanchelm did.'

Gervase weighed his promise to Inga against his duty to Ralph. The two commissioners were bonded so closely together in an act of deception that it was perverse to keep vital information from each other. Notwithstanding his friendship with the castellan, Ralph's discretion could be relied upon now that matters of state were involved. Gervase no longer felt that he was betraying Inga by releasing details of what had passed between them.

'I will tell you why I need to see Olaf,' he said.

'To pursue a career as a horse thief?'

'No, Ralph. Be patient and you will hear.'

Gervase explained in detail. Ralph heard but without any pretence of being patient. He spluttered throughout and was puce with indignation at the end.

'Why on earth did you not tell me?' he demanded.

'I gave my word to Inga.'

'And is she more important than me?'

'She was in this instance.'

'Gervase!'

'I am sorry, Ralph, but I could not take the risk.'

'What risk? We are *friends*!'

'I hope so.'

'Then why lie to me?'

'Because you are also a friend of my lord Aubrey.'

'Ah!' He was stopped in full flow. 'I begin to see.'

'You might have told him.'

'Not if you had impressed upon me the need to say nothing. Not if you had confided the full truth.'

'You know it now, Ralph.'

'Do I?'

'Every syllable.'

'You should have trusted me.'

'I did. Inga did not.'

Ralph smarted in silence.

'Not a word of this must reach my lord Aubrey,' Gervase continued. 'If he learns the identity of the intruder, he will have the remains dug up and further abused. Then he will turn his rage on Inga.'

'I know how he feels!' said Ralph grimly.

'She is not to blame for any of this.'

Ralph sat forward with his face in his hands as he tried to take in all that he had heard. The name of Olaf Evil Child occurred too often in the story to be overlooked. Why had he stolen their horses but returned their apparel? Why had Tanchelm tried to contact him and what had he hoped to gain from the outlaw? Was it conceivable that Olaf was involved in something far more deadly than robbery on the highway? What was the cause of the feud between Olaf and Aubrey Maminot? When Ralph sat up, his head was spinning.

'We must reach him somehow, Gervase.'

'I will go without you.'

'But you will need me there to protect you.'

'That would only frighten Olaf away. A troop of Norman soldiers is not an olive branch.'

'I want to capture the man, not sue for peace!'

'That is why I must be the emissary here.'

'You are dealing with a vicious outlaw!'

'Then why does he seek legal redress? His name is listed among our claimants. That shows he has some faith in the power of the law.'

'He'll feel the power of my sword when I catch him!'

'Let me handle him more civilly.'

'At least take some of my men.'

'No, Ralph.'

'A small escort. There are other outlaw bands at large. You might be set on before you got anywhere near Olaf.'

'I will have to take that chance,' said Gervase. 'I can slip away from York without being noticed. If you and I set off together with your men-at-arms it will be remarked upon, and secrecy is of the essence here.'

'That is certainly true.'

'While I am gone, you can pursue other lines of enquiry here. My lord Tanchelm learned something of great import and was silenced by an assassin. You must retrace his steps to find out what he did. But stealthily, Ralph.'

'I know the dangers.'

'We must both tread warily from now on.'

'Do not worry about me,' said Ralph. 'Think only of your own safety. I have a troop of men within call. You have none. This could prove an act of suicide.'

'I must see Olaf Evil Child.'

'Alone?'

'No,' said Gervase. 'I will take Inga.'

Brunn the Priest was fearful when he learned her intentions.

'It is too hazardous, Inga.'

'I will have Master Bret beside me.'

'One man cannot protect you.'

'We will travel with caution.'

'Sunnifa will be distraught when she hears the news.'

'That is why it must be kept from her,' said Inga. 'I tell you so that you may invent a story to cover my absence. Mother has worries enough. Spare her more anguish.'

'What if you do not return?'

Inga refused even to consider the possibility. She had brought the priest from their lodging for a special purpose. When they reached the churchyard, she pointed out the place where Toki's remains had been buried.

'Say a prayer over his grave,' she begged.

'There has already been a service of burial.'

'Not for Toki. A nameless man was lowered into the earth. The chaplain did not know him as you do. Toki deserves to be laid to rest by his own priest.'

'He will be.'

'I have a larger favour to ask.'

'What is it?'

'Toki lies in the shadow of the castle where he was killed,' she said. 'Every time I look up at it, I think of the agonies of his death. He will never sleep easily here.'

'We have no choice in the matter.'

'I want his bones to lie beside our own church.'

'But that is impossible,' said Brunn in consternation. 'Toki cannot be exhumed. That would need the permission of Archbishop Thomas himself. Do not ask what is beyond my power to give you, Inga.'

'There has to be a way.'

'Believe me, there is not.'

Inga looked sadly in the direction of the grave. Toki belonged near her. Huge obstacles had first to be negotiated, and Gervase Bret was the only person who could help her to do that. She squeezed Brunn's arm. 'I must away. Say nothing of this to mother.'

'It would break her heart. I implore you not to leave!'

'The decision is made.'

'Consider again!' pleaded Brunn. 'Olaf Evil Child is an outlaw. He and his band live in the trees like wild animals. They will show no respect to a woman, Inga. You may be—'

'Look to mother. That is all I ask.'

He shook with trepidation. 'God go with you!'

'I am not afraid. We will soon return to York.'

'You may be gone for days. Olaf Evil Child could be anywhere in the county. How ever will you find him?'

'We will not,' she said. 'He will find us.'

Ralph Delchard chafed at the bit of his task. While Gervase Bret rode off in search of an outlaw, Ralph was left to work covertly in York. Their roles were reversed. He felt that the quiet and inconspicuous Gervase could more easily glide into the shadows where Tanchelm of Ghent had gone, while he himself would be more suited to an adventuresome encounter with Olaf Evil Child. Recrimination was pointless. The duties had been assigned and Ralph set about his at once.

'Come and join us!' invited Aubrey Maminot.

'I will stay on this side of the bars.'

'Romulus and Remus will not hurt you.'

'They will not get the chance.'

'You are perfectly safe while Ludovico and I are in here. Step inside, Ralph. Be a lion yourself.'

It was feeding time. The castellan and the Keeper of the Beasts were inside the cage with the animals. Romulus and Remus did not even look up when Ralph came down to watch them. They were too busy devouring their fresh meat with growling relish. Aubrey patted each one of them before strolling over to his visitor.

'I have never known you to shirk a challenge.'

'Your lions already have a meal.'

Aubrey chuckled. 'Do you hear that, Ludovico?'

Hands on hips, the Italian turned to appraise Ralph. 'My lord Ralph is a stranger,' he said. 'They would not like that. He is better where he is. Romulus and Remus would only be unsettled.'

'They were highly unsettled this morning,' noted Ralph. 'When you tried to get them back into their cage.'

'That was most unusual,' said Aubrey.

'Yes,' added Ludovico. 'They have been punished for it. They were like naughty children. They will not misbehave again. I will see to that.' He crouched beside Romulus and stroked his mane.

'Look at them,' said Aubrey. 'My twin sentinels. The

other castle has a huge moat to defend it, built at enormous expense. I have Romulus and Remus. They are my moat.'

'They do not stop intruders getting into the castle,' reminded Ralph. 'You would have to give them the run of the courtyard to ensure that.'

'They are here to protect the keep.'

'Is that why you brought them to England?'

'It is part of the reason.'

'You said that they were a gift.'

'Yes, Ralph. In Rome.'

'What took you there?'

'I was visiting friends. Seeing the city.'

'Were the cubs born in captivity?'

'They were,' said Aubrey. 'Their mother was brought to Rome from Africa. A fierce animal. She did not like it when we took her cubs away. Ludovico still has the scars.'

The Italian scowled. It was not a memory he cared to have discussed. Aubrey let himself out of the cage to stand beside Ralph. The murder enquiry was now his priority.

'My lord sheriff arrives in York this afternoon.'

'I would speak with him.'

'We will do so together, Ralph. I wish to lodge a strong complaint against his deputy. The fellow has not been pursuing the killer with sufficient zeal. I had to take him to task about it this morning.'

'What if the murderer has already fled the city?'

'Search parties have gone out from my own garrison. I mean to find this villain, whatever the cost. A man who strikes at an honoured guest of mine strikes also at me. I have taken further steps to apprehend him . . .'

Aubrey explained in detail how many of his own soldiers had been committed to the hunt and what their precise duties were. Ralph was only half-listening. Out of the corner of his eye he saw something which he had not noticed at first. The floor of the cage was strewn with rushes, but they had been flicked about by the prowling occupants and bare patches had been exposed. One such patch intrigued Ralph.

The edge of a trap door was visible.

It was only when they left the city that they realised how fearsome a task they had set themselves. Plans had been easy to make within the encircling safety of York, but they no longer had its high walls and its garrisons to protect them. Gervase Bret and Inga were two lonely travellers who were hostages to fortune. Impelled by hope and sustained by faith, they rode north.

'When were they sighted?' he asked.

'Yesterday.'

'In the Forest of Galtres?'

'That was the rumour.'

'How reliable is it?'

'I do not know.'

'So we may be heading in the wrong direction?'

'Olaf Evil Child will have scouts all around the city. We must pray that one of them sees us and takes us to him.'

They rode a couple of miles at a rising trot. Those

who passed them on their way to York travelled in groups for safety and shot them surprised glances. Gervase was armed with sword and dagger – though one man would be no match for a band of robbers – and Inga carried no weapon. The further they went from the city, the more reckless their venture seemed. They tried to keep up their spirits with conversation.

'How did you learn to speak our language?' Gervase asked.

'Brunn the Priest taught me.'

'But you have a readier command of the tongue.'

'He showed me how to read and write,' she explained. 'The rest I picked up from my lord Nigel and his men. They haunted our land while my father was alive. I have a good ear. Whenever they came, I picked up something new.'

'What made you take an interest in the first place?'

'My father.'

'Did not Thorbrand wish you to learn Danish instead?'

'No, Master Bret. He feared that you had come to stay. We had to fight the Normans with their own weapons.'

'I am not a Norman,' he reminded her.

'You serve a Norman king.'

'That makes no difference.'

'It does to me. You sit in judgement on my people.'

'I am not doing that now, Inga.'

'No,' she said. 'And you do not have soldiers to give your voice authority now. You are a brave man.'

'I need to see Olaf Evil Child.'

'Why?'

'For the same reason as you. To ask after a friend.'

'Pray heaven that we find Olaf.'

Gervase looked ahead. 'I think that we may have done just that, Inga. Keep riding and be of good heart.'

Trees and bushes fringed the track, and Gervase caught a glimpse of movement off to the right. Inga had seen nothing but she heard the whinny of a horse behind the foliage. Resisting the impulse to flee, they trotted calmly on with hearts beating and palms moist. Gervase felt a stab of guilt at having brought her with him, but it was far too late to amend that mistake now.

The ambush was swift. Harnesses jingled, bushes parted and the track was suddenly boiling with bodies. Eight armed men surrounded them in a matter of seconds and held them in a ring of steel. Roughly garbed, they wore long hair and grinned through thick matted beards.

Gervase tried to ignore the swordpoints all around him. 'Take us to Olaf Evil Child!' he asked.

The men burst out laughing. One of them grabbed Inga and lifted her bodily from the saddle. When Gervase tried to intercede, the hilt of a sword was smashed down on his head. Knocked from his horse, he lay on the ground in a daze with blood oozing from his wound. Inga's screams soon faded in the distance.

As he strode across the courtyard, they were riding in through the gate with an escort of six men. Ralph Delchard stopped to greet them with a wave. Herleve and Golde brought their horses to a halt in front of him.

Grooms immediately ran up to take each animal by the reins. Ralph helped his hostess down from her saddle with a courteous hand. Golde was taken by the hips and swung gracefully to the ground.

'Where have you been?' he asked.

'For a ride,' said Herleve. 'Golde is a breath of fresh air to me. It is months since I left the castle for any reason, and it might have been months before I left it again. Your dear Golde encouraged me to go and it has been a joy.'

'She is a persuasive lady,' said Ralph.

'I have found that out.'

'We visited the Abbey of St Mary,' said Golde.

'Outside the city walls?'

'Yes. Little is yet built but the site is vast.'

'It will be a landmark in years to come,' said Herleve.

'Castles are better landmarks than abbeys,' argued Ralph with a provocative grin. 'They impose a stability and tell you much more about the character of a place. Besides, why do you need an abbey in York when you already have a Minster and too many churches?'

'No city can have too many churches,' said Herleve with a sweet smile. 'An abbey performs other functions. It is for those who prefer the cloistered existence.'

'Brother Simon!'

'Each man serves God in his own way.'

'I could take issue with that remark.'

'But you will not,' said Golde tactfully. 'Especially when you are talking to one of the patrons of the abbey.'

'Patrons?'

'Oh, I merely lent my name to the endowment,' said

Herleve. 'It is my husband who has supplied the money.'

Ralph raised an eyebrow. 'Aubrey, a religious man?'

'I have enough interest for both of us.'

'You are certainly well informed about the abbey,' said Golde. 'You knew as much as the masons working on it.'

'The project fascinates me, Golde. I have been involved from the start. My husband has been generous to a fault. Not only has he provided funds for the abbey, he has found other patrons to make endowments.'

'This is a side of Aubrey I have never seen,' said Ralph, 'and I will tease him mightily about it. I did not know that he raised money for a monastic establishment.'

'At my prompting, I must confess.'

'Did you have to hold a dagger to his throat?'

'It was Aubrey who held the dagger,' replied Herleve. 'In a manner of speaking, that is. When we had a banquet here at the castle some weeks ago, he bullied our two guests into pledging their support of the abbey.'

'Were they reluctant patrons?' said Golde.

'Very reluctant.'

'How did he talk them into it?'

'Aubrey knows how to get his own way.'

'Who were the two unfortunates?' said Ralph.

'Nigel Arbarbonel and his half-brother.'

'Robert Brossard?'

'Yes. You know him?'

'I know of him,' said Ralph, 'and I have met Nigel

Arbarbonel. He did not strike me as a man who would rush to endow an abbey several miles from where he lives.'

'Such is the power of my husband's tongue.'

'Aubrey opens his mouth and an abbey rises up!'

The women laughed, then took their leave and headed for the keep. Ralph was about to collect his horse from the stables when he thought of something.

'One moment,' he called after them.

'Yes?' said Herleve, stopping to turn.

'I wondered if you knew Brother Francis.'

'Very well.'

'Has he ever been to the castle?'

'A number of times.'

When he came out of his daze, Gervase Bret pulled himself up into a sitting position to take his bearings. Inga and the two horses had vanished. He remembered the ambush, but had only the haziest recollection of the men involved. One thing was obvious: they were not part of Olaf Evil Child's band. The thought of what they might do to Inga made him rise quickly to his feet, but he soon regretted the sudden movement.

His head pounded and he began to sway violently. His hat had taken the sting out of the blow but it had still opened his scalp, and blood was streaming down the back of his neck. Folding his hat, he held it against the wound to stem the flow. His mind slowly cleared and his legs began to declare their loyalty. Straightening up, he tried to consider his options. They were not appealing.

It was too far to walk back and too dangerous to go forward. If he went in the direction of York, he would be abandoning Inga to the mercies of her captors and would have to face anguished questions from Sunnifa and Brunn the Priest. If he struggled on, he could get lost in the wilderness of the North Riding and fall prey to other outlaws. On foot, he had no chance of tracing Inga. He needed help and he needed a horse.

Gervase could not stay where he was. His first move was to get off the road and conceal himself in the bushes. He and Inga had been too visible a target as they rode along. When he decided to press on, therefore, he picked his way through cover to the side of the road, looking furtively in all directions and keeping his ears pricked for the sound of horses. Sword in one hand, he tended his wound with the other.

He had gone just over a mile when he heard the hoofbeats. He flung himself to the ground behind a bush then raised his head gently to see what was coming, hoping they might be soldiers or travellers. Gervase was out of luck. A dozen riders in tunics and gartered trousers came galloping hell-for-leather along the track with their weapons drawn. He sensed hostility at once and threw himself face down once more, not daring even to breathe until they had thundered past.

When he did try to get up, he found that he could not move. Something hard and decisive was pressing down on the small of his back. Before he could swing his sword, a spear sank into the ground inches from his face.

'Who are you?' said a voice.

'My name is Gervase Bret.'

'Where are you from?'

'York.'

'What are you doing here?'

'We were riding in search of someone.'

'Where is your horse?'

'We were ambushed,' said Gervase, one eye on the spear as it was pulled from the ground and used to flick his sword out of reach. 'They took the horses. And my companion.'

'Two of you alone on the highway?'

'Yes.'

'You are lucky to be alive, Gervase Bret.'

'I know.'

'Whom did you seek?'

'Olaf Evil Child.'

There was a startled pause, then a throaty laugh echoed through the trees. The foot which held him down was now used to turn him over on his back. Gervase looked up into a rugged face with a beard of reddish tinge.

His captor appraised him with amused interest. 'Why do you want to see Olaf?'

'To ask him about a friend of mine.'

'A friend?'

'Tanchelm of Ghent.'

Recognition dawned. 'You are one of the commissioners.'

'That is right.'

'This is a dusty welcome to give you.' He helped Gervase up and peered at the blood on his head. 'That wound will need dressing.' He took a step back and spread his arms wide. 'Your search is over. *I* am Olaf Evil Child.' The expression on Gervase's face made him grin. 'Are you so disappointed?'

'I expected you to be different somehow.'

'With horns, claws and cloven feet? Three eyes, perhaps? A forked tail? No, Master Bret. I am only human.' His spear pointed the way. 'Come to my camp and we will talk.'

'I must find Inga first.'

'Inga?'

'My companion. A young woman. She was abducted.'

Olaf was aghast. 'You travelled alone through this countryside with a young woman beside you?'

'She insisted on coming,' said Gervase. 'She believes that a friend of hers has joined your band and she is anxious to speak with him. One Ragnar Longfoot.'

'Yes, Ragnar is with us.'

'He knows Inga. Perhaps he will help me to search.'

'Where was she taken?'

'A mile or so back down the road.'

'How many men?'

'Seven or eight. Dressed much like you.'

'With swords or spears?'

'Swords. One of them knocked me to the ground. Inga was carried off.' He clutched at Olaf's arm. 'I must find her before anything terrible happens to her. Do you have a horse that I may borrow?'

'Twenty. With riders to match them. Come, Master Bret. We will all search for them.' He pulled Gervase along beside him. 'And I think I know where we should begin.'

Inga struggled hard but the men were too strong. When they reached their camp, she was thrown to the ground then bound hand and foot. As one of them tried to steal a kiss, she spat in his face and he backed away. His companions hooted with laughter.

'She likes you, Halfdan!' said one.

'That ugly face of yours excites her,' said another.

Halfdan wiped the spittle from his beard and leered at her. 'She is mine first.' He reached forward to grab her by the shoulders but Inga bit his hand. Halfdan flung her angrily to the ground and snatched at her tunic. Before he could tear it from her, however, a voice rang out across the clearing.

'No! Leave her alone.'

Halfdan was caught midway between lust and obedience. 'She is mine, Murdac,' he growled.

'She belongs to all of us,' said another.

'Yes,' said a third. 'I am next.'

Murdac moved in to push Halfdan away and confront the others in his band. He was a short, stocky man with swollen features and a ruddy complexion. His hand was on his dagger as he saw the mutiny in their eyes.

'You are all fools,' he snarled.

'She is booty,' insisted Halfdan. 'We share her.'

'And what will you get for your share?' said Murdac with disgust. 'Five minutes of grunting pleasure and some scratches down your face! The girl is worth far more to us than that.'

'He is trying to keep her for himself,' warned Halfdan.

'No, I am not. I am using my brain. You only see a woman here and your pizzle does the rest. I see a hostage.' He looked around his men. 'Do you know how much we might get for her? She will bring us gold.'

'Who from?'

'A certain Norman lord.'

Slow smiles spread across their faces as they realised who their leader meant. Even Halfdan was impressed but he was loath to forfeit his pleasure.

'I have a better idea, Murdac,' he said. 'We share her first and then sell her off.'

'No, you ox! If we touch her she would be worthless.'

'Why?'

'He will not pay for damaged goods.'

The men muttered among themselves before agreeing with the plan. Inga almost swooned with relief as they drifted away. Murdac was as callous as the rest, but he had at least delayed her fate. It was a small mercy.

Halfdan lingered. 'Go to him at once, Murdac. Get a good price for her. I will guard her while you are gone.'

'No,' said the other. 'You would ravish her before I was a hundred yards away. *You* will take the message, Halfdan. I will stay here to keep the prize safe.'

Halfdan protested but he knew he would have to obey. 'Will he be at his castle?' he said.

'Yes,' said Murdac. 'Give him my regards.'

'You are sure he will buy her from us?'

'Very sure. She will not be the first girl who has vanished behind those walls. My lord Nigel is a man of taste.'

When she heard the name, Inga went into a faint.

Chapter Ten

Tanchelm of Ghent had been methodical. As he retraced the man's footsteps through the city, Ralph Delchard came to admire both his energy and his application. Tanchelm had spoken with almost everyone of significance in York. Through the unwitting channel of Canon Hubert, he had even put indirect questions to Archbishop Thomas at the Minster. The Fleming had used the disguise of innocent curiosity and the information had come flowing in.

Some of what he had learned was irrelevant to his needs and much of it was too trivial even to remember, but Tanchelm had separated the wheat from the chaff as he went along. Ralph found his own work as a commissioner fatiguing and all-consuming. It was astonishing to him that his former colleague sat on a tribunal all day yet still found time to explore the city, to meet its denizens, and to garner intelligence from a wide variety of sources. Ralph talked to many of those who had talked to Tanchelm. They all told the same story. He was an astute and personable man with an insatiable interest in everything around him. Nobody seemed to suspect for one second that his interest might have a deeper purpose.

Hours of painstaking research left Ralph weary. He amazed himself by seeking out the company of Canon Hubert in the Minster precinct.

'My lord?'

'Is there somewhere we may sit down? My feet ache.'

'Step this way.' Hubert conducted him to a stone bench and they sat down beside each other, dwarfed by the Minster behind them. A fastidious man, the canon wrinkled his nose with disgust as he caught an unpleasant odour.

'Fish!' he said.

'I have been to the harbour. They were unloading their catch.'

'You smell like part of it, my lord.'

'Then sit further off if it offends you.'

'What were you doing by the river?'

'Watching the boats come in. Talking to the sailors.'

'Why?'

'My lord Tanchelm did the same thing, it seems. I was searching for someone who might have spoken to him and who remembers what he said. Even the tiniest clue may be valuable.' He saw Hubert's pained expression. 'Stop sniffing away like a dog at a rabbit hole.'

'It is such a pernicious aroma, my lord.'

'It will wear off.'

Ralph did not tell him what he had discovered at the harbour. Tanchelm's affable enquiries had been directed at fishermen who had sailed up the Ouse from the North Sea. He wanted to know about the movements of vessels off the coast and the state of the tides. His particular interest was in how long it would take a boat to sail around Spurn Point, up the Humber estuary and thence into the River Ouse.

Hubert slipped into his familiar mode of condescension. 'While you were conversing with fishermen,' he said, 'I was speaking with Archbishop Thomas. He sent for me.'

'To excommunicate you?'

'To ask about the murder of my lord Tanchelm.'

'It has reached the ears of an archbishop?'

'Everything of importance in this diocese reaches Thomas of Bayeux. The Church is a fount of knowledge. No man understood that better than our late colleague, for he made extensive use of the fact. That is how his name came into the hearing of Archbishop Thomas.'

'Tanchelm?'

'Yes, my lord.'

'Go on.'

'It seems that he was conducting an enquiry here.'

'At the Minster?'

'Apparently so.' Hubert sounded peeved. 'I have to say that I took it amiss at first. Brother Simon and I had already furnished him with so much information about the Minster. What need did he have of more?'

'I have no idea,' said Ralph artlessly.

'And why did he not mention it to me?'

'It?'

'His clandestine enquiry. When he had drained us of all that we could tell, he turned his attention, it now emerges, to other figures in the ecclesiastical hierarchy.

The Provost, the Dean, the Treasurer, the Precentor, even the Master of the Schools. All were quizzed about the comings and goings at the Minster.' He stared pointedly at Ralph. 'And the comings and goings in York itself. The Church never sleeps. Its eyes watch over the whole city.'

'What did the Archbishop say?'

'He told me of this startling curiosity.'

'And . . .?'

'He wondered if I could account for it.'

'What did you say, Canon Hubert?'

'The truth,' said the other. 'That I could not. I did not know my lord Tanchelm well enough to discern the real nature of his interest.'

'Did that answer satisfy him?'

'Yes, my lord. Archbishop Thomas asked what progress had been made in the murder investigation, then promised to include my lord Tanchelm in his prayers.'

'That is kind,' said Ralph seriously. 'I will mention that to his widow. It might bring a crumb of comfort.' He saw the shrewd look in Hubert's eye. 'Why are you staring at me like that? If you are going to tell me yet again that I stink of fish, I shall get up and walk away.'

'My nose detects something other than fish.'

'What do you mean?'

'You are keeping something from me.'

'Why on earth should I do that?'

'For reasons of your own. I will not pry, my lord. But let me say this: I am not a fool. You found my lord Tanchelm searching the harbour for information. I now learn that he was equally inquisitive here.'

'Why, so was Golde,' said Ralph airily. 'She visited the harbour with my lord Aubrey, then he showed her every nook and cranny of the Minster.'

'There is a difference.'

'Is there?'

'She saw only with the eyes of an innocent traveller.'

'What are you saying, Canon Hubert?'

'I believe that my lord Tanchelm's death may somehow have been connected with his strange curiosity. I do not wish to know any details. They do not concern me. But I would say one thing.'

'Well?'

'I am part of this, my lord. Use me.'

'In what way?'

'Any way that will help. I too can ask questions. And I can get to people and places beyond your reach. Use me.'

Ralph's face was inscrutable but his mind was whirring. He had underestimated his rotund colleague and that was a mistake. Canon Hubert had caught the whiff of subterfuge. Having come to get certain information by stealth from him, Ralph now wondered if a more direct approach was possible. Hubert might prove an unlikely ally.

'I have no comment to make on Tanchelm,' he said. 'His reasons for being here lie in the coffin with him.'

'I understand, my lord.'

'But there is a favour I would ask.'

'It is yours.'

'How trustworthy is Brother Francis?'

'Brother Francis?'

'Is he discreet?'

'I have always thought so.'

'Sound him out for me.'

'Why, my lord?'

'Just sound him out.'

Canon Hubert beamed. 'I will.'

'Thank you.' Ralph rose from the bench.

His companion sniffed again. 'The stink of fish has gone, my lord.'

'Has it?'

'Yes,' said Hubert. 'You smell of horse again.'

The castle was small but well fortified, and its position on the ridge allowed it to command an excellent view in all directions. Halfdan was seen a mile away by the sentry above the gate. Long before he reached the palisade, he was told to stop and state his business. When Halfdan announced that he would speak only with Nigel Arbarbonel, the guard was minded to send him on his way with an earful of abuse and a torrent of threats, but the visitor was persistent and held his ground, claiming that he had something to impart of a personal nature to the castellan. The guard decided that he might be one of the many paid informers used by his master. Nigel Arbarbonel was duly summoned.

'How do I know this is not some kind of ruse?' he said.

'I swear a solemn oath, my lord.'

'Only an idiot would trust your word.'

'Then keep me here as a hostage,' volunteered

Halfdan. 'If anything happens to you, let your men kill me.'

Nigel sensed that his unprepossessing guest was telling the truth. His offer was certainly an attractive one. 'Tell me more about this girl,' he said.

'She is very comely, my lord.'

'What is her name?'

'She would not say.'

'How old is she?'

'Seventeen, eighteen. Not much more.'

'The *right* age,' mused Nigel. 'Firm and healthy?'

'Yes, my lord. And of good family. She has breeding.'

'Is she a virgin?'

'No question of that.'

'I will not look at her else.'

'She is a maid, my lord. Take my word. She has the bloom still upon her. I envy the man who relieves her of her maidenhood. She is beautiful.'

'I will come,' he decided.

'And how much will you give us for her?'

'I do not know until I have seen the girl.'

'Murdac told us you would pay handsomely.'

'Why, so I will if she fits your description.' He took Halfdan by the throat. 'If she does not, I will cut your tongue out so that you cannot lie again. Is that clear?'

'Yes, my lord,' said the other, backing away.

Nigel Arbarbonel shouted orders to his men and six of them were soon in the saddle behind him. He nudged Halfdan.

'Lead me to her,' he said. 'You have whetted my appetite.'

★ ★ ★

Riding in the company of Olaf Evil Child was an education to Gervase Bret. When he travelled with his colleagues, they moved steadily along a main highway with a sizeable escort. Olaf and his band shunned the roads altogether. Scouts were sent ahead to reconnoitre. When the others moved they did so in short bursts, galloping across open ground until they found fresh cover then resting until the next stage of their journey had been ratified by the scouts.

They had been kind to him. Olaf had dressed his wound and loaned him a horse. Ragnar Longfoot had confirmed that Inga was a good friend and he was most anxious to rescue her. During the search, Gervase tried to stay beside Olaf.

'How did you get your name?' he asked.

'From my father.'

'Sweinn Redbeard?'

'He did not like me at first.'

'Your own father?'

'When I was born, I was puny,' said Olaf, 'so I am told. My father could not believe that such a strong man as he could produce such a weak son. It was an insult he could not bear. He gave me a name that made me sound frightening. Olaf Evil Child. There is strength in a name like that.'

'It does not become you.'

The other laughed. 'It serves its purpose.'

They were waiting in a grove until the scouts signalled their next advance. There was no sign of weakness in Olaf now. Gervase could see his physical power and his strength of mind. He was a natural leader. The others deferred to him at all times and he never had to enforce his primacy.

Olaf saw the wave from the distant hilltop.

'They have found something! Come on!'

Gervase was too slow to keep up with him this time. Olaf set off at a gallop with his men behind him in a tight cluster. They went up the wooded slope until they reached the crest. Gervase was the last to arrive.

The man was on the ground, cowering before Olaf's spear.

'Where is she?'

'I do not know,' blubbered the captive.

'Where is the camp?'

'I cannot tell you.'

'Would you rather die here?'

'No, no!' he pleaded. 'Spare me.'

Gervase was overtaken by the certainty of recognition. 'He was part of the ambush,' he said. 'Who is he?'

'One of Murdac's men.'

'Murdac?'

'Yes,' said Olaf. 'Pray hard for your young friend.'

'Why?' said Gervase.

'She could not have fallen into worse hands.'

Murder made him suspicious of everyone. Ralph Delchard was reading significance into every word and deed of those around him and it was hampering his investigation. Innocence should be presumed unless guilt was conclusively proven. He told himself to collect sufficient evidence before he rushed to judgement again. Aubrey Maminot was entitled to speak with Brother Francis if he wished. Nigel Arbarbonel should be allowed to endow the Abbey of St Mary without being mistrusted. The name of Robert Brossard should not be under a shadow simply because it was due to come before Tanchelm of Ghent in a property dispute. Men should not be condemned out of hand because they were half-brothers.

Ralph saw how sceptical he had become and it made him feel slightly ashamed. Aubrey was an old friend who was giving them the warmest hospitality, yet he was being repaid with deception and distrust. If Ralph had even the remotest doubts about him, the best way to dispel them was to raise them with Aubrey himself. He found his host in the solar.

'Our work suffers while this continues,' Ralph said. 'It will not be easy to take up the reins again once this crime is solved.'

'Then take them up right now,' urged Aubrey Maminot. 'My lord sheriff and I have resources enough to pursue the killer. Resume the work which brought you to York.'

'I could not do so with a clear conscience. Tanchelm was my fellow. I have an obligation to solve his murder myself.'

'Then let the others act in your stead. Canon Hubert and Gervase are worthy judges. They will manage alone.'

'No, Aubrey. We are all of one mind. Tanchelm's death must first be redeemed, then all three of us will sit together as before with Brother Simon as our scribe.' He clicked his tongue. 'The murder enforces a double loss. A valued colleague is taken from us, but so is Brother Francis. I will be sorry to lose his cheerful presence.'

'Yes,' said Aubrey. 'He is an amiable fellow.'

'You know him, then?'

'Exceeding well. Herleve is a patron of the abbey. I never thought to waste my wealth on a collection of black cowls but there's no help for it. My wife must be kept content. And the abbey was the lesser of two evils.'

'Evils?'

'Herleve was desirous of founding a convent.'

Ralph chuckled. 'I cannot see Aubrey Maminot in the company of holy nuns!'

'A defiance of nature! Such cruel waste!'

'So you chose the abbey instead.'

'Yes, Ralph,' said the other. 'The monastic ideal is no more use to me than a hole in the head, but I am interested in design and structure. When this castle was rebuilt I helped to plan it. That is why Brother Francis is so useful to me.'

'Useful?'

'He keeps me informed of the building of the abbey at every stage. And he does so with a touch of merriment. He is the only monk I have met who does not make me feel sinful.'

'Yes. Brother Francis is a tolerant Christian.'

'It comes from his having lived in the world before taking the cowl,' said Aubrey. 'The fellow bore arms in his youth. He is no pale imitation of a real man, like your Brother Simon.'

Ralph was reassured. He was glad that he had raised the subject of his jovial scribe. It encouraged him to touch on another matter which had aroused his suspicion.

'You helped to plan this castle, you say?'

'After it was destroyed,' said Aubrey. 'I did not move the site or alter the basic shape, but I introduced many improvements. The keep was reconstructed to my design.'

'Did that include the lions' cage?'

'Of course. It was built into the base of the tower so that Romulus and Remus could be released on to the mound. Fresh air blows in through the bars to combat their smell.'

'I noticed a trap door in the bottom of the cage.'

Aubrey grinned. 'And what did you think it was?'

'I have no notion.'

'A wine cellar? A treasure house? A secret room where I keep a bevy of mistresses? No, Ralph,' he said easily, 'it is no more than a vault where we store the herbs to lend some fragrance to Romulus and Remus.'

'I guessed it might have some such purpose.'

'They guard it well. My lions would allow nobody into that vault except Ludovico and myself. It is the most well-defended part of the castle.' He grinned again. 'If the keep were ever stormed, that is where I would hide.'

Inga lay on the ground in silent agony. Ropes bit into her wrists and ankles, her back was aching and she was starting to feel the first twinges of cramp. Her physical discomfort was mild compared to her mental torment. Everything was lost. Instead of finding Ragnar Longfoot, she would be sold off to Nigel Arbarbonel like a side of meat in York market, and subjected to the most unspeakable treatment. If rumours were to be believed, Inga would not be the first young woman to vanish behind the walls of his castle. Her fate was linked to that of her mother and Brunn the Priest. Intolerable pain would be inflicted on both of them.

Even as she contemplated her own hideous destiny, she found time to spare a thought for Gervase Bret. A fearful blow had knocked him from his horse. He might still be lying on the road, bleeding to death. Inga felt strangely culpable. If she had not been with him, it might have been different. He had offered her friendship but all she brought him was bad fortune. It was Gervase who had told her about Toki, and he had done so with a gentleness and concern that touched her. But for him, she might never have known what had happened to her beloved Toki.

Rough hands seized her and dragged her backwards.

'Sit up for him,' said Murdac gruffly. 'He'll want a proper look at you, girl.'

'Let go of me!' she protested.

'We'll have you here, I think.' Murdac propped her up against a tree and stood back to appraise her. Jeers came from the other men. Their ribald comments and lustful glances burned into her brain. She was entirely at their mercy and she knew that there was worse to come. When she heard the approach of horses, she froze with apprehension.

The outlaws rose to their feet as Halfdan led the way into the clearing. Nigel Arbarbonel and his men drew up in a semi-circle. When he saw his prize, trussed up and helpless, he burst into harsh laughter. 'I'll have her!' he insisted. 'Whatever the price.'

'She does not come cheap, my lord,' said Murdac.

'You'll get your money.'

'We knew she would take your eye.'

'She does,' said Nigel, dropping to the ground. 'You could not have found me a finer gift. She is *mine*!'

He strode across to Inga and stood over her with his legs apart and arms akimbo. There was a world of mockery in his voice. 'What are you doing here?' he asked. 'Keeping company with such foul ruffians?'

'Go away!' she exclaimed.

'But I have come to save you, Inga.'

Murdac blinked. 'You *know* her, my lord?'

'Oh, yes. I know her, but I intend to know her a lot better before I have finished with her.' The others grinned. 'Inga and I are old friends.'

'I am no friend of yours!' she protested. 'And you will not get away with this. They will come after you.'

'Who will?' he taunted. 'Your mother? The valiant priest? We would all quake in our shoes before him! No, Inga. Nobody will come. You are just one more traveller who disappeared on a lonely road. Everyone will think that you were caught and killed by outlaws.'

'Caught, my lord,' said Halfdan, 'but never killed. I'd have kept her alive to serve my pleasure.'

Nigel smiled. 'You see what I rescue you from, Inga?'

'The bargain, my lord,' prompted Murdac. 'It is not

yet struck. How much will she fetch?'

'This much.' Nigel detached a large purse from his belt and tossed it to the leader of the outlaws.

Murdac opened it and dug his hands joyfully into the coins. 'The deal is done, my lord. Take her.'

'Yes,' said Halfdan, standing beside the tree. 'And when you have done with her, bring her back to me. I'll ride her hard when she's been broken in!'

The outlaws guffawed but their amusement was curtailed. Thrown with venom, a spear came out of nowhere to pierce Halfdan's throat before sinking into the trunk of a tree and impaling him. Armed men converged on the camp from all sides. As Murdac reached for his dagger, Eric's club knocked him senseless. Before Nigel could draw his sword, two spears prodded his chest. Surprise gave the attackers a supreme advantage. Soldiers and outlaws were held captive.

Olaf Evil Child came into the middle of the clearing. 'Release her,' he said.

Inga was overjoyed when Gervase Bret ran across to sever her bonds and lift her up. As she looked gratefully around at the others, she saw the face of Ragnar Longfoot.

'I threw the spear,' he said proudly. 'He will never use that filthy tongue on you again.'

Olaf strode over to confront Nigel Arbarbonel. 'You surprise me, my lord,' he said with sarcasm. 'I did not think to find you paying for something. You and your half-brother have always taken what you want in the past. You stole Thorbrand's holdings while Robert

Brossard stole mine. No coins changed hands in those transactions.'

Nigel glowered. 'I'll not be taught morality by an outlaw.'

'It takes a thief to catch a thief.'

'And now that you have caught me,' challenged the other, 'what will you do? Put me on trial in York? They will clap you in irons as they set eyes on you, Olaf. Who would take the word of an outcast over that of a Norman lord?'

'I would!' affirmed Gervase Bret.

'Keep out of this argument,' warned Nigel.

'I belong in it, my lord. I was with Inga when she was abducted. Anything which concerns her safety involves me.'

'I say the same!' vouched Ragnar Longfoot.

'Take him to York!' urged Gervase. 'To face trial.'

'What is my crime?' said Nigel with a contemptuous smile. 'Paying for my pleasure with a woman? You'll not find many men to condemn me for that. They keep the city whores well fed with their own expenditures.'

'Inga is no whore!' asserted Ragnar, advancing on him with a dagger. 'You will pay for that insult.'

Olaf raised a hand to stop him. 'No, Ragnar. He is mine. I have waited long for this chance. When I chase a rat, I like to kill him myself.'

'Brave words when you hold the advantage,' said Nigel. 'How brave are you when we meet on equal footing?'

'Let us find out, my lord.' Olaf signalled to the men whose spears still pointed at Nigel Arbarbonel's heart.

They withdrew a few paces. Nigel gave a confident laugh, pleased to have tempted Olaf into a combat that the outlaw was bound to lose. Gervase tried to prevent the fight but Olaf would not even hear his argument. Everyone moved back to give the adversaries plenty of space.

Olaf wanted to clarify the rules of combat. 'Choose the weapons, my lord.'

'Sword and dagger.'

'What happens if I lose?'

'I'll throw you over a horse and drag you into York. Aubrey Maminot will pay well for your pelt.'

'Inga must not be touched.'

Nigel scowled darkly at the loss. To have Inga as his prisoner would feed all his fantasies. There was such a crude amalgam of lust and anger in his eyes that Inga could not meet his gaze. She was glad when Gervase put a protective arm around her.

'She will go free,' Nigel agreed. 'Along with all your men.'

'And if I win?' asked Olaf.

'There is no hope of that!'

'We shall see, my lord. But if I do, I want it known that you were not murdered. You were killed in a fair fight on your own terms. Order your men to bear honest witness.'

'That eventuality will not arise.'

'Make them swear or I'll not fight.'

Nigel looked across at his men and they grinned back. Confident of their master's success, they gave their word that Olaf would not be branded as a murderer.

'I too will bear witness,' said Gervase.

'There,' mocked Nigel. 'You have the word of a royal commissioner as well, Olaf. Will that content you?'

'No, my lord. Only your death will do that.'

The preliminaries were over. Both men drew sword and dagger before circling each other with menace. Gervase feared for his new friend. Olaf moved like a skilled warrior but he wore only a rough tunic and gartered trousers. Nigel Arbarbonel was in a mailed hauberk and a glinting helm, his face and neck shielded by a mailed coif. A glancing blow would only bruise Nigel but it would draw blood from Olaf.

Inga tensed as the Norman struck first, wielding his heavy sword with a practised arm to deliver a flurry of strokes. Olaf parried them with his own blade, but he was driven slowly backwards.

Nigel's eyes gleamed either side of his iron nasal. 'You should have killed me when you had the chance,' he said. 'I'd have shown you no mercy. You'd have been cut down where you stood. Like this!'

He launched another barrage but Olaf took only the first few blows on his sword before dodging out of range. When his adversary moved in to slice at his neck, Olaf ducked. As the sword tried to smash his legs from beneath him, he jumped over it and retreated to the other side of the clearing. Nigel cursed and lumbered after him but his opponent would not stand and fight. Olaf preferred to parry some blows, strike back with a few of his own, then skip out of reach of the scything weapon in the other's gauntlet.

'Turn and fight, you coward!' yelled Nigel.

'Come and catch me, my lord.'

Olaf's mobility was taxing Nigel's superior strength. As the Norman lunged and flailed again, he was panting stertorously. Olaf replied with a relay of blows from his own sword, one of which glanced off the other's shoulder. Nigel was enraged. Charging forward with renewed vigour, he swung and jabbed until he forced his man back across the clearing. Olaf's nimbleness was his own downfall. As he tried to hop back out of range, he tripped over the body of Murdac which lay behind him on the ground.

'No!' gulped Inga, trying to move to his aid.

'Stay!' cautioned Gervase, tightening his hold.

Nigel lurched after his man, bringing his sword down with a ferocity that would have cleaved his head in two had not Olaf rolled out of the way in time. The fall was costly. As the outlaw tried to rise, Nigel stamped hard on his sword to jerk it from his grasp. One small dagger now stood between Olaf Evil Child and certain defeat.

'Stop him!' shouted Inga. 'Someone stop him!'

But nobody moved. Nigel Arbarbonel let out a macabre chuckle, but the fight was not over yet. As he came in for the kill, he was wheezing more than ever and he had slowed down considerably. The flashing sword missed Olaf by a foot.

When he tried to run after his quarry, Nigel was far too ponderous. Olaf danced around him and jumped on him from behind, a forearm across his neck to heave him backwards. They hit the ground with a thud and rolled over. Nigel's sword was knocked from his hand but his dagger was slashing violently. Olaf grabbed the wrist which held the weapon and tried to stab on his own account. Nigel was a resourceful opponent, twisting around to grab Olaf's wrist then squeezing it hard with his mailed palm.

It was now a trial of strength. Each dagger drew wild circles in the air as the men tried to attack and defend at the same time. Nigel was now on top and his weight was tilting the balance his way. Olaf was gasping as he strove to hold back the other's jabbing wrist. As Nigel thrust harder, the end of his dagger scored Olaf's face and blood gushed down his cheek. Inga quivered with fear and the other outlaws braced themselves against the outcome. Their leader seemed to be doomed.

But Olaf Evil Child suddenly revived. Pain drew a fresh burst of strength from him. With a concerted heave, he pushed Nigel off and the two of them rolled over and over, pushing the onlookers even further back and remaining locked in position until they bumped into the trunk of a tree. Nigel Arbarbonel ended on top again, but it was he who emitted a cry of anguish before dropping his weapon and slumping forward. When they lifted him off, they found Olaf's dagger embedded to the hilt in his eye.

The wounded outlaw got slowly to his feet. 'You saw what happened,' he said to Nigel's men.

'So did we all,' said Gervase.

'Thank God!' said Inga, breaking free to run across to the victor. 'You're safe. You're alive.'

Olaf Evil Child had not only rescued her; he had

killed the man who stalked her so relentlessly. Throwing her arms around the outlaw, she kissed him impulsively on his bloodstained cheek.

Canon Hubert did not have to wait long for the opportunity to accost Brother Francis. They met in the cloisters not long before Vespers. Francis had his hands tucked in his sleeves and his head lowered in meditation. He looked up to find Hubert in front of him and the ready smile flowered. 'It is good to have you in York, Canon Hubert.'

'I would much rather be in Winchester,' said the other. 'To be candid, Brother Francis, I wish I had stayed in Bec where I was subprior. Brother Simon, too. The Rule was strictly observed at the abbey and that contented us.'

'I have heard Brother Simon on this very topic.'

'He is too meek for this sinful world.'

'But you seem more robust.'

'I thank God I have always had much energy.'

'And directed to good ends,' said Francis with a note of flattery. 'Brother Simon has told me how you sat in commission with my lord Tanchelm. You were a model of rectitude. You brought a moral power to the administration of the law. That is a commendable achievement.'

'Thank you,' said Hubert graciously. 'But you too, have earned congratulation. You served my colleagues well, by all accounts. They both praised your penmanship.'

'That gratifies me more than I can say.'

'Where did you learn your art?'

'At Lastingham, when I took my vows.'

'So far north?'

'I fled there from my former life, Canon Hubert.'

'Former life?'

'I was a soldier. I bore arms against the Scots.'

'Happy is the man who has renounced violence.'

'It changed me,' said Francis soulfully. 'Killing an enemy gave me no satisfaction, only revulsion. It changed me. I fled to Lastingham and the monks took me in. I have known the true wickedness of the world and so have sought the cloister.'

'Yours is a heartening tale.'

'I found redemption. Most do not.'

'What brought you to York?'

'The abbot's invitation,' said the other. 'It could not be ignored. He asked me to become involved in the building of the abbey. Inspiring work. I dedicate my life to it.'

'Do you have funds sufficient for the task?'

'Not yet, Canon Hubert, but we will. That is partly my task – to find what patrons we may in the city. I have had some modest success,' he said with a smile. 'It was I who drew my lord Aubrey in and, through him, others of distinction in the county. My days in armour were not in vain after all.'

'In armour?'

'That is how I met my lord Aubrey. As a soldier.'

'You served with him?'

'Beneath his command. He remembered me.'

'Was he not surprised to see a soldier turned monk?'

'Yes,' said Francis, 'but he did not take it amiss.

Between us, his wife and I persuaded him of the abbey's needs, and he has become our benefactor.'

'I am pleased to hear that. One more thing . . .'

'It must wait, Canon Hubert. Vespers is upon us.'

'The bell has not yet rung.'

'It will. This instant.'

Even as he spoke, the Minster bell began to toll. With a farewell smile, Brother Francis tucked his hands into his sleeves once more and shuffled quickly away.

Suspending the work of the tribunal was a regrettable decision because it lengthened their stay in York indefinitely. There was an incidental bonus. Instead of being preoccupied with charters and leases all day, Ralph Delchard had more chances of a casual meeting with Golde. It was she who brought what joy there was to his stay in the north.

'What else have you been doing?' he asked.

'We talked, we ate, we visited the chapel.'

'Herleve and you are bosom friends.'

'She trusts me, Ralph. And I would sooner be looked on as a friend than condemned as a harlot.' Golde sighed. 'That still rankles. It is sometimes painful to be seen as others see you.'

'All that matters is how I see you, my love.'

'And how is that?'

'Not often enough.' He caught her in his arms and kissed her on the lips.

They were sharing a moment alone in their apartment at the castle. Ralph had retired there to reflect on the day's findings and Golde had slipped in to change her apparel. She was pleased to see him again.

'I have not been idle here,' she said.

'It is foreign to your nature, my love.'

'Herleve has shown me every aspect of the household. If I am to live with you in Hampshire, I must know how to run a large establishment.' Fleeting doubts crowded in. 'Am I to come to Hampshire?'

'If we can once get clear of this hell-hole!'

'It is a fine household with far more servants than we will ever need. They have a pantry, a larder, a buttery and a kitchen, each with its own staff. I met the baker, the slaughterer, the fruiterer, the candlemaker, the poulterer and I do not know who else.'

'No brewer?' he teased.

'They only drink wine here.'

'We will do the same in Hampshire.'

'No,' she countered. 'You will learn to savour the taste of beer. When you live with a brewer, you must let her demonstrate the finer points of her occupation.'

'*I* am your occupation from now on, Golde.'

'That is all I ask.'

They embraced again and minutes slid happily past. When they parted once more, Golde continued her bubbling account of the household administration.

'Four hundred eggs! Can you imagine such a sight.'

'The hens must be laying without stop.'

'And fish in huge quantities. Mackerel, flounder, mullet, and a dozen other varieties.'

'Do not mention fish,' he said. 'I spent hours down at the harbour this afternoon wading through them.'

'The cook was the most interesting man I met.'

Ralph yawned. 'Tell me about him another time, my love.'

'But he was so amusing.'

'You are the only amusement I want at this moment.'

'He explained to me how he makes his most delicious dishes. I have the recipes to take back to Hampshire with me.'

'Golde . . .'

'My lord Aubrey makes him work so hard.'

'I do not really need tittle-tattle about a cook.'

'You would love this man,' she said. 'He gets so wild when he is angry, banging his pots and pans with his spoon and threatening to leave if his master does it again.'

'Does what again?'

'Wakes him up in the middle of the night and demands a meal for his guests. It has happened more than once. What sort of guests arrive at *that* time? How do they even get into the city?'

Ralph was listening attentively now.

They had pitched camp near a stream. Olaf Evil Child rested in the shade of an oak. The wound on his face had been bathed and the blood stemmed. Gervase Bret sat beside him. Now that Inga had been rescued, he could turn to the business which had brought him in search of the outlaw.

'We need to talk about Tanchelm of Ghent,' he said.

'I do not know the man.'

'But you know *of* him?'

'Yes,' said Olaf guardedly.

'And you know that he was murdered?'

'I do.'

'How?'

'I have eyes in York.'

'Did they manage to see *who* killed him?'

'No, Master Bret. Nor did they discern why. Do not ask me to solve this murder. I never met the man.'

'But you agreed to do so,' guessed Gervase.

Olaf was evasive. 'I may have.'

'Yesterday, by any chance?'

'I cannot remember.'

'How did he make contact with you?'

'I have not said that he did.'

'You are involved in this, I know it.'

'Do not pester me,' warned Olaf with irritation. 'I will mend your head and loan you a horse and even help to save your companion, Master Bret, but that is all. It was done in the spirit of friendship.'

'Has that spirit suddenly died?'

'You are a royal official; I am an outlaw. You live in one world, I live in another. There's an end to it.'

'No, Olaf.'

'You have your horse back. Take it and ride to York.'

'Not until I have heard about Tanchelm of Ghent.'

'We never even met!'

'But you were ready to!' said Gervase earnestly. 'You did at least consider his proposal. Why was that?' Olaf ignored him. 'My lord Tanchelm *believed* in you. When he looked at the evidence in our returns, he believed that you had been dispossessed by Robert Brossard.'

'I was. By force of arms.'

'You have redress through us.'

'Not now. Not when I am an outlaw.'

'My lord Tanchelm thought otherwise. Norman law can be harsh but pardon is not unknown. If you had presented your claim with charters to enforce it, Robert Brossard might well have been compelled to restore your holdings. We have that power.' Gervase leaned into him. 'Did my lord Tanchelm offer you a bargain? Was that it? A fair hearing in return for some information?'

Olaf Evil Child became restive. He scratched at his beard before turning to stare deep into Gervase's eyes. 'Why did you come here?' he asked.

'I had to.'

'What did you hope to get?'

'The truth about you and my lord Tanchelm.'

'He is dead. All that is past.'

'His killer is still at large. I will do anything to find him. You can help me.' Olaf fell silent again. 'How did he reach you? What did he say? Were you tempted?'

A long pause. 'Yes,' admitted Olaf, 'I was tempted. He wrote to me in Danish, a language I still cling to at times. My lord Tanchelm let it be known that he had a message for Olaf Evil Child. His request reached my man in York.'

'Do you still have the letter?'

'I destroyed it. A dead man's promise is useless.'

'Promise?'

'To consider my claim without prejudice,' said Olaf. 'In return, he wanted information. My scouts see every movement of troops and ships. We know who comes, who leaves and where they go while they are here. This was what he wanted for reasons he did not say.'

'Did you trust him?'

'No, Master Bret.'

'But you came to York yesterday?'

'With some misgiving.'

'You were to meet at the shire hall?'

'When his tribunal dispersed for the day,' said Olaf. 'He knew I would fear a trap and tried to reassure me. I watched him come out to dismiss his men. It let me take a close look at Tanchelm of Ghent.'

'What did you think of him?'

'He looked honest enough. And devious enough.'

'Devious?'

'To speak with me, he had to get rid of his colleagues and his escort. There were other soldiers outside the shire hall, belonging to someone else. He knew I would not dare to walk past them to go into the hall.'

'So he left the shutters open for you!' Gervase began to piece it together. 'That is why he was not disturbed when someone came through the window. He was *expecting* you.'

'But another came in my place.'

'Who?'

'I cannot say. All I saw was the commotion. When they brought out a body, I knew it must be him. I left York at once.'

'Would you come back again?'

'No.'

'I would guarantee your safe conduct.'

'Norman justice would never help me.'

'Not if you stay out here in the wilderness.'

Olaf Evil Child looked around at his men. Some were chatting, some were eating the last of the day's catch, some were sleeping on the ground. Eric was sharpening an axe. Beyond them, in a secluded corner, Inga was talking agitatedly to Ragnar Longfoot.

'Go now while you still have some light,' said Olaf.

'Will you ride with me?'

'No, but I'll send someone to guide you.'

'How can I reach you again?'

'There will be a way.'

Inga came across with Ragnar limping beside her. Gervase could see the deep sadness hanging upon her.

'Have you learned what you came to find out?' he said.

'Yes,' she replied sadly. 'It will not bring Toki back to me. But at least I understand.'

'Light is failing,' noted Olaf. 'Go now or you will not reach York before dark.'

'I will show them the way,' volunteered Ragnar.

Gervase thanked Olaf for his help but Inga had far more cause for gratitude. To be delivered up into the hands of Nigel Arbarbonel was a fate she could not bear even to reflect upon, and Olaf had saved her from it. She kissed him once more on the cheek. He grinned appreciatively. 'You may visit us again, Inga,' he said warmly.

When they mounted, Gervase looked down at him. 'Why did you return our apparel?' he asked.

'It did not fit me,' said Olaf.

'Why did you steal it in the first place?'

'I hoped the packs might contain the missing charters to my land. Stealing one's own property back is not really theft.'

'We must go,' urged Ragnar Longfoot.

'We will, I promise you,' said Gervase. 'I must just ask Olaf one last favour . . .'

Ralph Delchard was racked by guilt and apprehension. He blamed himself for letting Gervase Bret ride off without an escort, and he feared that some terrible accident had befallen his friend. Darkness was enveloping the castle and there was still no sign of Gervase. Climbing up the wooden steps, Ralph walked anxiously along the boards, peering over the palisade with more hope than expectation. It was too late. The city gates were being locked. Gervase would not come back that night. Ralph had a sudden premonition that he would never come back.

After pacing up and down, he screwed up his eyes to pierce the darkness. Nothing was visible save the stark profile of the city. The sounds of night were descending on York. Revellers were noisy. Music played somewhere. Dogs roamed and yelped. A single bell tolled. Ralph turned away. He wanted to mount up and lead his men in a search but he knew that it would be a hopeless exercise. They must wait until dawn.

He descended the stairs in a state of dejection; then a familiar voice rang out. Gervase Bret was hailing the guard at the gate. Ralph ran back up the steps and gazed over the palisade. He could just make out six shapes below him.

'Is that you, Gervase?' he shouted.
'Tell them to open up!'
'What have you got with you?'
'Another gift from Olaf Evil Child!'
'Gift?'
'Yes,' said Gervase. 'Five horses.'

Chapter Eleven

Gervase Bret had much to recount, but Ralph Delchard listened without interruption. He winced when he heard of the ambush and his jaw dropped when the death of Nigel Arbarbonel was reported in detail. Ralph's own day in York seemed dull and unproductive when compared to the adventures with Olaf Evil Child. Relieved to welcome his friend back unharmed, he was now feeling a distinct envy of him.

'You should have taken me with you!' he insisted.

'I would never have got near Olaf if I had.'

'Do not speak so fondly of the man.'

'He helped us, Ralph.'

'To curry favour.'

'Olaf Evil Child is wrongly maligned.'

'Stop apologising for him, Gervase. It annoys me. Have you so forgotten? The villain stole our horses.'

'No, Ralph. He only borrowed them.'

'I will only borrow his head when I meet him!'

When the sumpter horses were stabled, they went straight to Gervase's apartment in the keep to exchange news. Ralph was delighted that he would not have to explain his friend's absence to Aubrey Maminot and to account for the fact that he had allowed him to leave the city so unprotected. Envy soon turned to affection and Ralph reached out to embrace Gervase.

'By all, it is good to see you again!'

'It is good to be back inside four walls,' said Gervase as they parted. 'But what have *you* learned today?'

'That I never wish to get that close to fish again.'

'Fish?'

'Yes,' said Ralph with a grimace. 'I traced Tanchelm's footsteps to the harbour. Anyone in York could have picked up my scent when I left. Canon Hubert certainly did.'

'Where did you meet him?'

'At the Minster. I engaged his services.'

Gervase was astounded. 'You *told* him?'

'I did not need to. He has sharper wits than I have given him credit for, Gervase. He does not know what Tanchelm's main reason for coming to Yorkshire was, but he is certain that it was not to settle property disputes.'

'What did he actually say?'

'Very little. Hubert can be discreet.'

'And you employed him?'

'He offered to help. I set him on to Brother Francis.'

'Why?'

'A number of things puzzled me about the fellow,' said Ralph. 'Do you recall a tussle with Nigel Arbarbonel in which he always seemed to hold the whiphand over us?'

'It was almost as if he was primed in advance.'

'He was – by Brother Francis.'

'Our scribe? But he seemed such a helpful man.'

'So did Tanchelm of Ghent.'

'Are you *sure* of this?' said Gervase, shaking his head in disbelief. 'Brother Francis had no access to our papers.'

'He listened. We forgot he was there.'

'Only because we trusted him implicitly.'

'That was our fatal error,' said Ralph. 'Hubert sounded him out earlier and missed Vespers in order to bring me his opinion. Our genial monk was another spy.'

'Working for my lord Nigel?'

'Indirectly. Everything came through another source.'

'And who was that?'

'It grieves me to say this, Gervase, and I am still not entirely convinced myself, but . . . the man appears to be Aubrey Maminot.'

'Does he even know Brother Francis?'

'They are friends.'

'I cannot imagine him going anywhere near a monk.'

'Francis did not always wear the cowl. He served as a soldier under Aubrey's command. Old loyalties remain. He is a useful source of gossip and information.'

'But he was assigned to us through the good offices of the Archbishop himself.'

'Aubrey has great influence in York. My guess is that he arranged for Brother Francis to sit with us when he heard that we were in need of a scribe. Who would not trust a monk? I must confess that he took me in.'

'Canon Hubert has done well to expose him.'

'He has, Gervase. When I taxed Aubrey himself about our merry monk, he explained away their friendship in terms of the abbey. He told me that Brother Francis had once borne arms but made no mention of having served with him. Is that not strange? It was Hubert who dug out the truth.'

Gervase was alarmed. 'Everything we have said in the privacy of our deliberations has come back here?'

'So it would seem.'

'And then?'

'It was passed on to Nigel Arbarbonel.'

'No wonder he was able to frustrate our purpose,' said Gervase. 'Well, he will not do so again.'

Ralph gave a grudging nod. 'That is one thing I have to thank Olaf Evil Child for. He has rid us of my lord Nigel. What I still would like to know is why Aubrey was so thick with that smooth-voiced popinjay. What was there between them that made my good friend – as I thought him – betray us?'

'Something that my lord Nigel said may help us there.'

'Oh?'

'When he thought he would beat Olaf in combat, he talked as if he were about to slay an animal. He said that my lord Aubrey would pay well for Olaf's pelt.'

Ralph weighed the significance of the remark. It hurt him deeply to think that his host might have been working covertly against them and he was still hoping that he might have been mistaken. But the evidence was now overwhelming. 'Golde was our other ally,' he said.

'Ally?'

'Hubert delivered Brother Francis. She served up the cook. What better person to talk to about the guests at this castle than the man who has to feed them? Golde put me on to him by accident. I spent a fruitful hour in the kitchen.'

'What did the cook say?'

'All sorts of things, Gervase. Mostly complaints. Aubrey has a habit of waking him up to prepare midnight feasts for guests who have just arrived.' He raised an eyebrow. 'What sort of men only travel by night? The cook gave me dates and times and one other fact of note.'

'Let me tell you what it is,' said Gervase, anticipating him. 'My lord Tanchelm also spoke with him.'

'Yes.'

'So *his* attention, too, was directed to this castle. He found out what we are only just beginning to learn. And they killed him for it.'

There was a roar from below as Romulus and Remus were given a measure of freedom for the night. They ran down the mound then padded around the ditch at the bottom, baring their teeth in snarls of warning. Gervase crossed to the window to look down but the darkness hid them. He thought of the mutilated body he had seen in the morgue.

'Do you know why Toki came here?'

'That intruder?'

'Yes,' said Gervase. 'He and Ragnar Longfoot climbed into the castle that night. Only men with a powerful reason would take such a huge risk. Inga found out why they came here.'

'To kill Aubrey?'

'No. To steal something. Ragnar spoke of charters and of treasure. Toki was convinced that there was some kind of hoard at the castle and that it was vital to find it. So he came like a thief in the night.'

'And found Romulus and Remus instead.'

'Yes, Ralph.'

As if hearing their names, the lions roared in protest and raced around the ditch in search of prey. Gervase was still at the window as the noise reverberated. It set off a thought which had not occurred to him before.

'You say the cook talked of midnight feasts?'

'For late arrivals at the castle.'

'How did they get in?'

'What?'

'The lions patrol the ditch every night,' reminded Gervase. 'When they are released, nobody can enter or leave the keep. If travellers came into the castle so late, how did they get in here in order to be fed by the cook?'

Aubrey Maminot waited impatiently while the servants cleaned the cage. By the light of torches, the two men used brooms to sweep the soiled rushes into a pile before putting them in a wooden barrow. The floor of the cage was then sluiced with water. When that was dry, fresh rushes would be scattered. The servants departed with their barrow.

'I thought they would never finish,' said Aubrey.

'Blame me,' said Ludovico. 'I banged their heads together yesterday and told them to be more thorough in their work. Romulus and Remus must have a clean cage every morning. The servants will not be slack again.'

'Stand over them when they strew the fresh rushes.'

'I will.'

'They must never be allowed in there alone.'

Aubrey went into the cage with Ludovico behind him. Both were carrying flaming torches. With the floor now cleared of its bedding, the trap door was revealed in full. It was very large and secured by two heavy bolts. Aubrey drew them back and lifted the door. He went down a few of the stone steps before turning back.

'Lock it after me, Ludovico.'

'I always do.'

'You know the signal for my return.'

'I will be here.'

'Then I bid you farewell.'

'Good night, my lord,' said Ludovico. 'Give her a kiss from me.'

Philip the Chaplain knelt before the altar and offered up his final prayer of the day. With an indifference born of repetition he crossed himself, rose from the altar rail and genuflected towards the crucifix high above him. When he turned to leave the chapel, he was startled to see Gervase Bret standing in the doorway.

'It is late, Master Bret,' he said.

'I hoped that I would still catch you here.'

'I was about to retire for the night.'

'Then I will be brief.' Gervase stepped into the chapel and closed the heavy door behind him. 'It concerns the letter which you kindly gave to me.'

Philip was agitated. 'Do not talk of it. You promised that you would never mention where it came from.'

'Nor will I. The letter is destroyed. Nobody else will ever see it or connect it with the chaplain.' Philip relaxed visibly. 'I came first to thank you once again.'

'Your discretion is all the thanks I need.'

'We require some further help.'

'We?'

'My lord Ralph and I.'

Alarm returned. 'You told *him* of my part in this?'

'Not a word.'

'I have my place here in the castle, Master Bret.'

'I know.'

'Nothing must jeopardise that.'

'I fear that something may,' said Gervase softly. 'Though it will not be our doing. The threat comes from within.' The chaplain gulped slightly. 'That is why we need your assistance. You have been here for several years. You know the operation of the castle as well as anybody.'

'I close my eyes to what does not concern me.'

'In the interests of justice, I must ask you to open them slightly. You know what I speak of. Three bodies have lain in your morgue this past week. One was that of an old servant who had lived out his allotted span.'

'He passed away quietly in his sleep.'

'The other two were not as fortunate,' said Gervase. 'The first was mauled by lions, the second was throttled. Violent deaths in both cases.'

'But quite unconnected.'

'I begin to wonder.'

'Why?'

'Both men were searching for something inside this astle. Both were punished for their curiosity. What vere they after, do you think?'

'I cannot say, Master Bret.'

'Can you not hazard a guess?'

'I am the chaplain here and nothing more.'

'Your duty is to the castellan,' said Gervase. 'I understand that. You owe your place to him. But is there not a higher duty that overrides my lord Aubrey?'

'Higher duty?'

'To truth. To justice. To God.'

Philip took a step back and glanced around nervously.

'Should murder go unpunished?' pressed Gervase.

'No, it should not.'

'Should evil go unchecked?'

'No,' whispered the other, 'it should not.'

'Then tell me about them.'

'Who?'

'Visitors to the castle. Unusual guests who arrive at strange hours of the night. Men whose horses are covered in the sweat of long, hard journeys. Strangers.' He put a hand on the chaplain's shoulder. 'Tell me about them . . .'

Ralph Delchard waited until he heard the sound of her breathing change slightly. Golde was asleep. Detaching his arms from around her, he rolled her gently on to her back and slipped out of the bed. His mind would not let him rest. Aubrey Maminot was an old and trusted friend of his. The thought that his host might be

involved in deception and manipulation was abhorre
to Ralph. At one level, he simply could not believe i
When he considered that murder and even treaso
might be laid at Aubrey's door, his brain revolted.
was impossible. A perverse illusion.

Action was the only way to relieve his turmoil. If th
castellan was innocent of the charges, then that inno
cence needed to be established at the earliest opportu
nity. If he was guilty, then the appropriate steps woul
have to be taken. He had to find out. Even with Gold
beside him, Ralph could not lie in a warm bed and drif
off to sleep.

He fumbled for his apparel and dressed as quickly a
he could. Reaching for his dagger, he thrust it into his
belt. He let himself out of the room, shut the door
quietly behind him, then moved across to the candle
which burned in the alcove. With its modest light to
guide him he set off down the stairs, pausing every
time his weight coaxed a squeak out of the boards.

The apartment was high in the tower and it took him
some minutes to work his way slowly down past the
other bedchambers, the solar, the hall, the chapel, the
kitchen and the tiny rooms where servants slept four to
a bed. He could smell the cage before he reached it.
Even with its fresh rushes, it retained the unmistakable flavour of Romulus and Remus. He crept up to it
and peered through the bars.

Letting himself into the cage, he went quickly across
to make certain that the door to the outside was
securely locked. Ralph did not want the lions to return
and catch him in their lair. Romulus and Remus were

truculent hosts. When he was satisfied that they could not reach him, he knelt on the floor and brushed back the rushes, looking for the trap door he had seen earlier. His hand fell on a bolt and he cleared the floor around it.

When the trap door was uncovered, he knew at once that it did not serve as a mere storeroom for herbs. The door was too large, the carpentry too careful. It fitted snugly and firmly in place. Ralph eased back the bolts and lifted the door back on its hinges. His candle disclosed stone steps which curled down into the ground. He was circumspect. Leaving the trap door open, he went down the steps with patient curiosity, using the candle to illumine the walls on both sides of him.

Reaching the bottom, he found himself in a subterranean passage that obliged him to duck as he moved along. After only a few yards, his thigh touched something and he drew back at once, snatching out his dagger to ward off an attack. The candle flame revealed his assailant to be no more than a large chest, set into a cavity in the wall. When he saw the size of the chest and its formidable array of locks, he was reminded of Toki's visit to the castle. He had come in search of some kind of hoard. The chest was certainly capacious enough to hold it and no treasure could be more securely guarded than this.

Ralph pressed on along the passage, following its twists and turns until he had no sense of where he might be in relation to the keep. He walked on until he came to a metal door that was reinforced with thick hasps. When he tried to open it, the door would not budge a fraction. Since there was no sign of a key, he wondered if someone had been through the exit to lock it from the outside. He was convinced that he had come under the castle walls and that the door gave concealed access to the city. The problem of how midnight visitors entered the keep was now solved.

A noise behind him made him grab his weapon again and he had a sensation of panic as he thought it might be the lions. To be caught in such a confined space by Romulus and Remus would be a nightmare. Escape would be unthinkable and his dying cries would go unheard. He had a vision of Golde, waking to find the bed beside her empty, going demented when she saw his blood-stained remains hauled out of the tunnel. It made him hurry back the way he had come.

There was nobody there, and his confidence quickly seeped back. Stopping beside the chest once more, he ran a meditative hand over it before continuing on to the steps. He never thought he would be so grateful to climb back into a lions' cage, but he did so with a sigh of relief. Setting down his candle, he used both hands to lower the trap door into position and slid the bolts home.

The candle saved his life. As its flame danced violently in the sudden displacement of air, he was given a split-second warning of the attack. Someone had charged up on him from behind. When a coil was thrown around his neck, Ralph instinctively put up his hands to work his fingers inside it. His assailant was strong and determined; the noose tightened inexorably. The man put his knee in the small of Ralph's back to apply even more pressure.

There was a dagger in his belt but it was out of reach. Ralph needed both hands to prevent the breath from being squeezed out of him. He tugged at the coil but it was cutting into his fingers. Ralph knew that he was up against Tanchelm's assassin. The man had killed before with vicious effectiveness but he did not have a sitting target this time. Ralph was more powerful and resourceful than Tanchelm of Ghent.

Throwing his legs out in front of him, Ralph dropped to the floor and pulled his assailant down after him. The suddenness of the move deprived the man of his grip and Ralph was able to tear the noose away. But the escape was only temporary. As Ralph rolled over, the man dived on top of him to grip his throat in both hands. A thumb seemed to be burrowing deep into Ralph's windpipe and he began to choke. Punching at the man with one hand, he used the other to grasp the dagger and lunge upwards.

With a yell of pain the man rolled away, knocking over the candle and extinguishing its pale flame. Ralph had wounded him in the side, but it only served to enrage the attacker and he came hurtling out of the darkness. Trying to rise from the floor, Ralph was knocked flying again and the weapon span out of his hand. Powerful arms enfolded him again and they grappled wildly, threshing about in the rushes as they sought for the hold that would end the contest.

His adversary squeezed, punched, scratched, gouged and even bit him in an attempt to subdue his victim, but the advantage had been shifted now. Ralph had superior strength and a greater surge of purpose. A fight which had lasted for several long minutes was over in an instant. As they grappled once more, Ralph flipped him on to his stomach, put a knee in his back then used both hands to pull back his head. There was a loud crack as the man's neck broke.

Ralph clambered up and stood panting over his opponent. He needed no light to identify the man. The would-be assassin was Ludovico, the Keeper of the Beasts. His chosen weapon was the whip which had strangled Tanchelm of Ghent.

Olaf Evil Child had never had a decision challenged before and it embittered him. Men who owed their lives to his leadership were now daring to contest it. What caused him most pain was the fact that Eric, his closest friend, was now speaking against him.

The giant waved a massive fist. 'We will not go, Olaf!' he announced.

'But it is for our own good, Eric.'

'I will surrender to nobody!'

'Nor me!' said a voice. And a dozen more rushed to endorse its affirmation.

They were seated around the campfire at night. Olaf looked at them with disgust. Living as nomads had bonded them strongly together and taught them how much they relied on each other. Each man brought his own skills to the band, but it was Olaf who had turned those individual skills to the best use. Without his guidance, they would never have survived so long. It was time to remind them of their obligations to him.

'Who brought you all together?' he demanded.

'You did,' said Eric.

'Who fed you and watered you? Who planned our raids? Who kept us out of reach of every search party that ventured out of York in pursuit of us?'

'You did,' repeated Eric.

'And was my advice sound?'

'Very sound.'

'So why ignore it now?'

'Because it smacks of weakness.'

'Weakness!' He leapt to his feet. 'If anyone thinks that I am weak, let him test me here and now. That includes you, Eric. I am ready. Who will be first?'

Embarrassed muttering broke out among the men. None of them responded to his challenge. Most looked away.

Eric wiped the back of his hand across his lips. 'Nobody doubts your bravery,' he conceded.

'Thank you, Eric!'

'We all saw what you did to my lord Nigel.'

'I am glad that someone has remembered at last.'

'But we will not go into York with you.'

'Why not?'

'Because we are outlaws.'

'With a chance of pardon.'

'From Normans?' Eric was contemptuous. 'Never! They will hang us first and pardon us afterwards.' Murmurs of general agreement went up. 'You heard my lord Nigel. He would have cut you down without a second thought. They are all the same.'

'Gervase Bret is not.'

'He is only one man among many.'

'He gave us his word, Eric.'

'What use is that in a city as big as York? He carries no weight there. I'll not put my future in the hands of a man with a bandage around his head.'

'Will *nobody* come with me?' pleaded Olaf.

'Yes,' said Ragnar Longfoot. 'I will.'

'Then you are as mad as Toki,' said Eric.

Ragnar bridled. 'Toki was the bravest man alive.'

'He was a hothead who threw that life away,' countered Eric. 'Do you think we want to end up like him, Ragnar? No! I would rather feed off vermin out here than get eaten by lions in York.'

'Then you are a fool!' accused Olaf. 'Feed off vermin and you become vermin.'

'At least we will stay alive.'

'Roaming the wilderness? Stealing to survive? It has been bad enough already, Eric. How much worse will it be when winter settles in?' He made a last appeal. 'That is a time when we need a roof over our heads and warm food in our bellies. When we need to be with our families.' He walked across to crouch in front of Eric. 'Gervase Bret has offered us a chance. A slim one, I grant you – and, yes, there are many dangers involved – but I am ready to trust him.'

'I am not, Olaf,' said his friend.

'Will you not trust *me*?'

'Not this time.'

Olaf searched the faces around the campfire. 'Ragnar is with me,' he said. 'Who else?'

Not a single voice was heard. Olaf was deeply hurt.

'Very well,' he said quietly. 'We are done. You can stay here while I go to York to fight for my inheritance. If I die, you can all sneer at Olaf Evil Child and say how stupid he was. But if I win my land back – and yours too, for you have been dispossessed – do not come snivelling to me with your thanks and your congratulations. I will not even hear you.' He untethered his horse from a bush and swung himself up into the saddle. 'Gervase Bret is only one man, it is true. But he had the courage to come looking for me without a troop of soldiers at his back. I will now go in search of him.'

Olaf kicked his horse into a trot and rode out of the camp. Limping across the grass, Ragnar Longfoot mounted his own horse and went after him. By the light of the fire, Eric and the others looked at each other shamefacedly. Their leader had just turned his back on them.

Ragnar, meanwhile, caught up with his friend and rode alongside him. The journey had a special meaning for him.

'I go to see Toki's grave to ask for his forgiveness.'

'There is nothing to forgive, Ragnar.'

'I believe there is.' He glanced over his shoulder. 'If they had listened to Inga, they would be with us now.'

'Why?'

'She told me how fair-minded Gervase Bret was. He will not break a promise. Safe conduct, that was his guarantee.'

'For all of us, Ragnar. Not just you and me.'

'Do not take it to heart so.'

'Eric and I were like brothers. I cannot believe that he has forgotten all we have been through together. He and the rest of them will not last a week without me.'

'They are frightened, Olaf.'

'So am I.'

They rode on through the darkness at a canter with the stars to guide them. Two miles further along the road, they heard the first menacing clack of hooves. It seemed to come from their left. When they veered off to the right, another drumming sound met their ears. Pursuers were closing in from both directions. Olaf and Ragnar went up a hill at a gallop and crested it to find thick cover on the slope beyond. Reining in their horses, they sheltered in the bushes in the hope of shaking off the chasing pack.

Fifteen or more horses came pounding over the hill to converge on their hiding place. They seemed to know exactly where to find them. Olaf drew his sword and Ragnar had his spear at the ready.

A familiar deep-throated laugh rang out.

'Is that you, Eric?' said Olaf hopefully.

'Yes,' confirmed the other. 'You will never get to York alone. We thought you might need an escort.'

Olaf nudged his horse forward to embrace his friend. 'You are with us, then?' he said.

'A few yards behind you at least.'

'You will not regret it.' He waved an arm. 'Onward!'

They set off in a tight bunch, drawing strength from their leader, glad to be united again. Eric drew his horse up alongside Olaf Evil Child.

'We know the real reason for this journey,' he said.

'What is that?'

'You want to see Inga again!'

'I do!' admitted Olaf with a grin. 'Who would not?'

'And will this Gervase Bret really help us?'

'He swore as much.'

'I do not doubt his word, only his ability.'

'He and the others are royal commissioners, Eric. They are here on King William's business.'

'Yes,' said Eric, 'but King William is hundreds of miles away. His army is not here to enforce the decisions of his commissioners. We have another king here.'

'I know. Aubrey Maminot.'

'Can Gervase Bret and his friends prevail over him?'

'They must. Or we are all doomed.'

Aubrey Maminot took a last guzzling kiss from her before stealing quietly out of the house. It was a short ride across the city and the morning air was refreshing. He felt as blithe and vigorous as a man half his age. She was right about him. He was her lion.

The first cockcrow heralded the approach of dawn, and other voices were soon raised in welcome. Aubrey turned his horse towards a makeshift stable not far from his castle. When the animal was tethered inside, he let himself out and walked towards a clump of thick bushes nearby. Making sure that he was unobserved, he stepped behind the bushes to find a metal door set into a grassy bank. One twist of the key let him in. His horse would be collected as usual by one of his men. Another night of blissful madness had gone to plan.

He needed no light to guide him. Locking the door from the inside by feel, he waddled happily along the tunnel until he came to the steps. The trap door was wide open and two torches were throwing their light on to the cage. Standing ahead of him, ready to welcome his master, was the Keeper of the Beasts. Aubrey came into the cage and walked over to him.

'Ludovico!' he greeted. 'Good morrow, my friend!'

The dead man fell forward into his arms and knocked him backwards. Ralph Delchard had been holding the Italian up. When Aubrey saw that he was clasping a corpse, he dropped it at once and stared down at it in horror.

'What happened?' he gasped.

'Ludovico tried to kill me,' said Ralph.

'Never!'

'The same way that he murdered Tanchelm. With his whip. He picked the wrong man this time.'

'This is terrible,' said Aubrey with apparent concern for his guest. 'Are you all right?'

'No thanks to Ludovico.'

'He *attacked* you?'

'From behind.'

'He must have thought you were an intruder.'

'He knew exactly who I was, Aubrey.'

'What were you doing?'

'The same as Tanchelm. Being too inquisitive.'

Aubrey gave himself a moment to gather his wits. He was like a commander who has just suffered an unexpected reverse on the battlefield. A new strategy was required. Combat was out of the question. Ralph was wearing his armour and had a sword in his hand. Aubrey carried only a dagger. Guards could be called but they could not get into the keep past Romulus and Remus. His lions were separating him from help. His lion keeper would never be able to assist him again.

He stepped over the prone body of the Italian. 'Ludovico was stupid,' he said callously. 'I told him he would come off second best against Ralph Delchard.'

'So will you, Aubrey.'

'We are not in competition.'

'Yes, we are.'

'We need not be. What is it you want, Ralph?'

'You.'

'Why?'

'Tanchelm's murder, for a start. Ludovico was the assassin but you set him on. You ordered his death.'

'You will never prove that in a court of law.'

'I will enjoy trying.'

Aubrey chuckled. 'You will not even have the chance. Take a closer look into the courtyard. I have hundreds of men at my command. You have a handful. Arrest me if you must. But you will never get me out of here.'

'Yes, I will.'

'How?'

'The same way that you just came in.'

There was a long pause. Aubrey nodded in admiration.

'You *have* been inquisitive, Ralph,' he said. 'What else did you see down there?'

'Enough.'

'I beg leave to doubt that.'

'It's your secret entrance to the castle,' said Ralph.

'The one you designed when it was rebuilt. Guarded throughout the day by the lions so that nobody will come anywhere near it.' He peered into the gloom. 'By the way, I found no herbs down there, Aubrey. That is a pity. You need something to take away the stink of high treason.'

'Ralph . . .'

'Tanchelm of Ghent was the first to suspect you.'

'He is gone. Forget him.'

'He was our colleague. His death must be requited.'

'It has been,' said Aubrey. 'Ludovico paid in full. That account is settled. We must open a new one now.'

'No, Aubrey. It is all up for you.'

'I thought we were friends.'

'I do not consort with traitors!'

'Is that what you think I am?'

'We know it!'

'Do you?' Aubrey walked calmly to the side of the cage and leaned against it. Ralph covered his move with his outstretched sword. The castellan laughed. Taking out his dagger, he tossed it casually on to the floor.

'You do not need a weapon, Ralph. I am unarmed.'

'I will keep it drawn just the same.'

'Do you distrust me so much?'

'Yes.'

'And what charges do you bring against me? Murder? High treason? I must be the Devil Incarnate.'

'No, Aubrey. The Devil is more honest in his wickedness.'

'Let us examine the word "traitor", shall we?'

'You will examine it at the end of a rope.'

'I think not,' said the other, almost nonchalantly. 'A traitor is a man who betrays his country. Is that what I have done, Ralph?'

'We believe so.'

'Ah, you only believe. A moment ago you *knew*.'

'Do not prevaricate. I have talked to your cook. He has told me about demands for food at odd hours of the night. I have questioned other members of your household. They have heard Danish voices more than once in here.'

'What does that signify?'

'You were plotting with our mortal enemies.'

'With or against?'

'You will not wriggle out of this, Aubrey,' said Ralph. 'We know everything. Dates and times of your secret meetings. The nationalities of your guests. How they sneaked in and out of the castle without being seen.' He pointed with his sword. 'Do you deny this?'

'Not at all.'

'Tanchelm died because he learned the same.'

'No, Ralph. Your guesswork is woefully adrift there.'

'You had him murdered.'

'Ludovico killed him,' said Aubrey, unperturbed. 'That is all I will say about the event itself. I can enlighten you about the motive, however. Tanchelm was not murdered for being a spy but for not being a willing tradesman.'

'Tradesman?'

'Someone with an eye for a good bargain. You have it. Golde is proof of that. You will trade. He would not.' He indicated the sword. 'Make a gesture, Ralph. Put it away.'

After a moment's consideration, Ralph sheathed the weapon.

'That is better. Now we can talk on equal terms. Tell me about this high treason I am supposed to have committed. You and Tanchelm together have dogged my steps between you. What exactly did you find out?'

'The threat of a Danish invasion has been there for months,' said Ralph crisply. 'They have the ships and they have the men. What they needed before they sailed was an ally in York itself. Someone with the power to unlock the city to them when they sail up the River Ouse.'

'They come from the east, then?'

'Of course. Up the Humber estuary.'

Aubrey chuckled. 'That is your first mistake, Ralph. I fear that Tanchelm of Ghent made it as well. Both of you looked in the wrong direction. Turn your eyes to the west. That is where my guests hailed from.'

'Irish Danes?'

'They have ambitions too.'

'And you treated with them?'

'Several times. I confess it freely.'

'Then is your treason published.'

'Is it?' Aubrey strolled across to him. 'Who is the betrayer and who the betrayed here? I wooed the Irish Danes to draw their plans out of them. I did the same with the Scots. If you have talked to my fiery cook, you will know I have had guests from north of the border as well. They asked for my help, I offered to give it.'

'Why?'

'To insinuate myself into their counsels.'

'The King was not made aware of this strategy.'

'It is delicate work, Ralph. Winning the confidence first of the Irish Danes, then of the Scots. Patience is required. Commit it to paper and disaster threatens.'

'So you are no traitor. Is that what you claim?'

'I feign treachery to entrap our enemies.'

'Can you really expect me to believe you?'

'No,' said Aubrey with a grin. 'Follow me.'

He moved to take one of the torches from its holder and Ralph put a precautionary hand on the hilt of his sword, but the castellan did not try to use it as a weapon. Instead, beckoning the other to follow, he went back through the trap door and down the steps. Ralph went after him at a discreet distance. When he reached the chest, Aubrey produced a key from a ring at his waist then offered the torch to Ralph. The latter held it so that his host could unlock the chest.

'Not herbs, perhaps,' he said happily, 'but something that will sweeten any man's dream. Behold!'

He lifted the lid then stood back out of the way. Ralph was amazed. A veritable treasure chest stood before him. It was crammed with gold, silver, jewelled ornaments and dozens of bags of coins. Lying in amongst the wealth were piles of charters and sheaves of letters. Aubrey reached in to retrieve a large purse and an accompanying letter.

'Here,' he said. 'Read this. Written to me by an

emissary of King Malcolm of Scotland.' He held up the purse. 'This was the payment that came with it. There are letters and gifts from Dublin as well, but your Danish is probably not adequate. This is the sum of my treason, Ralph.'

'Leading on foreign powers for your own advantage.'

'I want some return for my cunning, of course,' said Aubrey. 'I may squeeze money out of them but I also squeeze their plans and their troop deployments.' He tossed the purse and letter back into the chest. 'Look at it, Ralph. I have grown rich playing our enemies off against each other.'

'That is one way of looking at it.'

'What is the other?'

'You are biding your time,' decided Ralph. 'Conspiring with the enemy in order to betray them yet ready to join them if their invasions promise success. You are watching the tide to see which wave will carry you farthest.'

'I am an opportunist, that is all.'

'No, Aubrey. You are a traitor-in-waiting.'

'I am loyal to my King and country.'

'But which King? And of which country?'

'Ralph . . .' coaxed the other.

'You have sold your soul, Aubrey.'

'At least I have something to show for it.' His face hardened. 'We came to the north together. We killed its people and burned its houses and destroyed its crops. Then you went away. But I stayed, Ralph. I saw potential in a ruined land. I rebuilt this castle, enlarged my holdings and used every means at my disposal to extend my power. It has made me the wealthiest man in York. I more or less *own* this city.'

'Not any more.'

'This is only part of my treasure.'

'It will all be confiscated and put to good use.'

'Put some of it to good use yourself,' said Aubrey, running his hand through some gold coins. 'We are friends, Ralph. Take your share to seal that friendship. Trade with me.'

'No, Aubrey.'

'Take it,' urged the other, offering the coins.

'No!' Ralph slammed down the lid of the chest with finality. Aubrey abandoned all hope of bribing his way out of his predicament. Pushing Ralph away, he darted along the passage and back up the stairs. Torch in hand, Ralph went after him, but the castellan was not trying to escape. He was only running for help. He unlocked the gate which led to the outside and stepped swiftly through it.

'Romulus!' he called. 'Remus! Kill him!'

Ralph followed him out but froze immediately. Obeying the command of their master, the two lions were bounding up the incline.

Olaf Evil Child led his men into the city with the farmers streaming in to sell their produce in the market. Having followed their leader thus far, Eric and the others dispersed to attract less attention. Olaf and Ragnar Longfoot rode on to the castle alone. True to his word, Gervase Bret had left instructions that they were to be admitted. As the guard swung back the gate, the newcomers went through to find the whole castle in a state of uproar.

Soldiers were yelling from the walls, women were screaming from the windows of the keep and every animal in the castle was swelling the chorus of alarm. Olaf and Ragnar gaped at what they saw on the mound. Torch in one hand and sword in the other, a man was trying to fend off two snarling lions. A second man, standing to the side, was exhorting the beasts to attack and dancing in glee as they did so.

Olaf's instinct was to help, and his brain worked fast. Swinging his horse around, he galloped out of the courtyard. Ragnar Longfoot responded differently. While Olaf saw only a man in distress, Ragnar saw the beasts which had killed Toki. He dismounted quickly and ran to the nearest staircase.

Ralph Delchard, meanwhile, was fending off Romulus and Remus as best he could, jabbing sword and flame at them while trying to keep clear of their flashing paws. The ear-splitting noise was a distraction to him, but it only served to incite the animals to greater ferocity. Herleve was screeching from one window, Golde crying from another and the rest of the household fighting to watch through every available aperture.

The contest was cruelly uneven but nobody intervened. Aubrey ordered his men to hold off and they, in turn, stopped Ralph's own soldiers from coming to his aid. The escort were forced to watch with revulsion as their lord struggled to stay alive. It was only a matter of time before his strength waned and the lions overpowered him.

Aubrey Maminot was in his element, urging the beasts on to tear their quarry to pieces and looking for the chance to assist them in some way. As Ralph backed towards him, the castellan jumped forward and pushed him off balance. A shout of horror went up as Ralph lost his footing and rolled helplessly down the mound to the ditch at the bottom. The torch was knocked from his hand and he was left with only a sword to defend himself.

Remus was nonplussed for a moment but Romulus went in pursuit of his prey. Running down the hill, he sprang into the air with paws outstretched. Ragnar's spear hit him directly in the chest and knocked all the life out of him. Ralph dodged out of the way as the lion's body thudded down beside him. Up on the wall, Ragnar Longfoot was cut down by half a dozen of Aubrey's men, but he went happily to his death. He had avenged Toki and proved his courage.

Remus went straight to his brother. Bleeding profusely and growling his last, Romulus was twitching about on the ground, the spear still buried in his heart. Ralph backed gingerly away but he did not get far. Remus came at him again, lashing out with his paws and searching for a moment to pounce. The sword was an inadequate defence and Ralph could do no more than poke it in his face as he kept on the retreat. When he lost his footing again he tumbled over.

Aubrey yelled in triumph, Remus moved in and the

crowd shrieked with terror. It was then that another figure joined in the contest. Bursting through the door of the cage, Gervase Bret came slithering down the mound with a lighted torch in each hand, waving them in circles at the top of his voice to attract attention. Remus was distracted long enough for Ralph to get to his feet and take one of the torches from Gervase as the latter came down to him.

The lion was perplexed. Fire, noise and the dying moans of Romulus confused him. Aubrey was enraged. He came skidding down the incline himself to take control.

'Kill them, Remus!' he ordered. 'Kill, kill!'

With the fiercest roar yet, the lion sprang in the air and flattened Aubrey with its impetus. Claws cut through his tunic and the angry mouth closed over his face. The women at the windows turned away as the creature mauled its master. Ralph and Gervase did what they could to draw it away but their efforts were in vain.

Some of the garrison opened the gate in the fence and poured through to rescue their master, poking at Remus with sword and spear. The animal rounded on them angrily, howling with pain as the weapons dug into it. Scattering the soldiers, it loped out through the gate and across the courtyard, setting off hysteria in the stables and the chicken coops. It was Olaf Evil Child who had the solution. Riding into the courtyard with a fisherman's net in his hand, he flung it over Remus with great accuracy and the animal was completely enmeshed. Before it could fight its way out of its prison, soldiers hacked it to death.

Ralph was wounded but alive. Gervase was breathless but unhurt. Aubrey Maminot was a bleeding remnant of high treason on the grass.

The lions of the north would kill no more.

Epilogue

Brunn the Priest officiated at the ceremony. The exhumation of Toki's body was carried out in the drizzle of an early morning. Two gravediggers worked sedulously with their spades while the priest and his impromptu congregation looked on. Supported by her mother, Inga was dry-eyed but deeply moved. Toki's bones would be translated to the tiny churchyard near their home. Her beloved would lie at rest beside his friend, Ragnar Longfoot.

The knot of onlookers included Gervase Bret and Ralph Delchard. Behind them stood Canon Hubert and Philip the Chaplain. They watched in silence as the rough wooden coffin was lifted out of the earth and carried across to a cart to be draped with a cloth. It would have a slow and respectful journey back to its new resting place.

The horse plodded and the cart moved off. Chanting a prayer, Brunn fell in behind it with Inga and Sunnifa. When the tiny procession was out of earshot, Ralph turned to Gervase.

'How ever did they get permission to move him?'

'It was not easy,' said Gervase.

'Only the relics of a saint are translated like that. I never met this Toki, but he does not sound as if he had the makings of a saint.'

'He is a martyr in Inga's eyes.'

'That is not the same thing.'

'We owe it all to Canon Hubert's kind intercession,' explained Gervase. 'He spoke in person to Archbishop Thomas and laid the case before him. When the chaplain buried him, Toki was a nameless victim of Romulus and Remus. Hubert argued that a second ceremony would really be a first proper burial and therefore permissible.'

'And the Archbishop acceded to the request?'

'Not at first, Ralph.'

'Why not?'

'He believed that it would set a dangerous precedent.'

'Did he need more persuasion?'

'Much more. But he softened towards the notion when Hubert told him of our decision to leave the confiscated treasure of my lord Aubrey at the Minster until the King decides what shall be done with it.'

Ralph chuckled. 'Good old Hubert! Putting Aubrey's ill-gotten wealth to a Christian purpose.'

'Do I hear my name being taken in vain?' said Hubert.

'On the contrary,' said Ralph. 'We are praising you.'

'Thank you, my lord.'

'You should have been a diplomat.'

'I am.'

There was work awaiting them at the shire hall. The three of them took their leave of Philip the Chaplain and walked away from the shadow of the castle.

'What news of Brother Francis?' asked Gervase.

Canon Hubert smiled. 'He is sorely troubled.'

'Expelled from the Order?'

'No, Master Bret. Kept within it to be punished.'

'He committed no real crime,' said Gervase. 'All he did was to eavesdrop on our conversations and report them back to my lord Aubrey.'

'That was crime enough,' decided Ralph.

'Yes,' said Hubert, 'and he has confessed it in the most abject way. Brother Francis did not realise to what foul use the information he supplied was being put. He was mortified.' His cheeks dimpled again. 'Father Abbot assures me that his mortification will continue for some time.'

'Is he to listen to your sermons, then?' joked Ralph.

'No, my lord. He is to be given responsibility for the latrines at the abbey. A lowly duty but one that will teach him to serve his brothers with all humility.'

'We shall miss his elegant hand.'

'It is being put to a more basic purpose,' said Hubert. 'Besides, we have Brother Simon to fulfil our needs.'

'The four of us are together again,' noted Gervase.

'Yes,' said Ralph, surprising himself with his enthusiasm. 'I am quite looking forward to it. Canon Hubert and I seem to have reached an understanding at last.'

Hubert allowed himself a rare excursion into humour. 'I will strive to educate you further, my lord.'

It was a paradox. In interrupting their work, the murder of Tanchelm of Ghent actually shortened their stay in York. The chest beneath the empty cage at the castle was found to contain charters and leases that had a direct bearing on the disputes under review. Armed with a fund of documentary material, the tribunal was able to pronounce judgement at a fairly brisk rate.

Pleased to be reunited, the four of them worked in greater harmony than they had ever achieved before. Events in York had given them a notoriety which lent them an added authority. Murder had been solved, high treason averted. Ralph Delchard and Gervase Bret were entitled to feel their visit to the city had been a successful one.

When they departed from York, the commissioners were waved off by the grateful Inga. With their land restored, she and her mother could live with more dignity now. Toki had gone, but Olaf Evil Child was allowing a decent interval to elapse before he showed his interest in her. In the meantime, he had work to do on the holdings which had been taken from Robert Brossard and returned to him by decision of the tribunal.

Ralph rode at the head of the cavalcade with Golde. When they were clear of York, she gave her curiosity full vent.

'And now may I be told what was going on?' she said.

'You already know as much as you need, my love.'

'I do not, Ralph. And it is vexing.'

'Ask what you will, then.'

'Why did my lord Tanchelm travel with us?'

'For the pleasure of our company.'

'Give me a serious answer.'

'He was only doing what we do. Obeying orders.'

'But what kind of orders?'

'It matters not, my love. They died with him.'

'And that is another thing I do not understand,' she continued. 'He was strangled at the shire hall because he unbolted the shutters at the rear of the building. How did Ludovico know that he would be alone?'

'It was on Aubrey's advice.'

'And how did lord Aubrey know?'

'He knew everything, Golde,' said Ralph. 'When a man is that powerful, he attracts many parasites. Tanchelm's letter to Olaf Evil Child was intercepted then sent on. It was vital that our Fleming was killed away from the castle, and Aubrey had the perfect chance. He knew the time and place when the victim would be alone in the shire hall with a private mode of entry already set up.'

'So Ludovico was dispatched as the assassin.'

'Yes,' said Ralph. 'He scattered the charters on the table to make it look as if they were his target and throw us off the scent. Aubrey hoped to snare Olaf at the same time, but he was too cunning for Aubrey's men. Too cunning for me as well, I might add. I still think it was a mistake to award that land to a horse thief.'

'Gervase lured him back within the law.'

'That is a matter of opinion.' Ralph heaved a deep sigh. 'York was a story of gains and losses, Golde. The gains were immense but the losses are very painful.'

'What hurts you the most?'

'Losing Aubrey's friendship. I cannot believe a man could change so much yet seem exactly the same. That affability never left him. Yet all the time he was involved in his own personal Harrying of the North.'

'My sympathies are with his wife, Herleve.'

'She will survive.'

'I will never forget what she told me.'

'When?'

'That time she saw us in the chapel,' said Golde. 'She said we looked so right together, like husband and wife. That touched me deeply, Ralph.'

'Why?'

'Why do you think?'

He reached over to kiss her softly on the cheek. 'We have a chapel back in Hampshire . . .'

While intimate matters were being discussed at the front of the column, legal concerns dominated at the rear. Gervase Bret rode between Canon Hubert and Brother Simon. The scribe had still not come to terms with the enormity of Aubrey Maminot's crimes.

'I have never known such villainy!' he said.

'Pray God you never do again,' observed Hubert.

'My lord Aubrey was a fiend in human shape.'

'No wonder he chose lions for his pets,' said Gervase. 'He was truly one himself. He had the lion's share of wealth and power in the city. And far beyond. Stealing land and the charters that went with it before leasing it out to the likes of Nigel Arbarbonel and his half-brother. He held them all in the palm of his hand. Aubrey Maminot was the true landlord of Sunnifa and ıll those others dispossessed. Toki climbed into the astle in search of the charters that would prove that.'

'How did he know they were there?' wondered Iubert.

'Ragnar Longfoot explained that to me. Toki would lo anything to regain the inheritance for Inga and her nother. Because my lord Nigel held the land, Toki ıssumed he would also hold the charters relating to it. Vhen my lord Nigel and his men were away, Toki lipped into the depleted castle and threatened the teward with death if he did not surrender the documents. Men usually tell the truth with a dagger at heir throat. The steward confessed that the charters n question were held by Aubrey Maminot and that *he* vas the true landlord.' Gervase sighed. 'The success of hat escapade was Toki's undoing. Because he had ;ained entry to one fortress so easily, he thought that ıe could do it again in York.'

'I am so pleased that we stayed at the Minster,' said Simon. 'We were spared this atmosphere of wickedness ınd deceit. To be in the same castle as my lord Aubrey ınd his beasts would have stained my soul.'

'Evil contaminates all that it touches,' noted Hubert. But goodness purifies. I like to feel that we leave York a nuch cleaner place for our visit.'

'Oh, yes, Canon Hubert,' said Simon.

'My lord Tanchelm did his share towards that.'

'Amen.'

'We will commiserate with his widow when we reach Lincolnshire. Her grief will be profound.'

The three men suddenly found that they had two

new companions. Ralph and Golde had dropped back to join them. To Brother Simon's consternation, Golde drew up beside him and her cloak all but brushed his habit. The proximity of womankind made him blush to his roots.

'We have come to apologise, Brother Simon,' said Ralph.

'To me, my lord?'

'Yes,' said Golde. 'We have caused you offence.'

'No, no,' he lied.

'The simple fact is this,' said Ralph. 'We are not wed. That troubles you. And Canon Hubert has also suffered discomfort.'

'Spiritual anguish,' said Hubert. 'Profoundly unsettling.'

'It will not happen again,' promised Golde.

'When we travel to another county,' said Ralph, 'you will not have to ride beside such blatant immorality. Golde and I are resolved on that. We have repented.'

'Your words move me, my lord,' said Simon joyfully. 'I feel as if a great stone has been lifted from me.'

'Yes,' said Hubert. 'We applaud your conversion to the path of righteousness. How did the miracle occur?'

'In the chapel back at the castle.'

'One moment,' said Gervase, disappointed. 'Do I understand this aright? Golde has been such a delightful companion. Are you saying that she will never travel with us again?'

'No,' said Ralph. 'I am not saying that at all.'

'But I thought you were, my lord,' said Hubert.

'Yes,' agreed Simon. 'You promised even now.'

'Golde will *always* travel beside me now,' said Ralph.

A smile of true contentment spread across Golde's features. Ralph held her hand proudly and beamed at the others.

'But less sinfully.'